Games with the Orc

MONSTER SMASH AGENCY
BOOK ONE

KATHRYN MOON

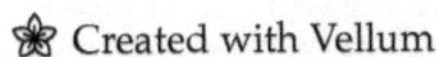 Created with Vellum

To my Patreon babes,
who joined me in this new adventure!

Contents

This story was originally shared with chapter by chapter updates in rough draft form on my Patreon in starting in December of 2021.

Warnings and information include:

Dominant and submissive role-playing, sex-work, primal play etc. Overall a great deal of consensual kink and smut. Oodles of after care. Please check out my website kathryn moon.com for a comprehensive list!

Games with the Orc

MONSTER SMASH AGENCY 1
BY KATHRYN MOON

CHAPTER 1
Sunny

THIS WASN'T *how I wanted to do this*, I thought, staring down into the upturned face of my boyfriend of three years. He knelt on the pretty tile of the upscale restaurant he'd chosen for our date night, the busy room's attention slowly drifting in our direction. I'd been surprised by Harry's suggestion for dinner out. In the three years of our relationship, Harry was rarely the one who wanted to try a new restaurant or activity in our casually arranged routine.

Now, it made sense.

Harry's breaths came quick and nervous, eyes filling up. "Sonya, I know you said we should wait, but we're ready. You make me feel like the man I want to become."

That doesn't make any sense, a snarky little voice chimed in my head as my gaze flicked over Harry's head, skirting away from the stares of the diners on us.

Why did people always want to be loved for who they *could* be? Didn't it make more sense to be loved for who you already were? Was that just a juvenile fantasy I'd been clinging to? Harry loved me for who he thought I was, and while that woman wasn't a lie—productive, cheerful, mild, and agreeable—she wasn't the complete picture, either.

Shit. A bright and glittering tear rolled down from Harry's eye, and a young harpy one table over cooed in response, her feathers rustling.

"Marry me," Harry said, and I tried not to flinch. It sounded more like an order than a request, but maybe that was because it was the third time he'd repeated the phrase.

All around us, the restaurant held its breath, the moment seemingly suspended as Harry and the rest of the room waited for my answer. Except time hadn't stopped.

I had to speak.

It was on the tip of my tongue to just say yes. Everyone was staring. Harry was *crying*. Yes would be easier. Yes would be nice, cheerful, agreeable.

But yes would be months, years, a lifetime of routine, of continuing to hide the parts of myself that made Harry's eyebrows raise, of coasting on the little concessions he made. In Harry's book, "adventures" included driving somewhere without the GPS, trying a new spice profile on the chicken breast, and watching a television series without him reading comprehensive reviews aloud to me beforehand. Those were the things Harry found daring. Those would be the boundaries I would push gently against for the rest of my life if I said yes.

I wondered what Harry would think of the ideas, the fantasies, that kept me awake at his side while he snored softly next to me—those secrets that helped me finish the job he rarely completed during sex.

I should've told him. Then maybe it wouldn't have come to this.

I opened my lips, not sure what answer would fall out, when I realized that my silence—far too long in the face of his eager proposal—had already answered for me. The hope that had glowed in Harry's pretty blue eyes had vanished, and now he was wearing that soft bruised expression I met sometimes when my mood wore thin and I snapped at him.

"I'm sorry," I whispered as Harry's bottom lip began to tremble.

The words were barely audible, but the restaurant had grown silent. All at once, with my not-quite answer, the restaurant sprang back into life. A slender, scaled waitress gave up her disguise as a statue and rushed back into action, delivering plates of food to a table of human diners. The accidental audience around us now displayed a new and polite determination to ignore the rest of our scene.

"But...it's been three years," Harry said, still kneeling, now frowning.

"Please, please sit," I answered, reaching down to tug at his elbows, careful to avoid his outstretched hands still holding the ring box.

"Do you...not believe in marriage?"

"It's not that, it's—"

"Me? It's me," Harry said, voice growing a little too loud.

He deserves to be angry, I reminded myself. I should've done this earlier. I should've broken up with my comfortable but not satisfying boyfriend of three years... I wasn't sure when.

No, I was. It was as soon as he'd started talking about marriage a few months ago and it had filled me with a clammy, nervous dread. I'd known I was bored for too long, yes, but I hadn't realized I was actually afraid of a future with Harry until that first coy mention.

"It's me too, Harry," I said softly, eyes blinking away the sting that rose. I was the one doing the damage, which meant I was not the one who deserved to cry. "It's us. I'm sorry."

Harry finally rose from the floor, but he didn't take his seat at the table. Gazes were flicking back and forth between us more rapidly again, a new curiosity heightening the tension in the room. Would Harry explode? Would we fight?

Sadly, I already knew the answer to that question. Was it

perverse of me to wish my unfailingly sweet boyfriend had more of a temper?

"Do you… Is that going to change?" Harry asked, his brow tangling and an elegant hand going up to push his golden and carefully coiffed hair back from his face. He didn't wait for my answer. "Do you even want to be with me?"

Sometimes, yes. What kind of person would I be if I'd dated someone for three years and had been waiting to leave the whole time? No, Harry was sweet. He was considerate. He was a good—if not varied—cook, and he'd always treated me as his equal. He gave me back rubs when I had cramps, without being prompted, and took time to get to know my tastes in music and books. I did love Harry.

I just didn't want to spend the rest of my life loving Harry.

"It's not a yes or no," I said.

Harry's eyes widened, and I took in a deep breath.

"Not always. Not forever," I admitted softly.

It was almost true. A part of me hadn't been ready to give up the ease of my life with Harry. It wasn't fair to him, especially not now. No matter what discomfort came next for me, I knew I was the villain of the story in this moment.

Harry's golden skin turned pale and ashy, and his eyes lifted to the full room around us for the first time since he'd taken that horrifying bend to his knee minutes ago. Suddenly aware of our audience, Harry sank into his seat.

No, Harry wouldn't make a scene. His temper wouldn't flare.

"You said…" Harry blinked at me.

I'd said we weren't ready. "I should've said more. Sooner. I just… I didn't know if I was sure." I bit my lip immediately. No excuses.

"Sonya, you're never sure!" Harry spat in a whisper.

I flinched back, gaping at him. "What?"

"You hate making decisions, you always leave things up to

me! I thought... I assumed—" Harry paled again after the outburst and shook his head.

Was that true? No, I made decisions all the time! I ran my own social media brand and independent business, offered advice to others, directed my own career. It was only that with Harry, the options offered were never very interesting.

Harry's eyes narrowed on me. He knew me well enough, even with all I'd kept from him, to read my expression.

"Well? What do you want to do now?" he asked.

And there it was, on the tip of my tongue. *I don't know. What do you want to do?*

Huh. Was he right? Did I shy away from big decisions? A year into dating, he'd asked if I wanted him to move in and I'd...left the decision up to him.

"I'm going home and I'm packing a bag," Harry snapped.

My shoulders sagged with relief. Okay, so maybe Harry was right.

"You're paying for dinner. And calling a ride. Give me... Just give me an hour to get my things without you there. Enough for a few days. I'll move out as soon as I'm able," Harry said.

I shrank slightly in my seat, aware I deserved this anger and just slightly disappointed I'd never seen this authority in Harry before now. Still, I wasn't completely fickle, and his rightful command over the events of our unraveling breakup wasn't enough to change my mind.

We were over.

You're free, a little whisper in my head hinted shyly.

Harry rose from his seat, staring down at me a moment longer, a brief flicker of sorrowful hope on his face. I ducked my chin, heard the huff of his breath, and watched his feet march away from the table.

Free to do what?

Across from me, Harry's plate was half-eaten, and I noticed a shaggy yeti eyeing the steak with faint interest. A smile quirked my lips, and then a tear coursed down the side of my cheek, curling into that smile and bringing the taste of salt to my tongue.

There was a meal in front of me too, a duck confit Harry had remarked on with surprise, but I'd entirely lost my appetite. I didn't want to eat, didn't want to remain here staring at Harry's empty seat like nothing had happened.

A shadow appeared at my side. Oh, an actual shadow. I blinked up at the murky face of the wraith waiter and wondered if I imagined a twist of sympathy in their smoky expression.

"Would you…like boxes?"

Boxes of the last meal, moldering in my fridge, reminding me of this mess I'd gotten myself into every time I opened the door?

"No, thank you," I said, my voice sounding somewhat shredded, thin and tight. "Just the check."

The wraith floated away, and I sighed. Maybe I would walk home. It was a long walk, through at least four Chicago neighborhoods, and I was wearing an unfortunately high pair of heels, but it would give Harry time to grab whatever he needed.

You're not even going to fight to keep him?

No. I wasn't.

I'd spent almost three years trimming little pieces of myself away to fit into a life with Harry. Not because he'd asked me to, but because I was scared of what I secretly wanted. Because what Harry offered was safer, simpler. I told myself that I was cultivating a life that made sense for me.

Without Harry, I would have no excuse not to let those dangerous parts of me grow. Already, my skin tingled, as if new sprouts would suddenly burst forth right here in the trendy restaurant, thorny vines newly vengeful for their years of being stifled. I wanted them to cut through the shell of me, yet I was terrified at the idea of discovering what really grew beneath.

I would learn soon enough.

"DO you think your subscribers will even notice he's gone?" Natalie asked, watching me hold up a piece of art to the wall in front of me, examining it against the rest of my collection. She had her son, Emmett, on her hip as she bobbed in place, rocking back and forth in the steady movement of motherhood while Emmett cooed and yanked on a stray braid of black hair.

"Umm…" It was true, I hadn't made much use of Harry in my social media. Harry hadn't seemed interested in being a part of my "brand." In fact, he'd been more confused about my work than anything.

Why an illustrator and *an interior decorator influencer?* he'd asked.

"I don't think I'm going to make a thing out of it," I admitted with a shrug, pulling down the art I'd been considering and staring at the new blank space on the wall—the spot where a portrait I'd drawn of Harry reading had been placed. There were little pockmarks all over my small carriage house now. The places I'd made room for Harry's interests, now subtracted. He'd been texting me instructions of what to pack up for him for almost two weeks since our disastrous dinner.

"Is he taking the portrait?" Natalie asked.

I sighed and turned to face her and the table where a few unhung prints of mine were resting. "I have no idea. He's… He went to stay with Jimmy and Kenley. He texted to tell me he found a place. He wants a week to be able to move out."

"What do you mean?" Natalie asked, frowning, her warm brown eyes zeroing in on me.

I flicked my gaze up and darted it away just as quickly. "A week without me here."

Technically, Harry had asked for "at least three days, no more than a week." Considering the situation, I thought being generous and offering as much time as he wanted was only fair.

"No way," Natalie scoffed, pulling her hair free from Emmett's grip with a wince. "What if he trashes this place? Or takes stuff that doesn't really belong to him?"

"It's Harry," I reasoned with a shrug.

Natalie snorted. "True."

Harry was mild. Responsible. Fair.

"You don't *deserve* to have your place trashed just because you broke up with a nice guy," Natalie said, voice lowering.

"What?" I gasped, staring at her.

Her lips quirked. Emmett was falling asleep in her arms now, her steady, repetitive motion slowing down.

"I know you, Sunny. I know why you stayed with Harry for so long. Maybe I don't know why you felt like it wasn't the right relationship for you," she said, one eyebrow raising, an invitation for me to fess up. I pressed my lips firmly together, and she continued. "And I know you feel guilty for finally being put in a position where you *had* to be the one who broke things off. But just because you hurt Harry, doesn't make you a bad person," Natalie whispered.

Natalie did know me. We'd been friends growing up in the suburbs together, friends through college, friends here in the city, constantly marveling that we were now adults living somewhat adjusted versions of our childhood dreams. I'd only really been able to make a living through my art after my PicsApp account grew popular with my daily decoration and documentation of this carriage house. Natalie wasn't the famous fashion designer she'd predicted, but she was a stylist for the young wives of the financial district. We'd grown into our new dreams together.

And maybe a little part of me had found Harry comfortable because Natalie had just married her husband Theo—a friendly werewolf who burnt off his pre-full moon energy at the same gym as Natalie. Natalie had taken the next adult step, and I hadn't wanted to be left behind.

"I just felt like...I wasn't totally myself with Harry," I admitted.

"Harry was boring," Natalie reasoned without batting an eyelash. "Nice-boring. Like what other people think normal is."

"I'm not normal?" I asked, voice squeaking slightly.

Natalie huffed a soft laugh. "You're lots of things. You're the girl who screamed at those gargoyles for me when we were ten. You're a twee and charming social media influencer. And you're the woman whose imagination sometimes produces images that I can't even begin to understand where they came from."

She nodded her head over at one of the frames on the wall, an illustration of a strange tangle of figures and weeds and teeth and chains. It was one of my favorite things I'd ever drawn. Harry had 'genuinely disliked' it, as strong a term for hate as he would use. He'd found it disturbing and confusing, and I'd caught him studying it occasionally with a twist of disgust on his usually placid features.

"I'm..." My cheeks were hot. Harry wasn't the only one I hid things from. "I'm not even sure I really *want* the things I think of, or if I just...like thinking about them."

Natalie stared blankly back at me for a moment and then blinked. She glanced down at Emmett in her arms before turning to tuck him gently sleeping into his carrier before facing me again.

"Are we talking sex stuff?"

I made a soft, strangled sound at the back of my throat, and Natalie answered with a stifled squeal.

"We are!" she gasped, obviously delighted. "Sit, sit, sit."

I pulled out a chair from the dining room table and realized this was one of Harry's pieces of furniture, and in a couple weeks it might not even be here. Strangely, or cruelly maybe, the realization thrilled me. I would find new furniture and get great material for my work—mercenary, but a refreshing change.

"It's not *just* that. Harry never wanted to try anything new, but that was food and going to new places as much as it was..."

"Positions," Natalie finished for me, elbow propped on the table and her chin in her hand.

Positions were barely the tip of the iceberg, but I shrugged and nodded.

I wasn't sneaky enough, and Natalie knew me too well. Her eyes narrowed and her grin grew sly. "*Scenarios,*" she purred, eyebrows waggling.

My flaming face and throat was answer enough.

Natalie laughed and relaxed in her seat. "Sunny, it's me. Don't be embarrassed. I've told you all about Theo's full moon appetite. If you think we aren't up to some kinky shit while my mom takes Emmie, you are underestimating me."

I knew Theo had Natalie chain him up in their reinforced basement, sometimes a generous amount of time *before* he shifted.

"Did you know before you met Theo that you would... enjoy that kind of thing?" I asked.

Natalie frowned in thought. "I mean...I guess not. I definitely hadn't considered the idea of chaining and collaring any previous boyfriends. I don't know that Theo really had with any of his partners, either, to be honest."

"I'm worried it's just...in my head. And that what I had with Harry really was *enough*."

Natalie shook her head and smiled softly at me, reaching across the table. "Sunny, babe, if it was enough, it would've felt like enough. Maybe not every day. There are moments where I think about what my life would be like if I'd run a little harder for being a designer. But a good chunk of the time I'm *really* happy, and I don't want things any other way but the way I have them."

I nodded and fiddled with a framed print. That sense of satisfaction had been rare and fleeting with Harry.

"Maybe…maybe you should just figure it out," Natalie said, her tone rarely delicate.

I stared at her and she stared back, her brown cheeks darkening just a touch.

"Figure it out?"

"Try," she said. "Try some of your fantasies. You have a week to spend away from here, right? I mean, you could come stay with us, if you wanted. Or your parents. Or take a cute trip for work. *Or*…you could see if this part of yourself you've been avoiding facing is a daydream or something you really want."

"I…I mean, I…"

That doesn't sound safe, I thought. But I hadn't told Natalie what I wanted.

To be claimed, chased, hunted. *So many ideas*, a little voice whispered.

But I couldn't just go on DateGrab and ask some stranger to lock me up and fuck me three ways from Sunday without potentially risking my safety. I'd given this enough thought to know that what I wanted was a delicious illusion. One I could walk out of if I wasn't enjoying myself.

"It just sounds dangerous," I admitted.

Natalie's gaze flared with curiosity, but I was surprised to see her take a deep breath and brace herself, thinking for a moment. She nodded slowly. "I see your point. But you're thinking about the general populace, right?"

I wrinkled my nose at the phrasing and laughed a little. "Uh, sure. Like…I'm not unwilling to have a one-night stand, but there's fucking and then there's—"

"Hire a professional," Natalie said, sitting up straight.

"A...a what?"

She snorted. "Hire a *professional*."

My jaw hung open. A *professional*. Hire a sex worker.

In spite of my blushing and my nerves, I was not ignorant. There were absolutely all kinds of services in the city for this sort of thing. Clubs. Agencies. The work had been legalized decades ago as more and more species had integrated into human society and brought with them their liberal views on sex, shifting the traditional human perspective with them.

"A werewolf would be great, actually," Natalie mused. "Not volunteering mine, but Theo said he used to be a member of this one..."

Natalie continued, but my ears were buzzing, my thoughts flying in a new direction. *This isn't even the first time you've really thought about this*, I admitted to myself, imagining a broad and massive figure over me, dark eyes glinting down, tusks gleaming.

"Ohhh, look at you."

I shook myself, and Natalie giggled. "Sorry, I was just—"

Just imagining being caught by a big, brutal, monster of an orc. I'd seen a few orcs and half-orcs in the city, doing mundane grocery shopping or meditating under massive trees in Lincoln Park. I didn't really have species-specific interests like some folks. A handsome vampire was as appealing to me as an attractive gargoyle. It was just that orcs tended to run...big. They featured in a lot of erotic content— naturally libidinous and impressively equipped. I'd only watched one, and it'd been tame, practically domestic, but the growls the orc had made and the way his huge hands spanned the woman's waist had taken up permanent resi- dence in my imagination ever since, although I'd rarely indulged in the fantasy.

"You know what you want, Sunny," Natalie said, smiling. "Give yourself permission to try it."

CHAPTER 2
Sunny

THE MONSTER SMASH Agency was located in the southern suburbs of Chicago—a bit surprising, considering the popularity of such places in the city. It had a near perfect five-star rating online and an overwhelming online catalog of workers.

It was one of only three places that offered an "immersive, curated experience." I'd stammered out my request over the phone, nervously outlining my desires to an absolute stranger, wanting to hang up at every second.

"We are perfectly prepared to provide everything you've mentioned," the young woman on the phone had soothed. "Your experience will be entirely at your discretion."

Now, sitting in the pretty office of the agency, with sun streaming in through a lovely stained glass window, a beautiful woman—a succubus, I suspected, based on her otherwordly beauty and delicate horns—smiled gently at me.

"You'll be able to stop, leave, or rest at any time. You have your safe word, as well as a remote that will assist you in controlling your scene or putting a stop to it altogether. You and your partner will be secluded, but we always assure our clients who ask for these kinds of dynamics of two things," the woman said, a familiar recitation for her. "First is that you will be able to reach us at any time via a number of security measures we offer you. And second is that your partner is a professional. If at any point you find yourself uncomfortable, unsatisfied, or frightened, *they want to know*. They want you to have a pleasant experience, regardless of what you've asked for. No matter how they behave in scene, their only goal is to offer what you desire."

I swallowed hard and nodded, my right hand holding down my knee to keep my heel from jiggling.

The woman—Astraeya, the name tag read—smiled sympathetically. "This is your first time, so your partner will be especially attentive to your boundaries. Five days is…it's quite a dive into the deep end."

I opened my mouth to answer but couldn't think of anything to say. The interview over the phone had been thorough as I'd made the appointment, but they'd told me the one in the office would be even longer. I couldn't decide if I wanted to stay here in this office, going over delicate logistics forever, or ask if we could skip the rest and let me dive into that deep end she'd mentioned.

"Then again, you have a great deal you'd like to accomplish," Astraeya added, grinning and glancing down at her notes. "First things first, no blood play."

"No, thank you," I gasped out.

"Do you still consent to your partner going without prophylactics?" she asked. "Both your test results are clean— I'll show you his—and you both have the necessary birth control."

She was so matter-of-fact, as if it could stop me from setting myself on fire with embarrassment. "Yes, I consent," I squeezed out.

"It really makes the most sense with orcs," she said, winking conspiratorially. She drew up a tablet from her lap and held it across the desk to me. "Now, I'm going to have you go through this file of images. You don't have to say whether you like something or not, although you are welcome to. It's not a bad idea to tell me if you aren't interested, though. Sometimes, the body has a different opinion than the mind."

She had another tablet in her hand, one that must've shown her what image I was looking at. So she was definitely a succubus, if she would be able to sense my interests without me saying so out loud.

I tapped the screen and bit my tongue at the first image, a massive green hand with lovely dark claws wrapped around a throat, squeezing gently.

"A bit," I breathed, and the succubus chuckled.

Bruises. Chains. Cuffs. A leash. Dildo. Butt plug. Just the mouth of an orc, tusks gleaming and protruding from thick, full lips. I stared a moment longer at that image, unable to understand *why* it made my whole body throb with need.

"Very?" I managed, my voice a little breathless.

Astraeya only nodded.

I tapped the screen and caught my breath, the sight of those black claws and thick fingers cupped possessively over a woman's pussy.

"Very," I squeaked out.

On and on it went. There was even a sequence of penises, each one larger than the last. Other obvious images—ropes, floggers, clamps, a handprint on an ass—were mixed in with more obscure but somehow equally arousing images like a moonlit forest, a barely dressed bed by a stone wall. I flipped through a few confusing inclusions of wine, a cheeseboard, and a candle, and then paused at the picture of an intricately arranged bathtub, full of flowers and dimly lit by candles. It was well out of the range of scenarios I'd asked for, but it *was* appealing.

"Very," I said lightly, looking up to meet Astraeya's approving smile.

THE MSA BUILDING was an attractive office, with plenty of windows and lots of greenery—not at all what I would've expected from the kind of place to hire out submissive captive fantasies. It was not, apparently, where said fantasies would be taking place.

Astraeya had offered to let me drive myself, but I'd opted instead to take the agency up on transport. My bright yellow suitcase, leather painted with strange and delicate daisies sprouting up from the base, was sitting cheerfully in the back of the black town car as we kicked up dust on a dirt road winding through the woods.

"You weren't kidding about secluded," I murmured, staring out the window and searching for any signs of civilization.

"Honestly?" Astraeya said, somewhat hesitant now. "It's not as secluded as it looks. But that's part of the experience, that sense of being alone with your partner, out of reach. I'm not supposed to spoil that for you, but—"

She paused and I waited, finally prompting her, "But?"

She grimaced slightly and offered me a sheepish, beaming smile. "You're *very* new to this. It's a big leap."

Two weeks ago, I'd been too embarrassed to tell my best friend my deepest, strangest desires. Now here I was, in a car with a stranger, feeling slightly embarrassed that I hadn't already acted on them. It was like Astraeya thought I was having sex for the first time. Except maybe that wasn't so far off.

"I just want you to know you're safe. You have a *really* good partner, so I know you're going to have an amazing time," Astraeya said.

My hands clenched on the skirt of my dress, my head whipping to stare at her. "You know him?"

Astraeya grinned, the car slowing. "Just from the office. And his reputation with clients."

I stared at her for another long, quiet moment, willing her to give me more information, but she said nothing until the car had stopped, the forest quiet around us.

"We're here," she said brightly.

Distracted from the mention of my *partner* for the week, I turned again and gaped at the sight before me. Being chased through the woods was one of my requests, and I'd halfway expected Astraeya to drop me off to be chased. Instead, we sat parked in front of a sweet cottage, with cream plaster and a thatched roof like something right out of a fairy tale. There was even a blooming vine crawling up the corners of the house.

"Appearances can be deceiving," Astraeya said coyly. "Come on, I'll get you oriented."

I licked my lips and hesitated. Astraeya had made sure to tell me that I could back out or cancel my appointment at any time, even once *everything* had started. For a moment, I considered asking her to drive me back to the office, to my car. I would lose the deposit for the session, but not the entire small fortune this was costing me, and Natalie would let me stay with her. Or better yet, I could go to a hotel with a nice spa package, like I should've done in the first place.

I pushed open the car door, while Astraeya already had my small suitcase in her hand from the backseat. I met her at the little door, and my eyes widened to see the keycode and smart screen rather than some antique knob and lock.

"Just go ahead and press your thumb to the screen. It's easier than us loading you up with a bunch of codes you have to remember," Astraeya said.

"Will I need to unlock the door?" I asked.

She shrugged. "Probably not, but we like for our clients to know that if they decide they want control of anything at any time, they can have it. You want to surrender and offer trust, and we want you to know that we take that very seriously. There, all set. In we go."

The inside was every bit as charming as the out, old-fashioned with softly grooved wood flooring and surprisingly tall ceilings. *Of course they're tall, because he's going to be...*

"Now, you'll see similar smart screens at every doorway," Astraeya pointed out. "You use your thumbprint there, and you'll be in contact with someone at the office. We don't monitor or invade your privacy, but we are always available if you need us. There, on the table, is a wrist cuff you can use similarly. It's up to you if you want to wear it. And finally, if at any time you speak your safe word, the agency will be monitoring just long enough to check on you, see if you need any assistance. Otherwise, you're not being monitored in any way. Again, these are offered as assurances to you, not as necessary safety precautions. Your partner's priority is your enjoyment and safety."

I nodded, absently noting all the details. The cottage was larger inside than I'd expected and incredibly cozy. There was sunlight streaming in through lace curtains, and in spite of the rustic table at the center of the room and the antique sink in the far right corner, there also was a very nice espresso machine and an updated stove. On my left, a massive dark blue velvet couch waited in the shadows. Ahead of me, a broad doorway revealed a darker room and the corner of an enormous four-poster bed.

"This...isn't quite what I was expecting," I admitted slowly, rushing to add, "It's totally lovely, I just—"

"Oh, this isn't all of it," Astraeya said with a wave of an elegant hand and a toothy grin. "I expect he'll save upstairs for your downtime. And actually, since we're getting closer to it being time, I should probably show you around downstairs real quick. Grab that wrist cuff. I'll set your bag down."

I lifted the small cuff—something like a smart watch—

from the large dining table set for two, and Astraeya put my suitcase down in the doorway of the bedroom.

The door to "downstairs" was tucked behind the vintage aqua fridge, and my heart thumped in my chest as Astraeya had me use my thumbprint again to open it. There was a light on below, but it was only enough to see by, enough to see the stone walls and bare floors. I stepped down slowly, watching the slow reveal of a long leather bench waiting in the bare room, a wall of paddles and floggers, and an enormous floor-to-ceiling mirror.

"More like what you were expecting?" Astraeya teased from behind me.

My mouth was dry now, so I swallowed again as we reached the end of the stairs.

"Good, we aim to please. But wait, there's more!" She stepped to my left, and I twisted to see a dark doorway behind the stairs. There was no light on inside, but I moved slowly closer, waiting for my eyes to adjust until finally I saw a glint of metal ahead of me, hanging from the ceiling.

Astraeya waited by the bench as I stepped inside the dark room, my arm outstretched. Metal clinked as I found the chains, my breath rushing in and out of my lips as if I'd been running, fingertips sliding into cold links.

"Your partner has your brief. He knows everything you're interested in and everything you're *not* willing to do. He'll start slow, take cues from you, ask questions, that sort of thing. It's totally up to you where you'd like to be when you meet him. It can be upstairs at the door, in the bed, or down here," Astraeya said, her voice so deceivingly simple, as if there weren't an enormous world of options, scenarios, mysteries in what she was saying.

"When does he get here?" I asked, a tremor in the words.

"Ten minutes. Do you have any questions, Sonya? Anything you need from me?"

I needed to know what would happen next. Would I enjoy

myself? Did my fantasies only make me wet and wanting when they were safely tucked away in my head? Was I strong enough to go through with this?

Astraeya couldn't answer any of those questions. I wrapped my fingers around the chains and turned slowly. There was more in this room, more I couldn't see in the dark. It seemed to go on endlessly. And there in the doorway was the little blue smart screen, waiting if I needed help, or if I was too scared.

"No, I'm ready," I said to Astraeya, forgiving myself for not really sounding so.

She smiled at me and nodded. "I'll leave you alone. You know how to reach us. And, Sonya…have fun."

CHAPTER 3
Khell'ar

I WAITED under the shade of one of the great old oaks in the woods, staring at the front door of the cottage. I'd watched Astraeya arrive with the woman—average height for a human female, with bright gold hair. A new client booking me for five days was surprising, if not strange, and I expected her to look more…prepared. There was no rule of thumb on what kind of person wanted an orc to hunt and ravish and fuck them until they couldn't stand. The lusty ones came in all appearances.

Still, the little cotton sundress, peachy pink against sun-flushed skin, was refreshing.

Astraeya, our succubus client relations manager, appeared in the doorway again, and I found myself somewhat surprised not to see the young woman—Sonya—with her. I stepped out from the shade of the oak, and Astraeya's eyes found mine immediately, a slight smirk on her lips as I bounded through the trees. She met me partway, out of view of the cottage windows.

"Is she really as new as her file says?" I asked.

"Nice to see you too, Khell," Astraeya quipped, glancing

back at the cottage over her shoulder with a puzzled smile. "And...yes, she is."

I nodded, bracing myself. "I'll tread lightly."

I was more patient and less inclined to follow mating urges than most of my kind and almost always assigned to the new ones. They spooked easily, and not all of them wanted to go through with their full requests. And those were the ones who booked me for a night, not nearly a *week*.

"Good. I like her, though," Astraeya said, her eyes narrowing at me, sizing me up. "She was very enthusiastic in her arousal gauges."

I'd seen the report. If the numbers were accurate, this human had the sexual appetite of an orc. But even so, they would be no guarantee of what she liked in person.

"I left her downstairs," Astraeya said.

I nodded and shrugged. "I'll find her." Even from outside the cottage, I could still catch a little tart whiff of her from the car.

"Khell...be careful with her," Astraeya said.

I frowned at the succubus. "I'm not Rezzik. I know not to scare the new ones."

Astraeya rolled her eyes. "I mean, yes, good, but... Look, if I'm right about her, you won't need to be careful for *her* sake. She's ready. She's practically orc bait. So just..."

Ah. I snorted and ground my jaw, my tusk pressing into my upper lip. "I've worked for MSA for eight years, Ast. I haven't mated a client yet. I won't start now."

Mating would be a death sentence for my work at the agency—work I actually enjoyed. Fucking was natural, fun, easy. The games some clients concocted were curious and not always to my own pleasure, but I could play the parts they needed. I had no interest in risking my place at MSA just for a more than usually agreeable human client.

Astraeya's lips pursed, and then she shrugged and turned

on her heel, heading back toward the town car. "Fine. Fair enough. Have fun. Be nice."

I grunted and watched the succubus get into the car and depart from the cottage. I glanced at my watch. I had three minutes. There was a small storage shed at the back of the cottage that was secretly a locker room for us partners. I ducked inside, frowning as the top of my head nearly brushed the ceiling.

The little human wanted primal play and to be my captive, and costumes were an unfortunate part of my job. No one wanted to be thrown over the shoulder of an orc in a gym hoodie, apparently. I shrugged out of my street clothes, tucking my watch into the pocket of my jeans, and scowled down at the outfit Astraeya had assigned me. A red shoulder cape and a miniscule leather armor skirt. It would've made more sense for an orc to charge into the cottage naked, but human women often found the size of our cocks overwhelming. Perhaps the flap of leather offered a reassuring disguise to the fact that I would fill them to the brim with my girth.

My phone chimed in the locker.

It was time.

I left the shed and walked softly around the cottage toward the front door. Most women waited nervously on whatever seating in the scene looked the most innocent, so I was surprised not to find the young woman perched on the blue velvet couch or anywhere in the main room. Next most likely was the bed, but even from here, I could see she wasn't inside the bedroom. Her yellow suitcase was still by the bedroom door, an artificial but not unpleasant floral fragrance emanating from inside.

She was downstairs.

Brave little human.

I rolled my shoulders and grinned at the open door to the basement. It would be a nice change of pace not to have to tiptoe too much at the start, make small talk. We would have plenty of time for that later, when she needed to be brought down from the high of our play.

Her scent was stronger on the stairs but still airy, not attached to any of the surfaces. I could hear the first whispers of her breath, quick and sharp, aware of my heavy footfalls on the steps. She wasn't in the room, not waiting on the bench, and my claws extended slightly, a rare sense of anticipation rising in me.

A flicker of shadow and a soft gasp called to me, and I turned to the open doorway to my left, my body tensing. There she was, deep in the shadow of the dungeon playroom. She was staring at me, brown eyes wide in a heart-shaped face, lips parted, no doubt assuming I was unable to see her in the dark. But my kind had keen eyesight from living in underground dens, and she was perfectly clear. I stepped slowly closer, watching her long fingers tighten around the chain in her grasp, her breasts heaving with her great gasps of breath, pressing to the collar of her dress.

I paused in the doorway, filling the frame and blocking some of the dim light, shadowing her slightly from my view. Her scent was rich now, growing stronger by the second, clinging in my nostrils and coating my throat in tangy arousal. That was a good sign. I was close enough to hear her heartbeat hammering, the catches of her breath soft and excited.

How to approach? New human partners liked to chatter nervously, to fill the silence as I stared at them like the predator they wanted to pounce. But this one, Sonya, only watched, waited.

"Take off your clothes. I have plans for you."

There was a squeak of sound strangled from her throat, and the chain in her hand rattled softly as she startled. For a second, I prepared to backtrack, give her another option like joining me on the bench, go over the usual introductions. And then her hand released the chain, twisting behind her back and arching her chest forward as she hunted for the zipper on her dress. Her eyes were still wide, searching in the dark for me, and a pretty red tongue flicked out to stroke over her bottom lip.

I flexed my hands to retract my claws.

Interesting. She was eager, but silent.

"You're mine for this week, pet," I said, my voice heavy and low, bouncing off the stone around us. I stepped back and reached to the wall panel, slowly drawing up the light in the electric candles positioned at the corners of the room. Her hands paused on her hips, heavy breasts still in her bra, with pert and tight nipples pressing to the lace, rounded stomach sucked in self-consciously. She was staring at me, pupils dark and full. "Five days to do whatever I like with you," I tried, wondering when or if she would want to break the scene.

They usually did on the first try.

But not this little treat of a human. Sonya pushed her dress over soft hips, catching her panties with her thumbs and taking them down too. She kicked her flimsy sneakers off with the dress and reached back to the clasp of her bra, holding my gaze.

I opened my mouth to tell her to lower her gaze but let out a growl as she dropped her bra. Those breasts were proper orc handfuls. I would feast on them later.

"What next?" Her voice was thin, breathy, but sweet too.

I had a number of ideas, many of which she'd suggested herself in her requests, but Astraeya's warning rang in my head. As ready as Sonya seemed, this was her first experience in submission. It was time to check in with her.

"What would you like, pet?"

She blinked and held still as I stepped close, close enough for the heat of my skin to stroke against hers. "I..." Her brow furrowed, and her lips pressed together as she arched to stare up at me. "I want you to tell me what to do," she said, with just a hint of a bite in her tone.

I chuckled at that. "Are you ready for chains, pet?"

Her frown eased slightly, head nodding, and she held her breath as my hand reached out to her. I moved slowly, waiting for any shrinking or retreat, but instead the pretty little human swayed in my direction, her hair stroking against my fingers, soft, golden, coiling around my hand.

"Arms up," I said, fighting my smile as her arms flew up over her head without so much as a pause. I grabbed up one slender wrist and fastened it into a padded cuff, using the pulleys to lift her arm high and taut, still resting on her feet but stretched fully.

Sonya leaned in, her chest brushing against mine, peaked nipples teasing lines against my chest. She whined and repeated her sway, pressing harder against me.

"Naughty pet," I warned, cupping her shoulder and pushing her back, letting my gaze glow down at her upturned face. "Hold still for your master."

She sighed as if relieved and nodded gently. Delightful. Untrained, but it would be so easy with her if she behaved so well all the time. I fastened her other wrist in another cuff, sliding it down so that the one MSA had given her was still available.

"You'll be able to reach that," I said, drawing her wrists together over her head, guiding her fingers to the smart watch. "And you can use your safe word."

She only held her breath and stared back at me.

If she had been a recurring client, or at least one new to me but not to the role of a submissive, I would've had her bent over, sucking on my cock, or riding it. Even now, it was growing thick, my blood called south by her scent, the sight of her, the way she held herself frozen and awaiting my instructions.

Orc bait, yes. Also a new client. Be careful.

I stepped slowly around her, rattling the chains hanging from the pulley system, watching the way the sound drew a shiver up her back. I flexed my hand again, drawing in the claws that wanted so badly to stretch and dig into her pretty flesh, leaving just the tips out to scratch carefully at her skin. I didn't sharpen my claws like some orcs, too risky in my work, but even dulled, my fully extended claws could do damage if I wasn't careful.

Sonya stretched up onto her toes and softened her upper body, arching into my touch, head falling back.

"Are you wet for me, pet?" I asked. I knew she was, I could smell it on her.

"Y-yes… Do I call you master?" she whispered, breaking out of that breathy surrender with a little squeak of nerves.

I grinned where she couldn't see me. Not usually right away, but since she was eager…"Yes, pet."

She sighed again, shoulders easing and body relaxing slightly. "Yes, I'm wet for you, master." She stumbled awkwardly over the word, some hesitance bubbling up.

My hand trailed down her ass, taking a firm grip, amused by the slight whimper she tried to bury. I slid my other hand over her shoulder, down her chest, to tweak at one nipple and then the other. She hummed, a soft and contented sound.

"Are you frightened, little pet?" She certainly didn't seem so.

"Not yet," she whispered, turning her head to glance at me out of the corner of her eye. Long, dark lashes kissed at her cheeks as she shivered and waited for my next move.

Play it safe, I thought. *Work up to her limits, don't try and find them from the start.* Except there was an energy surrounding this woman, almost feverish and impatient. And the predator in me, only allowed out in measured doses, wanted to make her jump and skitter as she ought to in my presence.

I checked my claws once more, just barely digging into the giving heft of her hip, before swiping my hand around to clasp over her pussy.

She jumped and jerked, rattling the chains above her head, as I growled in her ear. "Then open for me."

Her legs stumbled wide, toes stretching and digging into the floor as she made room for my thick fingers to stroke over folds of flesh, slightly slippery with arousal.

"Ohh!" She curved like a bow in my hands, one breast pushing against my left hand, softly curled golden strands brushing against my chest. Her eyes were wide, staring up at the cavernous ceiling. But she wasn't trying to escape my searching fingers that stroked against her sex, spreading her wetness. No, she was still eager.

Good.

I burrowed one finger against her, pressing to her opening without attempting to breach, and her eyes fell shut, that little furrow of concentration appearing on her brow again. Not quite an objection. Not surrender, either.

Perhaps I would need to draw it out of her slowly, so thoroughly, she would forget she had designed the games at all.

I was a patient orc. Surely, I would be the victor.

CHAPTER 4
Sunny

THE ORC'S skin was velvety and hot at my back, almost like suede, and I wanted to rub myself against him just to prove to myself he existed. One thick finger was circling around my cunt, teasing, and his massive hand was cupping over my breast, and it was almost like he wasn't really *here*. Like I might breathe or twitch and he would evaporate. I'd itched to be touched as I'd stood alone in this room, and now, with him here…

Some of the fever was cooling slightly with reality.

This is just…foreplay, I thought. *I mean, aside from the chains, Harry could've—*

The finger that had been teasing my entrance plunged suddenly in, drawing a garbled little moan from my mouth.

Well. Harry's fingers couldn't compete with the orc's, at least.

"Tight little hole," the orc muttered, pumping the shockingly thick finger inside of me.

I leaned back at last, my head tucked beneath his chin, and stared down myself at the dim and blurry view of his hands on me, gentle and impressively large. And yet…

Maybe what you want really is too strange, I thought. The touch felt good, but not exciting, and the orc behind me wasn't much more than pleasantly warm and fragrant furniture, smelling like the woods I'd arrived in.

Suddenly, the touch stopped, both hands pulling away abruptly with the orc, leaving me stumbling slightly. His hand caught my hip, fingers still damp from being inside of me. I gasped as he spun me, the chains twisting above me and forcing me to go taut and high on my toes.

The orc's eyes were black with fine points of golden fire in the center, and they glared down at me, the harsh angles of his face barely visible by the candlelight in the corners of the large room—much larger than I'd originally guessed, with curious shadows farther off.

"Tell me, pet," he said.

I blinked at him, certain I'd missed the question. "Wha—I am…wet?"

He scoffed down at me, and I was surprised by the almost nutty whiff of his breath, unusual but not unpleasant. I'd known the features of orcs from passing them in the city, but I'd never touched one before, never had one focusing on me so intently that the glow of their gaze widened in their eyes and seemed to scratch sparks on my skin.

"*Tell me*," he repeated in a warning growl, head tipping.

Perhaps there was more to orcs than their physicality, because the fix of his eyes on me seemed to draw the words out.

"This is too…"

"Too much? You are uncomfortable?" One hand reached up to loosen the chains.

"No!" I cried, and his bare brows relaxed slightly. "No. I just expected this to be more…intense, and it's not yet. Which is fine, it's very nice—"

"Nice," the orc repeated.

My mouth hung open as my eyes freed themselves from the lock of his gaze to glance around the room. I was naked, chained, in a dark and not *too* drafty dungeon. Maybe nice *wasn't* the right term.

"You're being very gentle, careful, with...touching and, you know, um, fingering me," I said, my voice tightening to a squeak.

"You want my cock?" he asked plainly.

What I wanted now was to be let loose so I could dress again and go hide somewhere. But if I did that, I would never really accomplish the whole point of this week.

I opened my mouth to try and sort out what it was *I was* trying to ask for, but he spoke again. "No, I see. You want to be my little pet," he said, voice lowering to a rumble. Dull, hard tips of claws peeked out from his fingertips on my hip and dug in, drying my mouth. His free hand reached up and grabbed at my hair, tugging slightly and capturing me in his hold, rough and firm, offering me no choice but to be a captive in his grip.

My heart began to drum.

"You want to serve me," he continued in that wonderfully low, vibrating tone. "You're too small for my cock, pet, so something must stretch you. But if you don't like my fingers—"

"I like them fi—"

"Hush," he snarled, and I gasped, a perverse and giddy joy rising in me as he twisted the fist in my hair, a little bite of pain in the burn of my scalp. "You do as I say now."

Yes, a soft voice in my head sighed.

I pressed my lips shut and nodded.

"Good pet," he said with a huff, and I thought I saw his lips twitch, but it was too dark to tell for certain. His hand on my hip patted me and then reached up, yanking the chains and making me yelp as they tightened, leaving me now barely touching the floor, the stretch intense, aching, satisfying. "Stay," he added, shaking me by my hair slightly, then releasing me and sinking back into the shadows.

My breaths came fast again, my cunt hot and breasts aching to be touched. "Master?" I called weakly, wavering on my toes and my eyes digging through the dark, strangely convinced I was seeing more movement than ought to be there.

"Needy little thing," the orc's voice growled from the dark.

I held my breath till he reappeared from the shadows, sighing as that golden gaze glinted at me. And then the object in his right hand caught the light, glistening slickly, and my eyes widened.

"What is—"

"You don't want my fingers," the orc said, throwing a pillowed platform to the floor at my feet and waving the ridiculously large and tapered dildo in his hand, clearly well lubricated. The head was a normal size, but it grew significantly larger down its length into a thoroughly intimidating fist bulb at the base.

"I didn't say I didn't—Mphm!"

Two thick fingers were stuffed into my mouth, dull claws catching my tongue and pinning it down. He tasted clean, a little salty, and my mouth sucked on his digits automatically, eagerly. Warmth bloomed in my core under his gaze.

"You need to be stretched. Show me you can be good and ready yourself for me. Get this wet with your cunt down to the base," he said, waving the dildo in my face. "And get me slick with your mouth down to my root, pet."

The awkwardness of minutes ago was gone now. *This* was what I'd wanted. And it didn't feel strange at all. It wasn't even very frightening. I was calm—calm and desperate at the same time.

"Yeth, mather," I mumbled around the fingers in my mouth, licking them greedily just to prove that I could do the task he'd set before me—give or take that dildo. Surely he didn't mean the *whole* thing. That suede texture of his skin was a little unusual against my tongue, abrasive one way, soft the other.

The orc hummed thoughtfully for a moment, glaring at me, and then nodded, pulling his fingers free of my lips. He knelt, pressing the dildo to the platform, tugging me to stand with my legs spread, feet barely balanced on either side. He paused there, his eyes focused on the stretched V of my thighs briefly before darting up to meet mine.

"You do as I say," he said, almost casually.

I nodded.

"Knee up."

My heart stopped for a moment, but my right knee went up to his shoulder.

He leaned in, broad nose and jaw pressing into the skin of my sex, hot breath huffing into my pussy. My lips were parted on a pant as I stared down at him just breathing me in, the smooth and firm press of his tusks framing my folds perfectly. I couldn't see it from above, but I moaned as a slick, scorching hot, *long* tongue stroked against me, teasing my opening again as his finger had.

"Pretty little cunt," he whispered, as if he were speaking to it directly rather than me, praising just one part of me in particular. He licked again and then folded his lips around a crease of skin and sucked on it like a kiss. My leg holding me up trembled, my arms growing sore from the stretch, but as gentle as he was being, I wouldn't have interrupted him for the world.

Harry had certainly never done *that* before. Sure, he'd gone down on me, even seemed to enjoy himself, but he'd never done so with such private reverence.

The orc mirrored the kiss on another fold, took a last lick, and then just as I thought I might go completely limp and use his face as a real seat, he pulled away.

His tongue, a dark shade of brown, was cleaning up his lips as he rose, not paying any attention to my whimpers or trembles, as he reached up to the chains with one hand and wrapped the other around my waist. I sagged into him as he loosened the chains, rubbing my cheek over the velvet of his chest as he lowered me to the...

Directly onto the dildo, which nudged almost rudely at my warm and tingling cunt, more insistent and clumsy than the orc's wonderful tongue had been. He folded my knees up to the platform, settling me in my seat and testing the height of the chains.

"Do I get to use my hands, master?" The name was still awkward on my tongue every time I used it and felt more like playacting than the chains or his mouth on my cunt.

"No." And then he stood again, and I understood the need for the platform. He was too tall for me to kneel on my own and still suck on his cock, but now my face hovered in front of his crotch, barely covered by the flippant little leather skirt he wore, massive thighs on either side of my cheeks. Large hands in front of my face reached for the clasp of the skirt belt. His thighs were radiating heat, and I wanted to press myself to their muscles, seeking warmth and more of that soft, dense texture of his skin.

And then the leather parted, and I sat back, notching the head of the toy inside of myself as I gaped at the cock in my face. It was not quite as thick as the bulb at the base of the dildo but certainly much larger than anything I'd navigated before. I wasn't sure I'd even be able to—

"Open." The orc stepped closer, and the smell of him here at his cock was rich and sharp as a leaf pile and just a hint nutty, like his breath had been.

My mouth seemed to press shut even tighter in response to the order, and claw-tipped fingers reached out to grip my chin, lifting it up until those fire spots in his black eyes were staring down at me.

"Pet. Ride the cock beneath you and *open your mouth*."

Of the two, the dildo was less intimidating, especially

since the snarl of the orc's voice only made me wetter as he glared down at me. The platform I knelt on was padded, allowing me to sink in and holding me steady as I bared down on the silicone until I felt it pinch and stretch at me. The orc's fingers tightened on my chin as I rose up again and opened my mouth at last, leaning in and licking around the broad, rounded head of his cock.

The bite of salt and the flavor of dark, bitter walnuts pooled on my tongue, and I hummed. He just barely fit between my lips, and he was only an inch or two in before my jaw and gag reflex started to protest at my mouth being so full. I pulled away with a gasp and stared at the length before me. I couldn't swallow that cock—it would kill me, surely? But I could be creative.

I'd forgotten about the toy I was seated on in my focus on the orc before me, twice as menacing now as he loomed above me.

"If you don't stretch your pretty cunt for me, we'll never get anywhere, pet," the orc growled, his bright tusks creating a false curve to his lips.

I glared back up at him and stretched my mouth open wide, tongue flat, leaning in to lick up the underside of his cock, bouncing myself on the dildo slightly. It felt a little fruit-less. I didn't have hands to help me with my work, or even to touch myself and ease the way down the dildo, and I wasn't aroused enough yet for the stretch to be anything but a sting.

The orc's hands reached out, his eyes sparking above me as thick fingers clasped around my throat, just tight enough for me to feel my own pulse drum against his digits.

"Shall I teach your body to take me?" he asked.

Goose bumps broke out over my skin as I nodded and relaxed slightly, pressing my mouth to the head of his cock and suckling slightly before pulling away to say, "Please, master."

The orc released a low rumble of approval, and his hands

pushed down against the slope of my neck, a strange tension I hadn't even noticed unwinding now that he had me in his grasp. The pinch shifted into a pleasant ache, and he arched his hips forward, sliding his cock against my lips. I suckled as it slid to the corner of my mouth, against my cheeks, covering every inch of thick length with sloppy kisses.

There was an unfamiliar structure beneath the velvet skin my lips and tongue teased, almost like the cock was moving within its own sleeve, a pulsing pump sliding up and down, and I was immediately curious as to how it would feel inside me. Interest eased my path another inch on the dildo, and I moaned as one of the bulbs seemed to lodge inside of me, pressing against my core.

"Your greedy cunt will be so full by the time I'm done with you, my pet, my prize." The orc's voice had a resonance as it grew deeper, two rich tones at once bouncing off the stone, pricking at my skin.

He started to lean away, the pressure of his hands easing on my shoulders, and I chased him immediately, raising myself up the dildo again, whimpering and swaying as the thick bulb pulled free. My mouth was hunting for the base of his cock, my lips tingling from the soft friction of his skin, hairless even over the incredibly large and rounded sac hanging at his base.

There was a sticky streak against my cheek, and I rooted against his rigid base with my eyes closed, equally self-conscious about my own shameless endeavor as I was...

...relieved.

A claw dug against my pulse, and my eyes opened on another moan, mouth open wide to try and envelop as much of him as I could.

"I'll teach that throat to take me too, pet. I'll teach your lungs to wait for my pleasure."

I sank back onto the dildo, down past the stretch I'd already embraced, the orc's cock rubbing and now streaking my other cheek with richly fragrant precum. He pushed hard on my shoulders, and I cried out, eyes widened and body rocking as he forced me onto the next width of the dildo.

"Look down, pet," he growled.

I glanced down from the weeping head of his dark cock to see that there was only one width left to take, although the sight of my body stretched taut against its shape made the feat seem impossible.

To distract myself from the challenge, I surged back up, wrapping my mouth around the orc's cock, fixing my gaze to his as I worked myself on the dildo and sucked roughly. He rumbled, hips flexing forward just a bit, and this time, he sank in against my tongue slightly easier, my eagerness easing the shock of his girth.

"What a hungry pet," the orc rasped, and my whole body warmed at the praise, heat stirring and pooling in my cunt. "Untrained," he added, and now my blush was scorching.

The idea that I might be *trained* to please a man like the orc was so outrageous, so outside the world I'd retreated from for the week, that it made me feel as though I'd fallen out of my own life and into this moment—as much the orc's invention as it was mine, because the sharpness of reality made even the simplest of my fantasies vivid and electric.

I ignored my own protesting reflex and forced the orc's cock to the back of my throat, that fire in his eyes flaring.

"Suck, pet, swallow me."

The suggestion was impossible, but it made me sing around him, saliva slipping onto his skin the same way slick arousal now coated the dildo I fucked myself onto urgently. I tried to hollow my cheeks but he was already filling them, tried to pull him deeper into me but there was nowhere left to go. A warm thread of precum leaked down my throat, working like some kind of spell to halt the gagging. I whimpered at my own inability to do more than the remarkable act I'd already managed.

"Beg for my help," the orc murmured, the words twining around me in that strange, layered voice of his.

I couldn't beg, not stuffed like this. My jaw ached and my lungs were already tight, my arms numb. But I bobbed myself onto his cock, eyes weeping as I gazed up at him, seeing only the sparks of his stare, the dense muscle of his arms rising into shadows, the ridged planes of his stomach flexing and jumping with every weak suckle of my lips.

He pushed forward and my eyes widened, body protesting the force even as my brain begged for him to conquer me. But his hands were cupped around the back of my neck, fingers flexing down to my shoulders, pushing me down to the floor at the same pace that he pressed himself into my mouth, head breeching my throat, more of that silky rich fluid soothing what surely should've been agonizing pressure. That pumping sensation inside of his cock was more obvious inside of my mouth, a complementing and contrasting pace to his own subtle thrusts of his hips.

There were only a few inches of his cock left to take, and I tried to soften my body, willing myself to swallow him, to burrow my nose to his base. But the orc knew my limits and my potential better than I did. His hands pushed me down, my arms stinging from a new stretch, thighs burning as I splayed wide, and the shocking explosion of an orgasm as the lips of my sex reached the base of the dildo and the final bulb pressed roughly into every inch of my opening.

I couldn't scream, not with my lips gagged by lovely, thick, velvety cock, but I heard the chains rattle above me as I shook, pinned in position by my full cunt and mouth. The heat surged through me, soft fire licking up my chest, right up into my cheeks where clawed thumbs were stroking, gentle scratches.

"Good little pet, so soft and wet for me now, so ready."

In the storm and bliss of the orgasm I'd forgotten there

would be more, but it came back with the lovely bloom of aftershocks.

I wanted my orc's cock. It was drawing free of my slack mouth, my tongue and lips and throat feeling not stretched and sore, but soothed as if I'd received a very specific and thorough massage. I licked my lips, found more of that rich and salty flavor at the corners, and blinked my eyes. I rocked my hips slightly and panted at the flutter of pleasure that came with the rub of the bulbs inside of me.

In front of my nose, the orc's cock was producing a thin dribble of fluid, pulsating with that internal pump.

I rose up, whining as the dildo seemed to retract out of me with the pulse of the bulbs against my opening. The orc's fiery stare was warm, almost orangey now, my eyes having adjusted enough to the darkness to see him more clearly. The blunt nose, nostrils flaring around a golden ring through his septum, sharp high ears also lightly decorated in gold, incredibly broad and angular features, a braid of hair drawing back from his skull, sides shaved. If he were a human man, he would not be considered handsome, I supposed, but he was stunning to me—feral and furious and hungry for me.

In the back of my head I knew this was a calculated game, that I had paid this orc to be here with me, to fuck me, to chain me and teach my body to accept his. I was equally sure in this moment that I'd pleased or impressed him in some way and that he wanted to fuck me. That pumping cock, dribbling onto my bare breasts, was enough of an indication, even if his expression weren't.

What we'd done was just foreplay, overwhelming and thorough. I wanted more.

I licked my lips again, searching for the last traces of his flavor, and then gave my orc an order. "Fuck me, master."

CHAPTER 5
Khell'ar

MY SNARL WAS loud in the quiet that followed the young woman's words. My cock ached, the stav pulsing in the shaft of my cock thrusting emptily and wasting my seed on Sonya's breasts.

My next task was meant to be nurturing, to check in with her and soothe the muscles I'd abused in the act. Her lips were wet from the little licks she'd been using to gather my taste, and on the floor, the toy used to prep her was glistening.

The altar and oil was waiting. I was in charge of our scene. She was *new*, needed to be eased—

"Please," she gasped, leaning forward and rubbing her breasts against my leg. "Please, fuck me."

My left hand stole the chains up in a firm grip as I bent and whipped my free arm around her ribs, dragging her up from the platform as I pulled the chains at the same time.

She gasped, but her legs bracketed me, clenching on my waist as if she were afraid I might drop her...or deny her. I did neither, fumbling only as long as it took to line her up at the head of my cock, then thrusting myself inside of her.

The stretcher had done the work of preparing her for me,

but my little pet still let out a high cry as I filled her, her head falling back and exposing her throat to my gaze, long and elegant and thrumming with a nervous pulse.

"Hold onto your master," I rumbled. "I plan on using that sweet cunt to completion."

Her arms were weak from the lack of blood flow, the chains cold as she draped her limbs over my shoulder. I moved my hands to her thighs, pulling them away from me, letting her feel for a moment just how vulnerable she was in my grip. She didn't have the strength in her arms to push me away, and I had her by the backs of her thighs near her knees. I lifted her up, my stav pumping furiously, and watched her eyes widen as gravity dropped her back down my length, helpless.

"Oh god, *yes*." She sighed, her stomach flexing as she tried to ride me, and she moaned as my stav stroked inside of her, fast and urgent, uneven with my slow and deep thrusts.

She was lovely heat and soft flesh and the sweetest voice begging.

"More, master. Please, master. Harder, master."

I should've pulled her off my length and taken her mouth again, taught her not to make demands in a game where I was meant to be conquering her. But her desire was sweet in my ear, and it was…refreshing not to be the villain. Most of my female clients wanted to fight, to resist, to be forced into their surrender. This little human wanted the latter, to be fucked, to be used, but she couldn't hide her own pleasure and eagerness, didn't even bother trying.

"Fuck, your *cock*," she gasped, falling suddenly forward, pressing her forehead to my jaw and breathing deeply, arms twining closed, chains clinking together. "God, it feels so good."

I growled in her ear, her new position easier to manipulate, my hands slamming her up and down my cock, giving into those pleas she'd issued. Harder, faster, chains rattling and skin slapping, until my stav and thrusts were at the same pace in opposite directions, the friction wild and addictive, even for me.

Dull crescent nails dug into the dense skin on my shoulder as Sonya let out a high, thin whine of steady delight, limp and pliable in arms, breaths hiccuping with every collide of our hips. My stav was growing thicker, swelling in its stiff sleeve, and Sonya's breath was hot and damp on my shoulder, her tongue flicking out to taste me.

"Filled or showered in cum, little pet?" I rasped out, although if I had my way she would be both before the end of the day.

"Yes," she gasped out, nails digging in deeper, hips twitching as if to meet me.

I chuckled in spite of myself, a thrumming purr rising up from my chest. Orc bait.

As pretty as this little golden human would look dripping in my seed, I couldn't leave the sanctuary of her cunt so soon, not when it sucked and begged around my swelling stav, clinging to my length and weeping its pleasure down to my sac.

"Oh god, I'm going to come again," she gasped in warning, as if only just realizing that her core was licking and fluttering around me.

"Yes, little pet, your cunt wants to please its master. Come for me and suckle my cock just like your mouth did," I snarled into her ear, grinning into the dark as she trembled and tensed in my arms. My claws were leaving pinprick bruises on the soft flesh of her thighs as I tossed her up and down my cock.

She drew her own orgasm out at my words, clamping down around me and burying her wet cry against my shoulder. Her cunt tightened around my stav, and the pressure of pleasure exploded with a bellow of relief, my cock pumping into her, silky heat rewarded with a flood of release until it seeped out again, leaking around my base and coating her inner thighs. I wrapped an arm around her hips, pulling her firmly against me as she shook, and I groaned into her fine, silky hair, a surprising amount of tension bleeding out of me with my release.

The woman in my arms sighed, head drooping down to my shoulders.

"God, that was good. Thank you," she said, voice soft and relaxed.

I hummed and patted the hip my arm was holding. "We're not done yet, pet," I said, surprising myself. We *could* be done, at least for a rest and a bit of aftercare, but now that I'd had her once, I wanted her again. And this was our game, wasn't it? I would use her at my whim, never mind that she could call a halt to our act at any moment.

She leaned back just enough to catch my eye, a lazy smile stretched across her lips, eyes heavy-lidded with pleasure. "Oh, good."

A growl ran through me at her easy acceptance, and I stepped back before the rattle of chains reminded me that I was *working*, had to be mindful and not surrender to natural impulse. I reached my free hand behind me and searched carefully for the cuff releases, finding them and letting the chains clatter free. I drew one of Sonya's hands around and was pleased to see only light markings on her wrists— nothing that would bruise after a good massage.

"What's next?" she asked, eyes still on my face.

"Hush, or I will fill your mouth again," I said, checking her other wrist. Out of the corner of my eye I could see her mouth open again, lips twitching, but then she closed it shut and relaxed against my chest as she had been. That was unusual too, sweetly intimate and familiar for barely an hour into our appointment.

I glanced at the altar at the far end of the room and then grew greedy. She would be too high up for me to mount, and

I was partial to the way she clung to me. I moved us into the other room, her body still wrapped around mine.

"I just realized you're not growing soft," she murmured, eyes widening slightly.

"I told you I wasn't finished with you," I said, arching a brow. An orc's cock only flagged without stimulation, and there was nothing unstimulating about the sweet and coated heat of this woman's cunt.

It was brighter in this room, her hair sparkling slightly in the golden light, skin dewy with sweat. I straddled the bench and sat, waiting for a moment as she shifted on my lap, squirming on my cock, her lips parted and breath growing short.

"I didn't know that meant..." She trailed off, eyelids sliding shut as her toes grazed the floor and she used the leverage to ride me with shallow thrusts for a moment. My stav responded, pumping slowly in my cock. "Oh, god —master—I..."

"Khell'ar," I said, ducking my chin to hide my grimace.

"Khell'*ar*," she moaned, taking my name onto her tongue without question, her riding growing a little more ambitious. My hands tightened on her hips to help her pace for a few more moments before I remembered my work.

I slid my hands up around her waist, over her ribs, to squeeze and grope her breasts briefly before settling on her shoulders. "Lie back, pet," I said, not waiting for her to obey but pushing her backwards.

She fell back easily, not fighting my order or my touch in the slightest. Such surrender. She sighed and stretched, voice hiccuping as I hooked her thighs and fastened her close to my hips so that I wouldn't slip out of her. In truth, I should've retreated to offer the massage her arms needed, but even now she was rocking and twisting on my length and I didn't have the willpower to resist fucking her, at least with my stav, not when her body was begging for me.

I reassured myself that I was not thrusting into her, only letting my stav pump slowly. I bent forward, digging my fingers into her shoulders, working them in slow and thorough circles up to her neck.

"Ohhhh, that's lovely," Sonya moaned, hips moving a little more quickly.

I reached one hand down and swatted at her inner thigh. "Enough, or I will pull out. You will be fucked when I say you will."

I would've like for us both to be fucked right then, preferably with her ass high and beckoning my palm to turn it red and tender, but she needed ministered to right now, a balance to the demand of the chains she'd asked for.

"Yes, master," she said softly, blinking up at me and stilling.

It was only a moment more, and her eyes were falling shut again, the subtle shifting of her body increasing with her breaths, sucking in as my stav thrust forward, breathing out with a little whine as it retreated to her opening. I left her to it this time, focusing first on dragging my hands up and down one arm, loosening the joints and encouraging her blood flow.

This was usually the part I enjoyed most, when the tension had finally passed and my client relaxed under my care. The sex was the work, and I preferred to remain in my head, concentrating on the mechanics and the performance. Or at least, I always had before.

My hands drifted under Sonya's back, digging into muscle, working my way down to her tense hips, her legs trembling over my thighs. If I paid any attention to that red and swollen clit at her center, I would have her coming around my length again. The thought drew out a growl from my chest, and Sonya shuddered and moaned on my lap, blinking up at me.

"Please," she whispered.

"You rush too much," I answered, but my grip was tight on her body, my thumbs digging into the tender crease of her hips, my stav starting to swell inside of her, even at its slow pace. My claws were out again, seemingly incapable of remaining sheathed when my hands were on this woman. Their tips marked lines like arrows on her pelvis, and I realized too late that I had underestimated Sonya's sensitivity.

My stav was in a downstroke, pressing to her front walls, my thumbs just brushing against her outer lips, when she arched and clamped around me in a fresh orgasm that seemed to shock us both. I snarled as she shook and squeezed around my cock, arms flying back behind her head to brace against the edge of the bench.

I released one hip, slapping my palm against Sonya's spread sex, and even I wasn't sure if it was meant to be a punishment or a reward, the sharp and sudden stimulus to her clit, but she screamed and arched, grinding urgently against my hips.

I was meant to be in control, meant to be measured, to be moving forward with our games gently. Did she mean to make it impossible? If so, I would leash her more tightly in the future. But not now.

Now, my cock burned with the urge to thrust. I lunged forward, hooking my arms beneath Sonya's knees and bending her for my use, fucking her roughly from above.

"Oh, god, yes!" she cried, just as the first subtle knife of caution tried to cut through my thoughts. It vanished with her words, her eyes wide and mouth slack with relief, breasts shaking with the force of my thrusts.

She was natural, lustful, and sexual. *She was perfect.* And I was pleasing her, serving her even as I used her like a toy for my own appetite. I let the haze of covetous hunger rise in me for the first time in years, just a fraction, and growled. I slid my clawed thumb to her clit and tortured it with rough swirls. She came again with a shout, strangling my swollen stav, strangling my cock, and somehow my own breath too.

We'd barely begun our work. I had five days to use this woman in every way she would let me, and the ideas began to stir faster now in my head, her wishes and my own cravings mingling. But first, I would surrender with her.

I dove down, releasing her legs to let them twine around my broad frame, and gripped her face in my free hand, still working her clit with my other. Her mouth opened on a cry and then was full of my tongue, my roar of satisfaction, stroking and releasing into her lips as I did the same into her sex. She moaned and suckled my tongue, tying her legs as tight as she could around my back and milking my swollen cock of the last of my seed.

The last of it for the moment, at least. I would have more use of her—*need of her*—soon. Of that, I had no doubt.

CHAPTER 6
Sunny

I WOKE on the mattress of the four-poster bed. Light filtered through linen curtains pulled shut, and the first thing I noticed was the padded cuff around my ankle as I tried to roll. It held me in place and my breath hitched, my tender sex giving a surprising clench of pleasure that refreshed my memory of the rather stunning orgasms I'd already had.

And so many.

I turned my face into the pillow beneath my cheek and sucked in a deep breath, grinning against the fabric. I'd done it. I'd...I'd *loved it*. From the sound of the chains, to the bite of his claws in my flesh, to the growl of his voice as he'd told me how to behave. To the incredible, explosive, toe-curling and muscle-straining pleasure as I'd come on that magical cock.

Secret moments of touching myself to these thoughts, finding guilty release in fantasies and not my actual partner, had not just been something to imagine, to cope with boredom, but real cravings. I'd wasted years—for Harry and for myself—but not a lifetime.

Water rushed nearby and I twisted slowly, searching the room. There was a wide, tall doorway left of the bed, and the orc—Khell'ar—was there, kneeling on a woven bathmat by a deep claw-footed tub. There was a set of leaning shelves on the other side of the tub by the wall, with a couple bouquets of wildflowers, two burning candles, and an impressive array of bath products. The orc chose from the selection confidently, pulling up a pretty cut glass jar, and poured in a generous amount to the tub.

I hadn't been very lucid when he'd brought us up from the basement, and he'd kept my face tucked against his shoulder. I vaguely recalled him placing me on the bed and starting another massage, this one working its way up my weak legs, but I'd been out before the cuff had been fastened around my ankle. It was strangely reassuring there now. I was trapped, unable to leave the cottage or even the bed. Maybe it would've, *should've* sent me into a panic, but instead, it made the moment simpler.

I had to remain in bed until Khell'ar came and released me. Remaining in bed meant remaining relaxed, idle. I could call for him, or even use the cuff on my wrist to reach MSA, but I was safe and this mattress was perfection, and there was an orc in the next room drawing me a bath. I was a little hungry, with just a bit of a hollow sensation in my core, but that was all.

"Are you sore?" he called, not turning his head.

The sound of his voice, so casual now, missing the growls and the sharp stare, still left me blushing.

I sat up, amused by the tucked in blankets around me and then slightly startled by my own nudity. When I looked back to the bathroom, he had twisted to stare at me.

"I'd thought I would be, but...no, not really." I certainly should've been. Harry'd never been very aggressive in sex, but he'd had passionate moments and I'd been sore after sex with him a few times, especially early in our relationship.

Khell'ar let out a satisfied grunt and nodded, rising from his crouch. His chest was still bared, but he was now wearing a pair of tight black athletic pants that served as a beautiful reminder for the incredible girth and length of cock that had been pounding into me just—

What time was it? I searched the room, but there was no clock in sight and I wasn't sure if I'd had a short nap or slept through the night. I hoped it wasn't the latter. I didn't want my first day to be over already.

Khell'ar reached the bed and plucked the blankets away from my chest, throwing them down the bed and exposing me to his stare. "Spread your legs, pet."

Were we still playing or was this—? I hesitated too long, and his hand grasped my leg closest to him, pulling it to hang over the edge of the bed.

You could tell him to stop, I thought as his eyes fixed to my sex. I pursed my lips flat, and he hummed, gaze hooding with satisfaction.

"I said I wasn't sore."

His eyes weren't as vivid in daylight, and it was easier now to see the way his irises spread brightly out in dark orbs, shades of gold and copper. "You said, not *really*. Women spend too much time pretending to be comfortable."

The hand that had grabbed my thigh slid up as he held my stare until two fingers were thrusting gently into me, my lips parting and chest rising quickly with harsh breaths. His touch was clinical inside of me, apparently checking for any damage from his roughness earlier, but I was busy watching the subtle shifts of his face. It was so muscular that I thought it must've been capable of more expressive movement, but instead seemed to hide information better. Still, he relaxed slightly and pulled his hand free of me just before I released a whine of need.

I sagged, and this time I fought any begging as he moved around the bed to the cuff that had fastened me to the bottom right poster of the bed.

"We're going to put 'master' and 'pet' away for an hour at

least now," he said, releasing me. "But I'm still in charge, so far as you grant me. Do you prefer Sonya, or—"

"Sunny," I said immediately. Almost no one had called me Sonya, no one I was close with at least. Harry had preferred my real name, even after meeting my family, who'd been shocked at the sound, as if my mother had forgotten what she'd named me in the first place. "And you're Khell'ar," I said, trying to catch the almost rhythmic pause in the middle.

He opened his mouth briefly and then shut it again, nodding. "Come, Sunny."

Except he didn't hold a hand out in offering but simply grabbed me by my thighs, dragged me to the foot of the bed, and hauled me up into his arms. He was a wonderful combination of hard with muscle and soft with that velvety skin of his, and my arms felt familiar already around his shoulders, my breasts warm against his hot chest. His pointed ear was at my eye level, and he held me to his hip as if I were a toddler, the pressure of him between my legs just a bit too good.

His left eye traveled to the far corner and he had a predator's periphery vision, perfectly able to see me blushing as I realized that I was already eager to have him inside me again.

"Why *aren't* I sore?" I asked him. It made no physical sense. He was huge and incredible inside of me. I'd had to *stretch* myself to take him, and that final width of the dildo had hurt. But now, I felt fine.

His lip curled slightly in the corner. "Orc cum."

My mouth dropped open as he ducked, lowering me too, upon entry to the bathroom.

"I...I'd never... I didn't know that," I said slowly, processing. My eyes narrowed. "It's... What is it doing?"

Was it making me bigger? Or—

He shrugged slightly. "Helping, healing, making you ready for more. Keeping you slick."

I twisted my face well out of his keen sight at the memory

of arousal and cum sliding out of me, out around his cock and down my thighs.

"You like it." It was a statement, not a question. Because he didn't need to wonder. I'd made it plain already.

"Yes," I whispered. For the first time since he'd broken through my initial nerves, I wanted to run from the scene. I was thinking about his cum in a way I definitely never had with anyone else *ever* before. Like it was a treat. Like I wanted it sliding down my throat and pumping into my cunt and covering my skin, in my hair. With a sudden, startling new thought, I twisted, digging my fingers into his shoulders and catching his eye again. "Does it affect my brain?"

The orc's eyes went wide, those wonderfully heavy features of his failing to hide his surprise, and he let out a loud shot of a laugh, head falling back. Oh, his throat was thick, and I had the warring impulses to rub my cheek against the tendons and muscle, or sink my teeth in.

"Your hunger for orc cum is no fault of mine," he said through heavy laughter. He pulled me away from him without effort and dropped me into the perfectly hot but not scorching water of the bath with a movement just shy of a *plop!*

I'd been too busy being humiliated by our conversation to take a good look at the bath until I was simmering with embarrassment in the fragrant water. There were flowers floating around me, marigolds and roses and lilies, petals in shades of pink and orange and red. The water was tinted a pale and foggy shade of green, and I could already tell that whatever Khell'ar had poured in was going to leave my skin silky smooth.

"Oh, this is so..." It was so *pretty*. The water and the candles all smelled fresh and rich without being overpowering, and there were no windows, so the only light was from the bedroom and the candles. It wasn't at all like anything I'd put on my request list, though.

Khell'ar knelt at the corner of the bath, mostly out of sight. "I'm washing your hair and your body, then I will feed you and put you back into the bed. No more games downstairs."

Which was not the same as no games at all. "Is this going to be one?" I asked, twisting my head. He grasped my jaw in his hand and turned my face away from him again.

"No. You need breaks, little one, or you will stress your body and your mind."

"I didn't find it stressful," I said. "It was…not relaxing, but —" It had been a relief. Partly to know this part of myself at last, to know it was real, to stop wondering. And partly because when everything was at his command, I had no more worries, no more choices. Just open wide, be fucked well, and come hard. "I liked everything we did."

Khell'ar pulled a shower head from the side of the tub and switched it on, the hand on my jaw moving to claim the back of my head, tilting me just so, aiming the water carefully into my hair and away from my eyes.

"I know," he answered.

Of course he knew. I'd been begging and shouting and barely able to keep still, even when he'd ordered me to. Claws appeared at the back of my neck, but they scratched gently and purposefully, digging into my scalp as the warm water rushed over my hair and into the bath. I sighed and let my eyes fall shut, barely feeling the shift of my head from one hand to the other as he rinsed my hair.

"You're very good at this," I murmured as he began to massage my scalp. There was a whiff of tea tree and lavender, and I hadn't even noticed him getting the shampoo. Did he have extra arms?

No. You're just not the first person he's done this for, I reminded myself. Of course he was good at it. He'd had plenty of practice.

My chest pinched at the reminder and I tried to sit up, but

Khell'ar's claws dug gently into the back of my neck, holding me in place.

"You surrendered to my control, now surrender to my care too," he said, but it was gentler than the commands he'd made in the basement.

It's not his fault the sex was so good you're feeling possessive, I reasoned with myself. In fact, that was his job.

"Let go of yourself, little one," Khell'ar growled near my ear, as if he were reading my thoughts. His hands moved up toward my temples, rubbing tension out of my head, even out of the roots of my hair.

He was right—even out of the excitement of the scenes I'd requested, even in these periods of rest, I needed to forget the world outside of this cabin, that even this moment of him washing my hair was part of the experience I'd paid for. I softened in his hold, and Khell'ar released a rumble of approval. His thumbs pressed circles into the base of my skull as his long, thick fingers reached every inch of my head, thorough and tender, doing the work once and then all over again until I was melting in the warm water of the bath, flower petals kissing my breasts and knees as they skimmed the surface.

I wasn't dozing, but I fell into a comfortable empty space in my own mind as my orc companion rinsed my hair again, my head tipped back and his larger fingers protecting my eyes and ears from the rushing water.

"Sunny suits you," he said, combing slick conditioner into my tangled locks and then starting the scalp massage all over again. "Bright, golden woman, begging for my cock and coming in cascades on my lap."

I was too relaxed to do more than smile and blush.

"I'm going to feast on that generous cunt of yours, Sunny."

"Now?" I asked, rewarded with Khell'ar's huff.

"That round ass of yours too," Khell'ar said, his whisper more like a growl with the depth of his voice. He slipped one hand down from my hair to my chest, tweaking my nipples. "These breasts. Every inch of you."

I let my hips rise up in the water, my feet propped at the far end, to encourage this line of thought, and Khell'ar's hand traveled south, covering my rounded stomach with an impressive span of his hand that made me look quite a bit smaller, before reaching my pelvis and pushing me back down in the water with another rumble.

"You are tempting, but I am in control," he reminded me, returning to the task of washing me. "Now lean forward."

I obeyed, tucking my grin between my knees, and groaned as Khell'ar ran those wonderful claws teasingly down my spine.

CHAPTER 7
Khell'ar

"I JUST DON'T SEE the point, I have hands and—" Sunny's eyes narrowed as I stuffed another bite of chicken between her lips, leaving my index finger in her mouth until she relented and relaxed again in my arms.

"I will tie them if it makes more sense to you, but your arms need rest," I answered her.

We were seated at the dining room table, and while I'd planned on dressing Sunny in a warm wrap dress for our meal, I found myself too reluctant to cover her. I'd rubbed her skin soft with lotions after the bath, taken care to touch every inch, all the little places I'd missed during fucking her. Of all the things she should've protested, it was being left nude on my lap while we ate. Perhaps she expected me to keep her naked for all five of our days together.

Perhaps I will, I thought, bringing her a sip of sparkling cider from my glass next. I kept one hand gripped possessively high on her thigh, close enough to her sex to sense its warmth on the backs of my fingers.

Feed her. Put her in bed. Give her another hour's sleep at least. I was reminding myself of the schedule I'd planned over and over again, but then Sunny would nestle her ass on my lap, making herself comfortable, or huff in annoyance, generous breasts reminding me of their presence, and the impulse to push her down onto the table and watch her ass bounce as I saw to my own pleasure would rise again. She would enjoy herself of course, it was to her taste. It was *not* what I had planned.

Sunny might ask the agency for an orc unleashed, a beast of a sex partner, might want a scene where I hunted her and acted out of control, but it couldn't be real. We were professionals, for all the promise of 'monsters'—an antiquated human term for those of us not of their race, a term chased out when the humans realized they were outnumbered and we were better met as friends, or at the very least neighbors.

"Did you cook this food?" Sunny asked, reminding me to feed her another bite, this time roasted squash.

"The agency provided this meal for us," I said. "I will cook for you another day."

"Are you a good cook?"

"You will have to tell me."

Her lips quirked and she twisted toward me, pushing my hand away as I tried to feed her another bite. With a glance at the plate, I decided not to chastise her for the swat—she'd eaten more than I'd expected and was likely truly full.

"You're different than I expected," she said, head tipping and that warm stare studying me.

I arched an eyebrow in answer, helping myself to the remainder of the food. The agency cooks could do with better seasonings, I thought.

"I suppose it makes sense that we're not...that you don't just have me in chains the whole time," she said, cheeks pinked.

I could collar her, if it was what she wanted. Put a leash on her throat and shackle her ankles and treat her as my toy for the whole five days, but it was such a narrow scope of the realm of sex she'd come to me for and barely touched the tip of the pile of things I wanted to do to her.

That thought struck me hard, and I stiffened. I *wanted* this woman. I wanted to go off script, make my own plans for her that served my own interests. She was a bit more mouthy than I was used to for a woman so eager to submit. Not a brat who wanted a fight with her master, and not a woman looking to cast me as a lusty abuser. She was a woman who craved release, physical and mental, to be taken beyond the brink of her own control and brought to immense pleasure.

Orc bait. Perhaps Astraeya was right and I *did* need to be careful. Mating came on by instinct and genetics and emotions for orcs, and was a permanent shift. An orc mating a human was rare, but not unheard of. I'd thought myself incapable of mating a client because work was work for me, even when it was sex. I was performing, meeting a checklist on someone else's behalf.

But Sunny…

Small fingertips cupped my jaw, and my eyes slid to hers.

Sunny was luring me towards uncharted territory in my work, her own desires so similar to mine that I was considering our time together for my own benefit. How much pleasure would it take for me to mate the delicious human? How many little conversations and surprised moments of humor?

Sunny was work. She'd come to be fucked within an inch of her sanity. And a mate would unravel my life, my job at MSA. It was certainly not what she'd paid for and would be a massive violation of the trust she placed in me on behalf of MSA.

"You're more—"

I reached a hand up and wrapped my hand around her wrist, not removing her touch but interrupting the gesture. "If there's anything I should adjust, feel free to ask. This is your time."

Sunny's lips were parted, her eyes growing wide for a

moment. I wanted to take her throat in my grip and draw that mouth to mine, lick her whimpers onto my tongue and twist her in my lap till my cock was buried deep and my stav swelled until it couldn't move. Which was not how our evening was meant to go. Sunny was not my lover or my mate, she was my client.

Those full brown eyes winced and she turned away, and I dropped my hands from her to prevent myself from yanking her focus back to me. Sunny was dangerous—she made me want to erase every line between us. Cutting through the ease of the moment was clumsy, but necessary.

"Of course," she said, words winded.

I CHECKED my watch for the hundredth time as I left the freshly cleaned and reset basement, my steps stalling.

Vitals: sleeping.

At last. I'd been working aimlessly for two hours after buckling Sunny back into the bed cuff, waiting for her to fall asleep. It should've happened quickly, but instead the readings from her cuff only gave intermittent indications of stress. My comment at dinner had effectively undone the work I'd put in since the basement. Leaving her alone in the bed furthered the stress.

"Aren't you going to join me?" she'd asked, but she hadn't raised her eyes from my hands on her ankle. She'd wanted to be fucked again. Impressive and tempting. I could've dragged her to the edge of the bed, hooked one ankle onto my shoulder, and fucked her through a few orgasms right into my own finish. I could've climbed onto the bed, straddled her, and jerked myself onto her bare chest, offering her nothing but denial and my release. I could've thrown her onto her stomach, lain myself on top of her, and stayed buried through the night, having my own pleasure—and

her's—every time the clasp and heat of her cunt became too seductive to resist.

Instead, I'd left her there to sleep. Which she hadn't done for *two hours*. I'd nearly abandoned my own schedule several times when her heart rate spiked.

This is better, I reasoned. *She shouldn't have her way through all five days. The stress will make tonight's torture sweeter.*

I hurried up the stairs now, treading as lightly as I could, uncertain yet how light a sleeper Sunny was. I would know soon enough. The cottage was dark and quiet, a few candles left burning from dinner which I blew out now. Sunny's vitals approximated she'd been sleeping for a little over twenty minutes, which was just enough time to be truly disruptive.

She was curled up on her side under the blankets, her short blonde hair swept over her face, one hand fisted up by her nose. I considered her position versus my own goals. She wanted to be seduced while sleeping. It was higher up on her requests, so it would be best not to wake her by pulling her onto her back. I would start slowly, cautiously, in case an instinctive alarm outweighed her arousal. I shucked off my shorts and left them on the floor, my cock perking up in relief after so much time denied its chosen target. I'd enjoyed Sunny's appreciative stares on my form in these pants, which gave them a new purpose, but in truth they were simply tight and constraining enough to keep my cock in line when it wanted to be inside of this woman.

I lifted the covers, charmed by the sight of her rounded ass peeking out from the shadows, the folds of her soft waist, creased from lying on her side. She remained breathing softly and deeply as I slid into the bed behind her, my weight on the mattress shifting her easily in my direction. I held my breath in, my groan restrained as her ass lined itself up perfectly against my cock. I reached between us, squeezing and pumping my own length, drawing fluid to my tip and waiting to see if Sunny awoke.

She was well suited to this act because she remained asleep, even as I tucked the head of my cock between her thighs, stroking myself with slow thrusts against her warm pussy. I cupped her hip, tracing the rise and valley of her thighs to her waist, and then back again. Her breath was growing a little uneven, but her pulse was steady. If she was awake, she was very good at faking and not at all disturbed by my presence. I scooted closer, my chest against her back, and took the risk of jostling her to wrap my other arm beneath her cheek, my left hand rising to cover her mouth.

Sunny was growing wet, the pump and slide of my shallow thrusts between her thighs easing—a pleasant clasp of her body around me, even if it wasn't the hot and silky hollow I wanted to burrow inside of. My claws were distending, creating gentle dimples on her hip and cheek. I wanted inside of her, I wanted to roll her down to her belly or up onto my cock to ride me. She needed to wake first.

I pulled my hips back, and the head of my cock found its way to her opening as if it had already eagerly memorized the spot. I pushed in and grinned at Sunny's moan vibrating against my hand. With my size and height, I was easily wrapped around her, able to watch her eye lashes flutter open, eyes widening as she tried to see into the dark of the room. I clasped my hand tighter over her mouth, waiting to see her response. Startled or excited?

I should've known.

Sunny whined and arched in my arms, pushing herself back onto my cock, inching me inside of her. Her eyes fell shut again, body leaning into my chest. Surrendering, as usual. Could I ever even coax her to fight? The idea of Sunny red with exertion and sweat, frustration, wrestling beneath me—she would giggle, I was certain of it, incapable of hiding her own enjoyment—caused the first pump of my stav. I slid my hand on her hip down to her pussy and then thrust roughly forward, burying myself to the hilt, Sunny's cry muffled behind my fingers.

"I'm going to fuck you right out of your sanity tonight, little one," I rasped in her ear.

Sunny's arm reached back, digging into my shoulder, anchoring herself as I slammed myself in and out of her with messy slaps of skin, her wet sounds behind my hand, my fingers pressing down on her clit but not stimulating.

"I'm going to have you so many times, you won't know what's waking and dreaming tomorrow. I'm going to take *my* fantasies out on you tonight."

Sunny howled, louder now that she was being muted, or perhaps still waking. I would have her screaming by the week's end, trying to share her pleasure with the whole world. I shoved my index and middle finger into her mouth, and she sucked on them eagerly, trying to ride me from her reclined position.

I shifted, scooping her up and settling on my back, Sunny spread on top of me like a hedonistic, squirming blanket. I pushed her up to seated, and she rose with a gasp and an eager pace, bouncing on my length. Let her ride me while she had the strength, I would still make use of her when she was limp and delirious before the morning.

CHAPTER 8
Sunny

KHELL'AR'S HANDS *in my hair, his cock stuffed between my lips, hips thrusting gently, a purr of approval from above me as I suckled until my mouth was numb and my jaw was sore.*

The easy way he tossed me from hanging my head over the foot of the bed for his taking, to face down in the pillows, my hips hiked up around his, that endlessly rigid length of his burrowing back inside my over-sensitive—but never too sore—core.

Falling asleep with his mouth on mine, waking again with it on my sex, his tusks firm and holding my lips spread for his tongue's greedy searching, slurping, and feasting upon me until I was whining with a reluctantly wrung out orgasm.

My hands shackled to the bar at the center of the headboard as Khell'ar fucked me so hard, the whole bed rattled and shook, my bones jangling in my body with every thrust.

Another massage, with one hand in and on my sex, the other tending tired muscles. Khell'ar's touch pulling me in and out of consciousness with fluttering and gentle climaxes.

"No more," I whispered weakly as a hand stroked up my back. I squirmed away from the touch, searching for a pillow to burrow under, and came up empty, my eyes opening with heavy effort as a pair of arms dragged me up off the mattress.

The sun was up, faintly glowing in the room. I knew Khell'ar had let me catch glimpses of sleep, but they were cruel and brief, the night more full of sex and waves of sensation than any rest I'd managed to capture could make up for.

His hand was on my cheek, my body cradled in his lap, and he shook with silent laughter. "Open your lips, little one."

I whimpered but parted my lips, my brain too exhausted to reason out that he couldn't be feeding me his cock from this position.

Instead warmth and sweetness hit my tongue. I moaned and managed to lift my head, drinking the coffee eagerly, creamy and foamy and *caffeinated.*

"If you really wanted me to stop, you would have to use a better word than that," Khell'ar said as I drank, reminding me of my safe word.

Did that mean he wanted to have sex *again*? Surely it had been more than a dozen times in the night? Had I imagined some of it? Maybe the soft frottage in the middle, but no, my stomach was still sticky from where he'd come on me. So were my thighs, my lips and cheeks and jaw and...

Khell'ar was grinning, eyes crinkled at the corners, as I grew more alert.

I was a *mess.* Every inch of me was sore and every inch of me had been licked and kissed and sucked. My ass was... He hadn't fucked it, but he'd spoken about it and stretched me there with his fingers, something Harry had been interested in but too nervous to commit to.

In fact, I wasn't the only thing that was a mess. The bed looked like it had been hit by a tornado, and I had no clear recollection who had torn the sheet at the corner or when all the pillows had been thrown to the floor. Even better, Khell'ar was *rumpled.* There were soft, dark lines on his skin that must've been scratches from me, and his lips were visibly swollen. He didn't look tired, but more relaxed than during dinner the night before.

I opened my lips to say the word that would call a stop to

any of Khell'ar's plans. I was too tired, too sore, too euphori-cally satisfied to continue. And then a delicate whisper of curiosity bubbled up in my head. But *what* were his plans? Did I really want to refuse before I knew? I could call a halt to our activities at any time, it didn't have to be *now*.

My lips shut, and Khell'ar's smile widened as if in reward of my silence.

"That's a good girl," the orc purred, gaze glowing.

That tear and scratch and growl of his voice, layered deli-ciously, had found its way under my skin and crawled through me like a secret nervous system, lighting up my body whenever he spoke.

"Pretty little blush," he continued, staring down at my body, hands squeezing and petting at me, one leaving my hip to come up and simply roll my breast against his vast palm. "Like a little flower. Not pet, but petal."

"You're going to kill me," I whispered, eyes growing wide even as my body seemed to follow a natural magnetism, arching into his touch.

"I'm too good at my job to let you die before I'm done with you," he said, smile hiding itself away but the tease remaining in the squint of his eyes.

"I can't have sex again," I pleaded, even though I knew it was a lie. I *wanted* to, no matter how weary I was.

"Not yet," Khell'ar said, shrugging a massive shoulder and jostling me in his lap. "First, you'll eat."

"And bathe."

He growled and lifted me from the bed, tossing me over his shoulder like a sack of exhausted potatoes. His hand came down with a crack on my bare ass, and I shouted and turned red at the shocking release of fluid that slid out of me.

"You're not in charge, petal."

I was, though. He was marching us out of the bedroom, careful not to jostle my sore body, as it struck me. I could make him stop, change the plans, do as I asked.

You don't want to be in charge.

"I like my scent on you," Khell'ar remarked casually, and I buried my hot face into the fascinating muscle of his warm back. "My thick seed running down your thighs."

"Oh god," I whispered into his skin.

"Your cunt is mine today. To fuck and fill and feast from."

Another humiliating and wonderful leak of cum slipped down my thighs as I squirmed, and Khell'ar pulled me down from his shoulder, setting me back in his lap, right where we'd been the night before. We were both naked, and there was a dark mark on the side of Khell'ar's throat. It took me a moment to realize that it must've been from *me*. I didn't remember biting him, but I could almost recall the taste of his skin and the texture of it on my tongue, friction and salt and a nearly sweet flavor.

"Sunny," he growled, and my gaze whipped up to his. "Eat."

Sunny. Focus.

Except I was focused—completely focused on this orc. I'd heard the phrase "the whole world fell away" like some romance movie moment where the soundtrack swelled and the cameras zoomed in on the couple. I didn't realize it might be so literal, so real. It was as if all five of my senses had removed everything but Khell'ar from me. I twisted, my breath hitching at the ridge of his cock under my ass, rising up to fit between my thighs, the rounded weeping head peeking out as I glanced down.

Fingers dove into my tangled hair, yanking gently and forcing my head up. I whined, and then my jaw dropped at the sight on the table. Plate upon plate of food, scrambled eggs steaming in front of me with generous sides of bacon and toast plated on either side. Now that I was staring at it all, the sight and scents made my mouth water.

Before, you were too busy drooling over the hunky orc, I hissed at myself.

Khell'ar's hands were full—with my hair and my breast—and he made no move to feed me again. There was cutlery laid out, and I reached for the fork automatically before pausing and glancing back at my orc.

"I ate while you slept."

"You let me sleep for more than two minutes?" I asked, turning back to the food and digging in with the fork in one hand and bacon in the other.

"I let you sleep for more than three hours…overall," he said.

I frowned at that. Three was…not much. Then again, now that I had coffee and food in front of me, I wasn't sure I would've traded any of the hours I *hadn't* been sleeping.

"Eat up, petal. You'll need your strength today."

Warned, intrigued, and a little nervous, I dove into my breakfast, shoulders squaring to face the day and Khell'ar's plans for me.

HIS HAND ENCOMPASSED mine completely as he led me down the steps back into the basement. I was dressed for the first time since he'd ordered me to take my clothes off the day before, but it was in a thin and silky peach shift that was only held together by three buttons down my stomach and had slits in the long skirt running up both thighs.

Khell'ar stopped us at the bottom of the stairs and near the full mirror of the wall, pulling me in front of him.

God, he was huge. I was not a small woman in any way, but I appeared so in front of him, his shoulders and head rising behind me, around me. Even his hips were a little broader than mine, a fact my inner thighs remembered vividly.

"Look at yourself, petal," he said.

I preferred looking at him, but I obeyed, meeting my own

gaze in the mirror. Khell'ar draped an arm over my shoulder and then flicked the long and low collar of the shift aside to reveal one of my breasts, his fingers scooping beneath the weight to heft and roll my flesh in his grip.

"Lush woman," he praised, and my reflection turned pink at the words. "Breasts meant for *my* hands."

I let out a rough breath and relaxed against his chest, pushing my own into his palm. "Yes."

He left the collar pushed aside and moved his hand to the other side, this time sliding under the fabric, the silk shining and shifting like pink waves as he pinched my nipple just firmly enough to remind me how much he'd enjoyed playing with me the night before.

"You're going to be my prize today," he said. "I won you in battle to do with as I please."

I bit my lips to hide my smile and nodded obediently, as if I hadn't written this into a little form on a tablet myself, wishing and hoping whoever my partner was would be interested in playing this scene out with me.

"You may touch me however you like. You can fight or you can beg. But, petal," he growled, drawing my eyes up to his in the mirror, making me shiver at the flash of color in the dark basement. "You won't touch yourself. Your body is *mine*."

Logically, I couldn't imagine finding a moment with Khell'ar where I *needed* to touch myself. He seemed to grow new pairs of hands while he fucked me, his touch everywhere at once. But the order left me squirming and curious about his plans, and I nodded more eagerly.

"Yes."

"Yes, what?"

I hesitated. I'd called him master yesterday, but yesterday he had felt more like a stranger, almost faceless. I twisted to look up at him rather than our reflection.

"Can I call you something else today?" I asked.

His eyes narrowed and his lips flattened, and I was certain he was about to refuse and remind me of our roles. Then he let out a huff and nodded, pulling his hand from under my shift to grip my jaw.

"It's not that I mind calling you master. I just—" I was cut off as his head dipped, mouth finding mine in an unexpected and firm kiss. I swayed into him, breathing the heat of him into my lungs, wanting to climb up into his arms to be held against his chest again.

"You may call me what you like, petal," Khell'ar growled. "Now show me your pussy."

I bit off my squeak of surprise, stumbling back a step before Khell'ar's hands whipped me around to face the mirror again, pulling me to his chest and flicking aside one strip of the shift's skirt. I shuffled my legs apart, and Khell'ar growled. There wasn't much of a view in the mirror, not with us both standing, and he glared at me through the glass until I raised one leg and turned it wide, arching my hips forward.

My sex was pink and dark and slightly puffy from all the sex we'd had in the past day—a genuinely insane amount. But Khell'ar's cum was still doing the trick. I wasn't uncomfortably sore. He'd been rough with me in the night, and it'd only felt powerful and thorough, not punishing or painful.

He reached down and spread me with his fingers, a slight gush of more of our release appearing at my opening. "My cunt," he said with approval. "Full and begging. Ready for me."

"Yours, beast," I said, more focused on the look of his hand on me, the earthy green contrasting against my pink flushed skin. A moment later, the word landed in my head and my eyes widened, heart stuttering.

But the orc was grinning, tusks biting into his upper lip, eyes hot on mine. Beast it was then, at least down here in the dark together.

Khell'ar reached to the back of his warrior's skirt, drawing out a long strip of cloth that matched my shift. I held my wrists out in front of me in offering, expecting him to tie them together, and he chuckled.

"You'll have to control yourself, petal," he said, instead drawing the cloth over my head and then holding it in front of my eyes.

"Oh," I said, staring back at the blindfold, stiffening slightly. I hadn't written this down on my list. I wasn't opposed, but…

But I liked to look at Khell'ar. Liked to know what he was about to do, to watch him touch me. I could refuse. Khell'ar wouldn't deny me the role-playing just because I didn't want a blindfold.

Knowing the choice was still mine, I took the time to consider the idea. I would miss watching Khell'ar, but the idea of knowing he was there and only *waiting* for him to touch me…well, that did have an appeal.

I leaned forward, and Khell'ar rumbled with approval, the blindfold cool on my skin, kissing over my eyes as he tied it firmly at the back of my head. The silk wasn't so dense that it left me in the dark. I could still see the glow of dim light bulbs bleeding through the fabric, the shadow of Khell'ar as he turned me to face him, warm fingers tilting my chin up.

"Now we begin," he growled, the resonance of his voice washing over my skin and leaving goose bumps in its wake.

CHAPTER 9
Sunny

I SHIVERED IN THE DARK, my hands itching at my sides to reach up and fidget with the blindfold, pull it away to hunt for Khell'ar in the empty room. The floor was smooth and cold under my feet, and I lifted one and wrapped it around my ankle, wavering in place. The dark and silence brought my exhaustion from the night back, blurring the line between dozing and waiting for my orc.

"Khell'ar?" I called softly when minutes seemed to pass with nothing happening.

A growl echoed off stone and cement from somewhere behind me, and the hairs on the back of my neck rose.

"Beast?" I tried again, a little louder.

The growl rose again, and a scuffing sound came from my left that might've been steps against the cement.

"You smell like cum, petal."

Yours, I thought tartly, shrinking in on myself. *And my own.*

"Did you like the way he fucked you? The one before?"

I swallowed hard at the dark edge in Khell'ar's voice, the way his words seemed to prowl like a predator around me in my still and floating place in the dark.

"Yes," I said easily, heat rising up my throat.

And in spite of the game and the roles Khell'ar had given us, his growl softened into that sweeter approving rumble. He liked my answer, and it made my lips curl.

"His cum is in *my* prize, his scent on my property," Khell'ar snapped out, jolting me at the same moment his hand circled my arm. I let out a small yelp as he yanked me forward, my feet stumbling where he led. "Will you scream his name when your new owner makes you come?"

Would he like it if I did? He'd certainly seemed to enjoy the many cries of his name I'd released the night before.

This is just pretend, Sunny. Every second of it.

It was a bitter and necessary reminder, but it left my tongue glued in my mouth, and Khell'ar snagged my hip in his grip, claws digging in as if in punishment for my silence.

"No, beast," I whispered.

The hand on my arm slid up to my shoulder and then grasped the back of my neck, bending me forward.

"We'll see," Khell'ar snarled.

He nudged me another step, and my hips bumped into a raised platform, high enough that the top hit my waist. He lifted me up, pushing my chest down onto its slightly padded surface, my legs hanging over the edge.

"You should've cleaned yourself for me, petal, but I'll do the work myself if I must."

And as if in response, or perhaps at some aroused encouragement of my core, release slipped out of me again, just as Khell'ar smoothed a hand down my ass to cup my sex.

"How many times did he make you come?"

I hid my grin against the surface of the platform, stretching my arms forward and finding the other edge with the tips of my fingers. "I lost count."

"Mmmm, then I will have to guess."

Khell'ar's touch was gone at that declaration, and for a moment, I thought I would be left on the awkward platform in silence again. A moment later, and with a soft whoosh of air from behind me, brilliant and shocking pain bloomed on my ass.

I let out a cry at the sudden spank, and the note swooped higher as two thick fingers plunged inside of me with a wet squelch.

Oh god. The implication of Khell'ar's questions hit me at once. He would clean me with his fingers, fucking our mutual release out of me. He would spank me for the orgasms he had already given me. *Surely not, there had been so many!*

"Too hard?" he asked, slightly winded.

I moaned, turning my head and wishing I might see him behind me, but the blindfold was still firmly in place. His broad hand was soothing over the spot he'd just struck, leaving a sharp heat behind.

"Not yet," I answered.

"Good." His fingers picked up pace inside of me, and the next slap of his hand on my ass was a relieving distraction from the little splashes against my inner thighs.

"Oh, beast!" I cried out.

"That's it, little petal. Again," he said.

And in spite of the warning, I did scream for him as he spanked me again, twice in quick succession on either cheek. He'd ridden me limp the day before. I suspected I would be hoarse before sunset today.

"RIDE ME, PETAL."

I burrowed into the hot chest before me, my breath uneven, eyes stinging, searching for just *one* moment of rest.

"No," I moaned, my hands trying to find purchase on my orc's chest.

The cock inside of me was pumping slowly, and my legs felt boneless where I knelt on the broad lap beneath me, ass still burning hot from my spanking. "Do as I say, or I will throw you to the other hungry orcs who want soft flesh to feast from and a wet cunt to sate their cocks."

I whimpered, and two hands snatched my own off the chest I was resting against, pulling my arms behind my back in a stretch that had me sitting up straight and arching, crying out.

"I'm tired, beast!" Tears seeped out of my eyes, sticking the blindfold to my skin, but Khell'ar only chuckled. The sound was warm, too sweet, and it cut through the haze of frustrated arousal fraying at my thoughts.

"Your beast is unsatisfied. *Ride me,*" Khell growled.

Liar, I thought spitefully, gritting my teeth and snarling back at my orc, who shook with another, more restrained bout of laughter. I was tempted to let my limp body melt off Khell'ar's lap and down to the cold floor—the stone would be a relief on my fevered skin. Even that surrender would take some measure of strength, so instead I let out a rough cry of frustration and forced my body to rise, my thighs burning with the effort.

Khell'ar had spanked me until my ass was flames and my cunt was more or less drained of all his cum. He'd taken me down to my knees to use my mouth, made me bend and grip my ankles as he held me on my toes and fucked me from behind. I'd satisfied him *plenty* already, monstrous orc.

"Good little petal," Khell purred as I whined, forcing my body into the rise and fall, his stav picking up speed inside of me. I'd never heard of a stav before he'd explained his to me at dinner, but I was spectacularly grateful for the pump and swell of the inner sheath in his cock, and immediately obsessed with the sensation.

One large hand circled both my wrists, tying them in place behind my back and holding me in the pose, breasts thrust forward. I gasped as cool points of pressure scratched their way up my stomach, making it jump, over my ribs, on a path toward my breasts, swirling slowly. Blindfolded, Khell'ar's claws could've been the dull edge of blades on my skin or the tips of black pencils, marking their patterns over my skin, decorating my breasts with their touch.

"Bastard," I breathed, fighting my own exhaustion, my burning, aching, weary muscles, to rush to the end, to finish my orc and be *done*. "Oh, god, Khell, please."

My thighs were trembling, the ache growing to an almost unbearable fire. New tears slipped down from under the blindfold, over my cheeks. There was no pleasure in this.

Liar, I thought again, but this time at myself. There was a soft tingling running down from where Khell's claws traced my skin, into my cunt. There was the heady high of Khell's purrs and growls in my head, the sound of his grunt as I landed heavily on his lap, the hiss as I rose wobbling to his tip. But my body was too hot and too weary, and my head was deep in the fog of lack of sleep, too distant and shy of my own body in this moment.

I was hiccuping with tears and little moans, pleading whines to be released, gasping prayers for him to finish, when a hot wet stripe licked up between my breasts. I sighed at the new sensation, shivered as it marked its way to my collarbone, tracing up my throat to my jaw to taste my tears.

"My little petal is crying," Khell growled, but I was sure he sounded pleased. "Crying for her tender cocked lover when she now has me to please."

I was going to laugh at the notion of the Khell of yesterday being remotely considered 'tender cocked,' but then he thrust up, meeting my weak motions, and my breath caught in my lungs.

"Please," I gasped, sagging as he took over the motion, making me bounce on his lap.

"Do you give up, little petal?" he asked, licking more tears off one cheek and then another. "Do you want rest more than you want to please your beast? Are you too weak to serve your master?"

The sound I let out was too tired to be a scream as I forced myself into motion again, matching his fucking in a weaker echo, meeting his hips with a soft crash. Khell grunted, nipping at my jaw and then returning to tracing patterns on my chest. His cock inside me was a dull drumbeat, but that didn't stop it from echoing through my body, my bones, my strung out muscles.

"Never, beast," I breathed out, my own voice thin under the sounds of our fucking. "My cunt is yours."

I just wish I didn't have to put quite this much effort into you using it this morning, I thought privately.

My answer made Khell stiffen beneath me, until the soft claws on my chest were gone and an iron-strong arm banded around my back. Khell'ar hauled me up from the throne he'd been sitting in with a snarl, and the gravity of being trapped in his arms sunk me down to the hilt of his cock, drawing out a shout.

"Wrap your legs around me if you can, petal," Khell barked.

My legs couldn't even notch themselves at his hips, but it didn't matter. Khell's arm shifted to holding my ass, my hands still in his other grip, and then he was using me like he had the day before, my body like a doll in his grasp, my cunt the vessel for him to fill. I let out a long howl of relief as he fucked me. He pinned my arms down, drawing me closer, his mouth sucking and kissing at my neck, burying his growls there, his tusks digging into the muscle of my throat and making my breath come in tight, short gasps.

The closeness rubbed my clit against his skin, his stav swelling inside me to stroke against my inner walls again, and the numbness of minutes ago was burning up under a new, more and more delicious wave of fire.

Khell'ar came with a great bellow into my neck, and the hot flood of him inside of me demanded my own release, reluctant and bitter and slow as it was. I sobbed, sick to death of orgasms and somehow relieved too, the sweetness of the shuddering climax dulling the edge of anger I'd let simmer. Khell's grip on my wrists was nearly bruising, but it loosened, his body relaxing against mine, and then he drew each of my arms up to his shoulders one after the other. He pet down my back and then up again, sliding into the sweaty strands of hair sticking to the back of my neck.

"I can't tell if you make playing the beast harder or easier, petal," Khell whispered in my ear, breath flatteringly ragged.

I was drowsy with my latest release, limp in his hold, but he didn't wait for my answer. We turned and he carried me back to the platform, clasped to his chest, his cock still half-buried inside of me with an interesting and gentle friction as he moved us. He slipped free—the hollowness that followed a relief for once—as he settled me on the altar, draped over the surface as if I were the slaughtered lamb, my sacrifice on display for his gods.

"Do you hurt, Sunny?"

I sighed at the return of Khell'ar as himself and shook my head, although in truth, I did hurt from all the exercise and ecstatic strain of the past twenty-four hours. Khell hummed as if he knew I was wrong and reached up to the buttons of the shift he'd dressed me in, opening the garment up and gently pulling my arms free.

"You were very good today. Stronger than I expected."

Since I'd barely been able to put much effort into anything, I assumed he meant he was praising me for not calling a stop to the game. His hands were soothing up and down my arms, and I noticed that the platform I was on was growing slightly warm, heated just enough to keep me from growing chilled as he exposed me.

"Soft little goddess," Khell'ar murmured, pushing my legs slightly apart and petting at the wet release clinging to my cunt, sliding his fingers through the mess. He didn't bother retracting his claws, and I shivered as they teased my scorching and sensitive flesh. "Goddesses must be worshipped, petal. Even by beasts."

I'd never felt more human, more frail, than I did in Khell'ar's powerful shadow. And yet somehow, there was strength in that too. I couldn't match him, but I could meet him, could push myself to climb to the same peaks with him, fall down into bliss with him.

Khell's kiss landed on my knee, and I sighed as warmth bloomed in the spot, not ready for what came next but knowing I *was* strong enough.

CHAPTER 10
Khell'ar

SUNNY WAS HUMMING WITHOUT REALIZING, little murmurs of pleasure as I dug my fingers into her muscles, apologizing with touch for my rough treatment of the morning. And for the night before, poor little human. And yet in spite of denying her sleep, of using her to my own satisfaction, of torturing her with pleasure, she'd borne the hours beautifully. She was gluttonous and determined in equal measure.

Her chest was marked with my scratches. They would fade soon, but they glowed under the false candlelight on the walls. If I'd had ink, I would've painted the marks in place—the map of my hands' path on her skin.

Dangerous creature, I reminded myself.

It was easier when her eyes were covered like this. I didn't have to hide from that pleading, probing stare.

"Khell?"

I growled at her voice, the sweet notes, the affectionate clip of my name.

"Can I sleep now, Khell?"

"No, petal," I answered, although in truth I had no real

way of stopping her. I was done playing cruel master for the moment. I wanted to enjoy Sunny's flesh with my own mind.

She sighed and nodded, then remained limp aside from a little tremble as I ran my hands up from the inside of her frail ankles to the soft pillow of her inner thighs. I used my claws to carefully spread the swollen and reddened lips of her sex. Creamy fluid spilled out, and Sunny gasped, the peaks of her breasts rising and falling.

"Is it being opened to me you like, or my claws?" I asked.

"Both," she admitted softly.

I stroked one long black tip against the side of one of her labia and purred as she released a whimpering moan. I repeated the action on the other lip, stroking up to her clit and down to her opening, watching Sunny's stomach jump and breasts jiggle, her toes curl. It was not fear, not as far as I could tell. Sunny trusted me beyond reason, trusted my claws, my tusks, my strength. She didn't tense as I circled her opening with one claw, just moaned and clenched and dripped.

I pulled away, and she caught her breath, grunting as I grasped her thighs and dragged her closer, just enough for me to be able to bend forward and reach that cunt with my mouth. I dipped my finger inside of her, kissed her clit with a swirl of my tongue, and Sunny's hands flew into the braid of my hair, weaving her fingers into the strands and holding me to her.

She hadn't asked for this, and she was too tired and sore and overwhelmed for what I wanted to really be considered care. But I wanted to feast on this woman. I wanted to pay tithe with my tongue on her flesh, inside of her, with my teeth massaging her muscle and my tusks pinching her skin and my claws drawing possessive marks on her.

"Khell, what—what are you doing?" Sunny gasped.

She didn't mean what was I doing with my clawed finger

pumping carefully inside of her, with my tongue lapping away our release as it seeped out.

"Worshipping you, petal," I rasped, diving back down and sucking at her clit briefly until she whined with the pain of being overstimulated for too long. I pulled away. This wasn't about her release. It certainly wasn't about mine.

"But…why?"

I should've had her on her knees for me, crawling after me on the floor on those weak little limbs of hers. I should've had her washing my feet, kissing my skin, telling me how much she liked my cock. That was what she had come to the agency for, hired me for, paid me for.

But Sunny was tired and I had appreciation to express to this body that had already performed such feats of ecstasy for me.

I pulled my finger out of her, kissing her inner thighs, her rounded hip bones, a line up to her belly button where I dipped my tongue in, lapping at the playful flavor of her sweat. Did I have an answer for her? A true one I could speak, or simply one that would satisfy her?

"Because it pleases your master to do so," I said, grinding the words out as I stroked my cheek against her thigh, sneaking another flick of my tongue out to taste her cunt before standing straight again.

I scooped my hands under her left side and rolled her over onto her stomach before she could ask more questions.

I dug my hands into her lower back, and Sunny squeaked at the first satisfying *pop* of her body and then went limp. "Be my pretty deity, petal. For your cunt is divine, and so is your mouth. Because you sing like an angel as you come on my cock and make me see the heavens."

"Fuck, Khell'ar," she sighed as I kneaded and stroked down to her ass, spreading her cheeks briefly to admire her rosebud hole I'd played with the night before.

I bent my head again, and Sunny let out a half-hearted,

garbled yelp as I licked up her crease here too, from her cunt to the base of her spine and then back down to that puckered hole again, burrowing in the sharp tip of my tongue.

"I must taste every part of my goddess, petal. I am a hungry devotee," I murmured against her ass, kissing and tonguing at her hole as she squealed and squirmed, and pinned my hands splayed on her cheeks.

"Oh my—"

"My goddess," I said, cutting Sunny off with a growl, lapping down to her cunt where she was growing sharp with new arousal, and then up again to the darker and earthier, secretive flavor of her ass. "Give me all of you."

Sunny gave up speech as I helped myself to my new feast, tongue thrusting and licking where my fingers had first searched last night. I was tempted to stretch her again, to take her here on my cock, but even I wasn't a good enough liar to convince myself that would be for her benefit. So instead, I sated myself on her flavor until the call of her cunt and the pleading, weeping fluid gathering on the altar begged for my fingers. She was heaving and gasping, facedown, hands leaving sweaty streaks as they searched for purchase.

She came, ass pinching the length of my buried, curious tongue, cunt barely able to clasp around my fingers but simply fluttering gently with relief, and her sobs of baffled release echoed off the altar. I relented as she relaxed and climbed onto the top of the altar, watching her shudder, her eyes wide and unseeing. She glanced shyly at me, cheeks flushed red with embarrassment.

Fuck her again, the beast in me snarled.

Instead, I settled back on my own heels, my heavy cock resting on her soft ass as I leaned forward and grabbed a bottle of massage oil, coating it over my palms.

"You're joking," Sunny whispered. "You can't just—"

I put my hands to her shoulders, digging my fingers into

the tense muscle, smiling as it melted immediately at the first touch. "Hush now, petal. I must care for my goddess."

Sunny moaned, either at my answer or at the massage, I wasn't sure, and her eyes fell shut, body unwinding from the confused excitement I'd put her through, surrendering to me again.

"YOU SHOULD GET IN WITH ME," Sunny mumbled, eyes heavy-lidded, cheek resting on the tub as I leaned over and washed her with a soft sponge.

"There'd be no room for the water, petal," I said, lips twitching as she hummed in answer. She'd fallen asleep on the altar, clung weakly to me as I carried her up the stairs, and refused to wake for any lunch until her stomach had made the demand a few hours later. "Lean back."

Sunny rolled in the water, my hands guiding her back to rest her head on the ledge. I'd already washed her hair and combed in conditioner to soften and detangle her strands. She'd been quiet since she'd woken from her nap, thoughtful as I'd fed her leftovers of our breakfast from my own fingers. She'd also been entirely loose in my arms. She'd given up control of her body in the basement and had forgotten to take it back again. No squirms, no objections to my feeding her, carrying her, bathing her.

The satisfaction was thick and heady in my veins. There was no pretense to Sunny. What self-consciousness she possessed at her desires was gone now. Even acceptance was forgotten. She was simply existing as *mine*. Mine to fuck. Mine to care for.

"Would you like to bathe me, petal?"

Sunny's eyes had fallen shut as I stroked the sponge down her shoulders, over her breasts and into the water. They fluttered open again with effort now, but the light in her gaze was bright as she turned her head to find me.

"Yes, please." Her hands lifted from the water, bracing against the ledge of the tub, and I hurried to push them back in.

"Not now. But if you behave for me tonight, and if you impress me tomorrow—"

"What will we do tonight? And tomorrow?" Sunny asked, eyes growing wider, struggling to sit up in the slippery water.

Her lips were slightly chapped, eyes a little red from so much interrupted sleep. I reached over her head to the top shelf by the tub and pulled down a few jars. Mud mask. Lip scrub. Deep moisturizer.

"Tonight you will rest, petal," I said, wondering if I could keep the promise. Probably not if I was in the bed with her.

A restful fucking. She is here *for fucking after all*, the back of my head reasoned.

Sunny's head tipped back, offering herself up for the mask with a soft smile. "And tomorrow?" she repeated.

Tomorrow, I had *vivid* plans for the little human. Plans she'd requested. Plans I would relish bringing to life, embellished with my own desires.

Dangerous, I reminded myself, smearing mud over pink cheeks and a smooth forehead, down the slope of an elegant and fragile throat. "I think you'll like being surprised," I said, watching her lashes bat softly with every swipe of my fingers on her skin.

"Mmm, you're probably right," she said, falling quiet. I washed my fingers in the milky water and then used the scrub over Sunny's lips, her tongue flicking out to sample the sugar on my fingertip. "I was so scared, you know?"

I fought the sudden prick of my claws in my fingers, the urge to arm myself, to attack whatever had frightened Sunny.

"Of me?" I growled, brow furrowing, throat tight.

She huffed a laugh and blinked up at me, and I forced my

expression to be smooth. "No! No...of myself, I think. Of coming here and...being wrong about what I wanted. Or even of being right. I don't know. But this is so easy. You're making this very easy, Khell."

She was meant to call me master, sir, beast. Why had I given her my name in that first hour? It wielded too much power on her tongue.

"That's my job, petal," I said easily.

The words were true, and unlike last night, I hadn't said them with the intention to remind her of our respective roles, but her eyes shut and her lips pursed under my touch. I wanted to correct myself, but I swallowed my tongue for a moment, focusing on my task, rinsing the last of the sugar off Sunny's lips and then dressing them with a thick coating of balm to help them heal.

"You don't need to be afraid of what you want, Sunny," I said slowly. "You are...you are exquisite. You please me, petal."

Her smile twitched, and I pretended that I was only soothing my client as I bent, pressing a kiss to the scant inch of clean skin at her hairline.

"Tomorrow, you may be afraid," I rumbled in her ear, watching her nipples pucker and her body ripple with her shiver. "Tomorrow, I will taste that fear in the air, and then I will lap it off your skin, right from your cunt. I'll make my petal scream tomorrow."

Sunny grinned, lips smeared with a thick paste that reminded me of the sight of my cum on her mouth. "I can't wait."

"You will wait," I growled. "You may suck my cock tonight after dinner. And you may leave your legs open for me to fill you up tonight as you sleep. But you *will* sleep tonight, petal. And you will wait until tomorrow for more games."

Sunny beamed at me like I'd just promised her a king's wealth and the night sky on top of it all.

CHAPTER 11
Sunny

I MOANED AS I WOKE, my cunt throbbing, stuffed by Khell's cock, my breasts aching as he sucked one roughly and rolled the other in his hand. He was barely thrusting, but his stav was pumping eagerly inside of me. There was a bitter aftertaste on my tongue, some of Khell's flavor lingering, and his earthy scent was dense from his position on top of me.

I whined, pulling my arms from under my pillow to wrap them around his shoulders.

"No, petal. Don't move. You are sleeping," Khell'ar hissed.

My hands itched to touch him, already addicted to the soft texture of his skin, but I went limp easily, still exhausted from the day. Khell'ar grunted in appreciation, picking up his pace and lifting his head to watch my breasts tremble with his thrusts.

"Close your eyes," he purred, and I whimpered in objection but let them fall shut. He rewarded me with a long, wet lick up my throat, his tusks nuzzling my jaw. My lips were parted on a stifled moan, and his tongue slipped in, stroking against mine, right to the back of my throat and out again. His weight sank into mine, the bed and his massive form enveloping me, the pressure breathtaking, his roll and grind on top of me contrasting with the urgent pump of his stav.

And still I lay limp, the first rush of arousal upon waking and realizing Khell was fucking me softening into a drowsy and powerful throb.

"Soft, pretty, little petal," Khell'ar growled, hips snapping sudden and rough. My cry was brief, and my hands clenched until he filled my palms with his own, pinning me still. "Sweet cunt, wet and tight and full of cock, just like you like it."

He was too tall as he spread out fully on top of me, and it left my face pressed to his hot throat, the vibration of his voice drumming in my ears. He spread his feet wide, pushing my legs open to the point of strain, and he grew rough and urgent between my thighs, his claws digging gently into the backs of my hands.

"I'll fill you up with cum, petal. Make you heavy with my scent." I gasped as he spoke, squirmed into the crescendo of his thrusting to meet him. "I'll keep you plugged with my cock while you sleep, watch my seed seep out of you as I hunt you tomorrow."

"Oh god, Khell," I gasped, but with him covering me and spreading me with his body, the words were barely audible over his own grunts and groans.

He was a crushing, desperate animal on top of me, and my whole body ached from the force of his. Still, I tried to stay limp, relaxed, his vessel to use. The orgasm came on slowly, heat expanding from my center, and then a soft wave rising up from my toes over my head. Khell's stav swelled to a fist, pressing in against my G-spot, and the pleasure sharpened, harmonizing with the sudden rush of his own release inside of me.

How much is too much? When will my body just give up? I wondered.

Khell'ar bellowed into the top of my head, his tusks scratching, catching strands of my hair and tugging lightly. My heartbeat was an uneven roar in my own ears as he sagged on top of me, until I realized it was his pulse chorusing with mine.

Khell snarled, and then his hands loosened, soothing down my arms to wrap around my back before he rolled us on the mattress. He held me fastened to his hips and tucked my head gently against his chest. I was his ragdoll, fucked and filled and then nestled close.

And I loved it.

"You're going to hunt me tomorrow?" I asked, my breath catching. I wanted to climb up his chest and quiz him for details.

In the basement? Or out in the woods like I'd described to the agent on the phone?

I tried to lift my head to find his gaze, but he guided it back down immediately, his chest pillowy under my cheek.

"Sleep, petal," he said.

"You can't just fuck the air out of a girl, tell her you're going to hunt her, and then put her back to bed," I muttered.

Khell was quiet for a moment, and then he started to shake beneath me. "I can."

"Beast."

I was bent backwards, twisted, Khell careful to keep his promise of plugging me while maneuvering us on the bed so his face loomed over mine, eyes fire bright.

"Your beast," he growled.

It was like he'd put all his weight right back on top of me, double even. I couldn't breathe and didn't care either way. The words were a lie, but I wanted them to be true. Not for the five days I'd hired him, but—

This is just a fantasy, this is just a fantasy, I chanted in my head.

"And I do as I please with my pet, yes?" he asked, reaching between us to twist one nipple, then sliding his hand down to where we were joined, tracing my tender sex with the tip of a claw.

"Yes," I breathed out.

He was mine for five days, a little less than three more. And I *was* his.

The claw burrowed against his cock to tuck slightly inside of me, and the room had just enough light from the night for me to see the sharp grin he wore as I whimpered.

"YOU'RE ENJOYING THIS," I grumbled, catching Khell'ar's gaze fixed to my bare ass as I bent and stretched my arms down to my toes.

"Of course," he said with a shrug, lounging on the blue velvet couch as he directed my stretches. He cocked an eyebrow at me as he added, "It's my right. Squeeze."

I pretended my face was flushed hot from being upside down as I clenched my sex, and there was a slip of my orc's release oozing warmly out of me. Khell'ar growled in approval, and his tongue swiped over his lips.

"On your knees."

I'd woken with Khell'ar still wrapped around me—although apparently, he'd slipped out of me at some point in our sleep. He didn't snore, but his heavy breaths had ruffled the hair on top of my head. His arm was heavy over my waist, and one of his legs was stuffed firmly between my own. The thick and dense muscle had been hot against my sex, and I'd helped myself to a bit of grinding before he woke, only to have him encourage me to my own finish with some helpful dirty talk.

And now, even though I had no right to still be horny—I'd never been this sex-crazed in my entire life, but it was as if I was suddenly making up for years of being vanilla—I sank to my knees, planting my hands in front of me and arching my back to offer myself to Khell in this position.

He only chuckled. "Spread your knees and sit back on

your heels. Bend forward with your arms stretched in front of you."

Oh. Child's pose, yoga. I stretched into position and sighed as my back stretched, spine elongating.

Khell'ar coached me through more poses—cat-cow, baby cobra, downward-facing dog.

"Am I stretching in preparation to be hunted?" I asked as Khell rose from the couch to adjust my hips back, his hands petting over my ass and one finger pumping briefly in my pussy.

"Don't spoil your own surprises, petal."

We'd had a slow morning after I'd gotten myself off on his thigh. Khell had let me help make breakfast, although I'd still sat on his lap as we both ate. Then he'd pushed the dishes aside, bent me over the table, and fucked me to his own finish—not mine, though, and I was still a bit wound up from the tease.

"You're the one who mentioned the idea," I said with a huff, yelping as a large hand came down in a playful slap on my ass.

"You were meant to be sleeping." Khell pulled me upright, raising my hands up over my head and encouraging me to stretch high as I narrowed my eyes up at his.

"Did you really expect me to sleep through a fuck like that?"

His grin flashed. It was rare, and he usually hid it away just as quickly as it appeared, but I loved the sight of it, transforming his ferocious face with charm and humor. "You should've been very tired."

"Did you *want* me to sleep through it?"

His eyes grew warm, and his head ducked to mine, his dark braid swinging over his shoulder. "And miss your pretty whines and 'Oh god, Khell'?" he said in a poor imitation of my voice. I blushed, and he growled. "No. I like you awake as you come and call my name. But I don't mind you holding still and taking it like a good girl."

I choked on air, and Khell stepped away. No, the bastard sauntered, giant and bulky as he was.

"Maybe not as much as I like you thrashing on my cock, trying to fuck me with that sweet cunt of yours every bit as hard as I fuck you."

Would I come just from the filth Khell'ar spewed from those absurdly thick lips of his? It was becoming a close call.

"Digging your nails into the table, tearing the sheets. It's a good thing MSA has a damages policy—"

"Stop," I squeezed out, my hands flapping in front of my face as if they could cool the fever this orc was stoking in my cheeks.

Khell'ar just laughed and wrapped an arm around my waist, hauling me up from the floor so we were at eye level, even as I tried to avoid his stare.

"The sheets... Was that really me?" I asked, staring at a blank spot on the wall over his shoulder. It needed a piece of artwork, and I could almost imagine it, something that looked serene at first glance but was explicit the longer you stared.

"I wouldn't let you tear my hair out as I tongue-fucked your sweet pussy. You took your frustration out on the sheets," Khell said, voice low.

I reached up and tied my fingers into his braid now, finally finding the strength to meet his stare. "I suppose they are a better casualty," I said, tugging slightly on his hair. I had a sudden urge to make Khell *my* pet. To have him be the one crawling on his knees for me, subjecting himself to erotic poses for my gaze. But I couldn't imagine being the master and not having him fuck me exactly as he'd already been doing.

"What is making my petal smile like that?" Khell'ar asked, head tipping to the side.

"I was trying to imagine pinning you down and..." I laughed and shook my head. "I don't know what."

I expected him to laugh at the idea too, but his expression was thoughtful. "You could clamp me, keep me from coming. Take my ass with a toy. Leash me and ride me. Orcs heal well, and my ass would bounce nicely for a cane." He paused as my mouth dropped open, eyes growing wide. "Too much?"

"No—Not—I don't... You've thought more about this than I have," I said. Now that he mentioned them, my brain was racing to follow. The first suggestion was the most immediately appealing, although they all had merit.

"You have plenty of imagination, petal—you only need to decide what suits you. For now, we'll start with all those clever ideas you've been brewing."

"Like being hunted?" I asked immediately.

Khell'ar grunted and nodded, turning us and carrying me back to the couch, settling me in his lap. "If you refuse to be distracted, then we'd better start, unless you'd rather wait for dark. First, are you sore anywhere? Ankles, knees? Anything that would bother you while running?"

"I don't want to wait. And I'm not sore," I answered immediately, and Khell glared at me, forcing me to take a longer stock. "I really don't think so. I'm not much of a runner, though."

"I could catch you in seconds if I wanted to, but this is a game, so it's not about how fast you or I are," he said, adding with a twitch of a smile, "but I expect you to *run*."

I nodded, my fingers tightening in his hair, slipping against the thick and silky weave. He'd had it tied back this whole time, and I wondered what it looked like, felt like, when it was loose.

"There's no one around, just us," Khell'ar assured me. "Do you want to wear your monitor band?"

I'd taken the little device off after the first night and hadn't put it back on. Did I want to be wearing it so I could reach out to the agency during the chase? "No."

Khell didn't seem surprised, and he didn't ask me twice. "Is there anything you didn't include on your form that I can't do to you once I catch you?"

I blinked at that, studying his expression, but it was too smooth and professional again, the teasing and flirtation from minutes ago sadly missing. "I can't think of anything."

He was quiet, watching me. Was there anything I wouldn't be willing to let Khell do to me? He'd already been teasing and stretching my ass since the first night. He could spank me, choke me, chain me up…

"I'm going to do my best to scare you, petal, to be the beast," Khell said, reaching up and holding my chin. "Do you think being frightened will make a difference? Do you want me to check in with you once I catch you before I continue? It can be just a little word, or a kiss, or a touch on the hand."

Oh. Would being frightened of Khell'ar change my enjoyment of being fucked by him? I thought back to when we'd met, how careful he'd been, how it had made me think too hard. How the grip of his hand around my throat had cut through the noise and cleared my thoughts, made me his, calm and thrilled.

"No," I said. "No, I want to stay in the game, even when I'm frightened."

CHAPTER 12
Sunny

I OPENED the cottage door at exactly one-thirty, dressed for the first time in days.

Khell'ar had chosen the garments, laying them out on the bed for me to find before leaving the cottage. It was just another sundress, dark blue with straps that tied at the shoulders, and a matching set of pink lace underwear and a bralette that he'd spread out with obvious attention. The bra would do next to nothing for support. Running through the woods with lace and underwire would be more uncomfortable than helpful, but I put it on dutifully all the same. He'd also left a pair of comfortable but thin flats at the foot of the bed. Not that I'd brought running shoes with me. Not that I was meant to be able to *escape*.

On the dining table, I found a plate of light fare to eat and a quick note with instructions. Stay in the cottage until one-thirty. I wasn't sure what Khell was doing in the hour and change since he'd left. *A costume change, maybe,* I thought, grinning and remembering the funny red cape and deliciously short leather skirt he'd been wearing the first day.

The woods were quiet outside of the cottage—a little birdsong, a breeze rattling branches of leaves overhead, but peaceful. Was this cottage really so secluded? Were Khell'ar and I the only people for miles? Astraeya had promised there was more to this area than meets the eye, but for now, all I could be sure of was an endless expanse of trees and underbrush.

My chest burned before I realized I was holding my breath, searching the trees for Khell. Was I meant to just start running? I opened my lips to call for him and then shut them again. *Be patient. Play the game.*

I stepped forward to peek around the corner of the cottage, when an iron grip suddenly snapped around my wrist where I held the doorknob. My heart crashed in my chest and I jumped, spinning to face the snarling face of…

Khell.

I caught my breath, uneven as it was, and for a moment I smiled, my heartbeat racing from fear into excitement. Khell'ar bared his teeth at me, tusks biting into his upper lip, and his brow furrowed, eyes almost entirely dark in the sunlight.

I opened my mouth to ask how he got back inside the cottage without me noticing, but he yanked on my arm, pulling me roughly to his chest so I had to crane my neck back to look at him.

"Where does this sweet little cunt think it's going?" Khell'ar growled, his free hand slapping down on my ass and gripping it roughly.

Back to bed with you, I thought cheerfully. But of course, that wasn't what we were meant to be doing.

"Let me go," I breathed, uncertain if I sounded nervous or simply aroused.

"Why would I let you go when I could drag you by those pretty gold locks down into the dark?" Khell's voice was full of all the roughest of his echo, and I pressed my thighs together, my sex squeezing. "I could stuff you full of cock and seed until you knew nothing else."

I squirmed in his hold and considered snapping at him that if he wanted me to run, he'd better quit with the dirty talk and start being actually *frightening*.

"Beast," I gasped out, and this time my arousal was obvious, Khell's nostrils flaring in answer, his snarl flashing into a brief grin.

"Do you know what tastes good to an orc? What flavors the cunt to our liking?"

I licked my lips. This game was failing terribly. I was ready to climb Khell, not *run* from him. "What?"

"Fear, sweat, panic," he hissed, expression growing stern and dangerous again.

Then you're shit out of luck, buddy.

"And I am hungry, little human. I am so hungry, I would sink my teeth into you. I'd drink you down and feast on you."

Khell's head ducked, and his teeth gripped gently at the curve of my neck and shoulder, tusks digging in more insistently until I whined at the dull pain.

He retreated and I was arched in his hold, breaths gasping, my hips pressing forward against his thigh for the comfort of pressure.

"You must run, petal," Khell whispered, the words vibrating over my skin, my eyes falling shut on a weak sigh. "You must run, if I'm to get my feast."

My body tightened all at once, and Khell's hands released me so suddenly that I might've fallen over if I wasn't immediately in motion. I don't know what direction I turned, only away, charging toward the trees. Khell'ar roared behind me, and a flood of birds took up from their nests with bright cries, my own winded shriek joining theirs.

He knew me so well. I was too giddy at every delicious and dangerous suggestion. I would never run, not unless it was *for* him. I was mastered so easily.

I was also *not* a runner. My lungs began to burn first, my

breaths heaving with effort, my feet burning and aching in their flat and weak shoes, drumming pain up into my calves. The trees blurred around me, the ground uneven, and I swerved in a new direction. Was he following? Was he hunting me? His cum from the morning and my own arousal were sticky between my thighs, the running chafing.

Khell appeared suddenly from around a tree trunk on my right and I screamed, more out of surprise than terror. I stumbled back and hit a root with the heel of my foot, my balance faltering and sending me nearly to my ass, tree branches spinning above me.

But no, Khell's hands caught me, his claws digging into my hips, his laugh ragged and snarling as he set me back on my feet, braid swinging and slapping against his shoulders. I twisted out of his grip easily and ran again, and the laugh grew richer behind me, somehow menacing and thrilling at the same time. There was another roar, one that I thought shook the earth beneath my stumbling feet, but I swore the sound was full of pride.

Sunlight was cutting through branches and trunks, the woods almost like static as I rushed. I could hear Khell behind me now, running on my left, his steps broad and heavy and thumping, catching up with me quickly. He was herding me to the right again, driving me toward whatever destination he wanted.

Playful defiance rose up in me, the sudden desire to be the brat rather than Khell's good little pet, and I charged in a sudden left turn, the exact opposite direction in which he was trying to chase me.

Khell'ar growled as I neared him, out of arm's reach and making *his* steps stumble this time. I was grinning, breathless and aching at every rough step, but for a moment I felt victorious in surprising him.

Then he launched himself at me, crashing into me and wrapping his limbs around my body. The world jostled and spun as he tackled me down to the forest floor, the last air in my lungs knocked out. He was careful with me even then, keeping me from hitting the ground, one hand cupped around the back of my head. We rolled until he was pinned heavily on top of me, the sky bright above us through the trees, his eyes glinting with humor.

"Did you want to be caught so soon, petal?" he huffed.

Orcs heal quickly, I remembered him saying. I brought my knee up to his groin, watched his eyes widen in shock, a sudden bark pulled from his lips, and he released me to the dirt and grass and leaves. I rolled away from him as he laughed and growled, and I climbed up to my knees.

A hand gripped around my ankle and pulled me flat again, Khell's laugh louder, my skirt rucked up to expose my ass.

"Naughty little human, rough and ready like her orc."

I kicked, and Khell'ar grunted as the heel of my shoe connected with some part of him, I think his chest. His hand pulled the shoe off, but my foot was free, and I lunged up and ran forward again, Khell howling with delight behind me.

I shook my second shoe off and continued barefoot, wincing at the sting of debris on my feet but delighted with my triumph against my orc. He *would* catch me, I was sure of it, but I wasn't making it easy for him.

I'm probably not allowed to kick and hit my partner, I realized, but Khell was following, growling and snarling and roaring behind me, letting me hear him race closer. He was pleased with me, I was sure.

We were nearing a truly enormous tree, the trunk so broad both Khell and I could've stood comfortably inside of it together. I planned to weave left and then right, hoping to fool Khell, when I felt the waist of my dress snag in his grip.

I yelped and slipped free once, but I made the mistake of looking over my shoulder.

He was there, more massive and terrifying than ever, face

wild with the chase, teeth bared. My breath caught in my chest, and then his arm snapped around my middle, hauling me off my feet.

"Keep fighting, little human," Khell growled. "I like to conquer."

And now that I was in the joy of being hunted, of running, it was easier to not just give in to his usual siren call over me. I thrashed, and Khell tipped us forward, catching the ground on his knees and free hand, still keeping me safe. He dropped me then, framing me against the ground with his body, laughing as I landed on my belly and tried to squirm forward.

He flipped me to my back easily, grinning down at me so brightly, I could only stare back for a moment. Then his hand reached between us, digging into the collar of my dress and ripping it down the middle. I shouted as cool, fresh air rushed over my breasts and reached a hand up to slap at Khell, but he only batted it back to the ground.

I twisted, fighting my way back onto my knees, and Khell flipped my skirt up, smacking me roughly on the ass and making me falter as I tried to stand, the burn on my flesh exquisite. My head hung for a moment as I caught my bearings.

"Khell," I gasped. My cunt was throbbing, and my nipples were tight.

"Do you give up, pet?" Khell growled.

I groaned and then let out a snarl of my own, throwing myself up and forcing myself back to my feet. Khell chuckled and rose with me, only letting me surge three steps forward to the massive tree. He snatched me up again, this time with his hand scooped up under my skirt, cupping my sex as he lifted me into the air, my back to his chest. My breasts were exposed in lace, my eyes falling shut at the wonderful pressure of his fingers on my sex, and I rocked into the touch.

Thick fingers twisted under the fabric, and I cried out at the brief scrape of dull claws over my clit and lips, the pinch and scratch of the taut fabric rubbing against me, then there was a rip, and cool air rushed over my feverish flesh.

Khell tossed me back onto my feet in front of him, steadying me only as long as it took for me to stumble forward.

I didn't want to give up. I didn't want to keep running. I was hot, and the woods were spinning. Khell was right behind me, looming and ready, toying with me like a predator. I ran for the shelter of the tree, for the massive trunk, gasping as Khell snarled behind me, his shadow hazy on the grass. Fabric rustled, my breath hiccuped, and the sun spun overhead.

I was nearly in reach of the trunk when he tackled me forward again, softening the impact of the roots and moss beneath us briefly. One hand clasped my throat, the other shoved my skirt up with rough urgency. I barely caught a breath, and then Khell was thrusting in.

I howled at the shock, the stretch, the sudden *fill*. I was more than ready, slick and prepped from so much time spent riding that perfect girth, but it was still a surprise, still rough. His hand on my throat pinched once and then released me, and some automatic instinct, the sheer momentum of the game, left me crawling forward, pulling myself off Khell's cock.

He snarled behind me, and I only got as far as bracing myself against the roots of the tree before he pounced forward and thrust in again.

"Oh god, beast," I hissed, the fresh drum and thrust of him inside of me setting off an explosion of electric heat—not an orgasm but something like it. My body's expectation of the pleasure to come.

"Where will you crawl to now, pet?" Khell's hand returned to my throat, then down to my breast to squeeze, his claws unleashed to make unique points of pressure.

My hands slipped in moss, scratching forward into the

bark of the tree and accidentally tearing it away as Khell's hips started to crash against mine. The impact was hot and deep, and I scooted forward, barely an inch, maybe two, but Khell rolled.

"No more running," he barked.

His arm banded around my hips, bunching my dress up around my waist, and he hauled me up from the ground.

"Brace the trunk," he said through gritted teeth, but my hands were already stretched forward.

His palm on my throat spread broadly, holding my head up, and then he straightened.

Fuck! Full! Oh god, Khell. My toes lifted from the ground completely, and gravity forced Khell so deep inside of me, I thought I lost the use of my lungs. I was dangling, pinned on his cock, his arm around my hips and hand cupping my throat.

He thrust once, skin slapping wetly, his heavy sac kicking and kissing against my sex, my clit. An animal cry escaped my lips, and my eyes fell shut. The texture of the bark was rough on my palms, while the pump of Khell's stav in my cunt was urgent. His thrusts were shallow, careful not to pull out far enough to separate us, but it only meant there was more contact. He was gentle with my throat, in contrast to his merciless use of my cunt, his hand not squeezing but supporting, claws teasing little bites of my pulse.

My legs swung and beat against Khell's as he fucked me, my voice senseless and noisy, lips babbling and gaze staring up at the bouncing branches of the enormous tree I was braced against. I could feel him in my veins, in my head, the *drum drum drum, slap slap slap, tug tug tug* of thrusting hips and pumping stav.

I love this. Why do I love this? God, it's so good.

Khell snarled and growled behind me. "Sweet cunt. Perfect little ass bouncing as I fuck you, petal. I can feel your pulse like a little rabbit's drumming against my claws."

"Yours, beast," I rasped, the first logical words I'd uttered since he'd speared me and lifted me into the air.

Khell's roar was soft and velvety, his hips kicking faster. His arm around my hips adjusted so his hand could cup my clit, the other on my throat tightening. He rubbed me with the flat of his fingers, then walked us forward and shifted his hand on my throat until he was wrapped around me.

His heartbeat was hard against my back, a comforting echo of my own heavy and needful tempo.

"Fuck, Sunny," he hissed in my ear, undeniably desperate, his face nuzzling at me, tusks tangling with my hair, tongue flicking out to lick at my pulse.

I was pressed between him and the tree trunk, my torn clothing and Khell's embrace protecting me from some but not all of the friction of the bark, the scratch a new layer of sensation until it all blurred together. His fingers grew clumsy and demanding against my clit, the sensation there a fuzzy but scorching burn. I knew this feeling, the too-much that sometimes made me give up when I was trying to get myself off, that felt like I would never reach the peak. Ecstasy would either break through, harder and more overwhelming than ever, or it would wait there at the edges until frustration made me too weary to continue.

But Khell would not give up.

"Come, Sunny. Come for your beast," Khell rumbled, words ragged, demanding.

He stayed buried, rocking into my ass, grinding his cock inside of me, stav stroking and pleading. His teeth and tusks bit at my shoulder, his growl vibrating down into my breasts. And still, he rubbed and pressed and coaxed roughly at my clit.

The first burst struck at last, unexpected and without warning, but Khell and I both felt the sudden clasp of my cunt on his length. He roared into me, his release sudden and explosive, expanding and amplifying my own until there was only light in my eyes and Khell's voice in my ear and a sharp, jagged bliss coursing through my body.

CHAPTER 13
Khell'ar

YOU ARE SCREWED. *You should take her back to the cottage now before this goes any further. You should talk to Astraeya.*

Instead, I wrapped myself tighter around Sunny, growling at myself for suggesting the idea of turning away now. She was shaking, still fluttering on my cock, her breaths short and just a bit too frantic. I eased us slowly back from the trunk, tempted to stay buried in her but knowing she needed to be able to breathe, to separate herself from the intensity of the act. Especially given what I had planned next for us.

She'd been exquisite. Better than I'd imagined. I wanted to throw her back down to the forest floor, wrestle again, watch her eyes go wild as she kicked and thrashed and bit me, all while looking forward to that moment when I *won* and caught her at last.

I waited until her aftershocks had faded and she was limp in my hold before moving. Sunny whimpered as I pulled free, turning her to face me and scooping her up into my arms, her own reaching up to cling weakly to me. Her eyes were open but glazed, and I shuffled her gently in my hold until I was able to brush her cheeks with my finger.

"I'm awake," she murmured, sounding very much at the edge of sleep.

"I think you'll want to see this part, petal," I said.

She hummed and nodded, but didn't look much more aware. No matter, I would show her the magic trick on our way out if she was too dazed to take note of it now. I walked us around the trunk of the tree until the dark slit appeared in the trunk. Sunny hummed, her cheek against my shoulder as I carried her forward, squeezing her against me so we could fit through together. It was orc-sized, so we just managed. Inside was dark, too dark for Sunny's eyes, but I found the spiraling staircase turning down into the roots easily enough.

"An orc den," Sunny murmured. "Is it yours?"

I resisted the urge to laugh. Most orcs didn't live in dens these days, too in love with modern amenities like Wi-Fi and indoor plumbing. I had a garden apartment at the edge of Chicago, still comfortably underground but much more in line with contemporary living.

"It's ours for the day," I said instead.

In truth, this den was more of a clever disguise than a traditional den, with support beams crafted to appear like tree roots running down the curved walls, a real bathroom hidden around a curve at the far corner, and a nest that was pillowed and padded to suit much softer human tastes. A chest stood at the foot of the nest, filled with all the tools I could think of for entertaining both Sunny and myself. But with one glance at her in my arm, limp and dizzy with her release, I had one goal in mind, and it would take very little support from the toys.

I carried Sunny to the rounded nest at the opposite side of the den, and she sighed as I lowered her onto the dense mattress, surrounded by piles of pillows. She sank into the cushion, her legs sprawling open, torn lace panties still shredded around her waist, offering me a perfect view of her tender red pussy and my seed leaking out of her.

Couldn't have that.

Sunny's eyes fell shut as I rose from the nest and turned to the closed trunk, lifting the heavy lid and digging into the contents. With a few toys and a generous bottle of lube juggled in my hands, I turned to the nest, climbing in. I settled myself cross-legged on the mattress, pushing aside some of the copious pillows and lifting Sunny's sprawled legs to drape over mine. Her lips curled as I stroked my hands over her thighs, and then parted on an O as I took the thick, curved plug and dipped it into her weeping cunt.

"Khell," she breathed, blinking up at the root vaulted ceiling, stomach jumping and breath hitching.

The plug sank into her easily, and Sunny moaned, her eyes opening again as I settled it deep, the blunt curve teasing her sensitive interior.

"I want you nice and full of my cum, sweet petal," I growled.

Sunny squirmed weakly and sighed, nodding, trying to pull her legs together as if to help me plug her. Her inner thighs met my hands, soft flesh pressing into my palms as I held her open and snarled in warning.

"I said full, Sunny. I'm not done with you."

"You're never done with me," she answered softly, smiling as my claws bit into her thighs in answer.

I would be. In two days, our time would be up and Sunny would leave the cottage and my service. But I wouldn't be done with her until that time, I was certain of that.

"Sit up for me, petal. I want you bared to me."

Sunny groaned as she obeyed, her hair a mess and her clothes torn. I picked a few leaves free of her bright locks and purred for Sunny as she waited for me to undress her. I lifted the dress from over her head, tossed it to the floor of the den, and unbuckled the front clasp of her bra, tweaking her nipples with my claws until her breathing grew heavy.

"I think we'll leave this," I said, petting the waistband of the lace underwear where it tucked into the curve of her stomach. I liked the proof of it, that she'd let me tear them off her, had shouted in joy when I caught and filled her.

Sunny lay back into the mattress at my nod. I patted her legs to remind her to stay still and then took the second tapered plug and bottle of lube, working from my lap where Sunny couldn't see what I was doing. There was a little trail of cum running down from Sunny's cunt to her ass, and I used the tip of the plug to tease it closer, fucking it against her hole.

"Oh!" Sunny stiffened, and I huffed as she tightened, pressing the plug out.

"Did you think I wouldn't want you here too, petal? Open to your master."

Sunny's red tongue flicked out to wet her lips, her chin lifting briefly to meet my eyes. "For…all the way this time?"

I couldn't resist my grin at her bright blush, and I nodded in answer. "You're going to take my orc cock here too. My cum. And then I'm going to plug you up and leave you full of me for the rest of the day…or until I want to fuck you again."

Sunny gaped at me for a moment, her lips parting and closing shyly before she finally softened into the mattress. "Will it hurt?" she asked in a tiny voice.

I set the plug against the mattress so that it remained touching her without pressing in. "Yes," I said. It would do no good to tell her otherwise. Orc cock was ample, and my Sunny was lusty but only human. "But I promise you I will cause *no harm* if you grant me this. Did my two fingers hurt?"

Sunny relaxed as she considered the question. "It stung, but…I did like it. You took your time."

"You know I like to savor you," I answered, drawing out a bright smile from her lips. "And I want you relaxed as I fill your lovely ass."

She blushed again, but this time, she softened and settled,

wiggling down to bump herself against the plug waiting for her. "Okay."

I bent forward, kissing Sunny's stomach through lace, licking her through the strange texture until she squirmed. I found the spot of her underwear that had covered her sex, now rich with her scent, and sucked her flavor off the fabric. Sunny's hands stroked over my shoulders, groping softly, playing at the soft rub of my skin that I knew she liked so well.

My hand found the plug, stroking it against the crease of her ass, from the hilt of the plug in her cunt and over her asshole, back and forth until Sunny moaned. This time, as I pushed against her hole, the plug sank in an inch.

I purred my pleasure and sat up, Sunny's hands falling into the sheets of the nest, fisting and twisting fabric as she gasped, and I fucked her ass with the plug. She was barely taking two inches, but the taper was broad and every little millimeter made a difference in readying her for my girth.

"What do you like better, my fingers or the plug?" I asked.

"You!" Sunny cried out immediately, even as her brow furrowed and she tried to push herself onto the plug. "Always you."

The words alone tempted me to roll her onto her belly and fill her roughly, but my better sense reigned. I pulled the plug back, drawing my claws in, and Sunny cried out as I pressed my finger into her hole, pumping and stroking as she wiggled and rode my digit. I hitched her higher onto my lap, giving me more space to maneuver, and then pressed the thumb of my free hand onto the base of the plug in her cunt, making it grind inside of her.

Sunny's breath caught as I wiggled my second finger into her, and she froze in place for a moment before slowly releasing her breath and relaxing again, making my tease of her ass smoother.

"Good girl," I growled, leaving the plug in place as I

squirted more lube onto my pumping fingers. I was tempted to try and stuff a third finger into her, but the plug would be easier on her body. Instead, I savored the moment of her body squeezing and pinching on my fingers.

"You are made for orc cock, petal," I murmured.

"Yes," Sunny breathed, her answer more a response to what I was doing to her than the words.

"You were so good for me today. Such a perfect pet."

Sunny's response to praise was beautiful, the words driving her into a wild height in her mind, a base and subconscious response. She rocked on my fingers, her eyes drifting aimlessly around the room, her mouth open to sigh out whimpers and moans and cries. I stroked her clit with a slippery thumb and chuckled as Sunny squealed in response, trembling on my lap.

"Your ass is going to open to me, submit to your master's cock, just as the rest of your pretty little body has."

"Yes, beast!"

"Spread your cheeks for your beast, petal."

Sunny whined and shuddered, but her hands flew from above her head down to her hips, grabbing rough fistfuls of her ass and pulling her cheeks apart. I purred for her, pulling my fingers free. Sunny sobbed, her face scrunched in frustration, until I replaced my fingers with the freshly lubed, larger plug. She moaned and relaxed, sinking on its width to about an inch and a half above the base.

Sunny was musical as I fucked her ass with the plug, all whines and whimpers and then slow, guttural groans. I teased her clit enough to keep her at the edge, leaned down to lick circles around her nipples, and scraped the undersides of her breasts with my tusks.

"Oh god, Khell, I—"

I sat up at Sunny's breathless words, glancing to see my fingertips just poised against the crease of her ass, the plug spreading her beautifully wide. My cock was nuzzled against her stuffed sex, oozing more lubrication down to her ass. She was ready for me. My stav would stretch her further once I was inside her.

"Pain?" I asked, my own voice tight and my head cloudy with just the idea of filling my little Sunny's ass.

"Yes," Sunny said, nodding rapidly. "And more. Good. Please, I want you."

My purr grew thick with her jumbled words. I gave her clit one last gentle rub with my thumb before pulling away, slowly dragging the slippery plug out of her ass. Her hole gaped at me, a mirror of Sunny's open mouth, robbed of language and gasping for air.

I moved her hands from her hips, replacing them with my own, not even bothering to try and restrain my claws. Sunny liked them and the little marks they left on her body when I gripped her. My cock found the space I'd made for it unerringly, nudging at Sunny's open ass, kissing and wetting the spot with sticky arousal. My gaze couldn't make up its mind, flashing between the spot where I was slowly filling her to the arch of her back and upward thrust of her breasts as she let out a garbled cry.

I had prepared Sunny's entrance for me, and the steady flood of precum inside of her helped the slow progress of pushing in, but I kept my pace measured. Sunny's body tried to retreat, twisting away, and I let out a growl that froze her and sent her collapsing again, her eyes finding mine with an unspoken plea. But her body relaxing allowed gravity to help me fill her, until her opening met the resistance of my swollen stav.

My own breathing was labored, my muscles strained and jaw clenched as I resisted the urge to slam inside of Sunny's ass. Patience would be my reward. That, and the look on Sunny's face as my stav's slow pumping stretched her that last margin.

Our voices chorused in shouts as I sank inside to my hilt,

the vise of Sunny on my cock booming an electric shock at the base of my spine. My stav was pumping, stimulating me in her tight channel, and for several seconds, neither of us breathed. Sunny's rapid heartbeat sang through me, a bright little drum beneath the steadier tempo of my own pulse.

"Khell," she gasped out, and my vision sharpened.

Sunny was spread before me like a feast, the base of the plug in her cunt winking at me, the sharp tips of her breasts begging for attention, her bottom lip captured between her teeth, golden hair tangled in the sheets.

Mine, I thought.

I flexed my hips, and Sunny's soft cry praised my effort.

"Touch your breasts, petal," I said, words all grit and gravel.

She gasped relief at the instruction as I started a slow, gentle motion inside of her, rubbing upwards until I could feel the resistance of the plug. Sunny sobbed, her hands ferocious on her own breasts, no doubt distracting herself from the pressure in her ass.

"Tell me what a good girl you are," I said. Sunny whined, and I reached out, flicking roughly at the base of the plug and making her yelp. "Tell me, petal."

"I'm—I'm a good girl," she whispered. I growled, and Sunny whined. "I'm such a good girl...for you."

"Yes," I said, lifting Sunny's hips with my own, creating a broader stroke, teasing her opening with the thrust and stretch of my stav.

"I'm so good for you, beast," Sunny cried out. "I would... Fuck! I would do anything you asked me to. I'm a good girl. I'm yours, please!"

I snarled, my stav growing urgent, my blood hot in my veins, and leaned down, sucking and kissing at whatever skin I could find—the soft round of her tummy and ribs.

"Oh, god, Khell, I'm your good girl, I—I—"

The hiccup was familiar, the sound of Sunny at the cusp of

an orgasm, and I shifted one hand to gently rub her clit, rewarding her for this gift and knowing the stimulation would—

I roared into her skin as she clamped around me, body biting down as the orgasm swallowed her beneath the wave, demanding my own sacrifice too. I came with a sudden, explosive momentum, my arms wrapping around Sunny, pulling her firmly onto my cock, to my hilt, like I was trying to force her body to consume me or vice versa. I bit at her rib and released the spot quickly before I could hurt her. Her hands tangled into the braid running down the back of my head, holding me as we shook and shuddered, my cock pumping her ass full of seed that would soothe the stretched muscles.

We were tangled together, contorted and uncomfortably clasped as Sunny milked me for every last drop, while I kept her speared on my length. When the pulse of pleasure slowed, softened, and shivered gently into stillness, I sighed into Sunny, reaching my hands back to untangle her fingers out of my hair, then sitting up to admire the wreckage. There were two red marks on her side where my tusks had nearly broken skin, and I rubbed my thumb over them gently.

Sunny's expression was still slightly strained, her breath short, and I bent once more to kiss each of her breasts before relenting. I scooped up the large plug from the mattress and held it in one hand as I slowly withdrew from her ass. Sunny hissed at my retreat, brow furrowed, but she sighed by the end. A slow rush of my seed followed my cock out, and I stopped it short, replacing the head of my cock with the plug and holding Sunny's gaze through her brief wince.

"How long?" she asked.

How long would I keep her plugged? Probably not long. I wanted to clean her before we retired for sleep. But instead I answered, "Until I want to fill you with my cock again."

And Sunny, because she was so good, such a perfect fit for

an orc's—no, *my* appetites, just giggled and squirmed experimentally.

"Fine, beast. Will you hold me?"

I growled and dove down to Sunny's side, scooping her up in my arms and hooking one leg over her hips to hold her legs together and add to the friction of the plugs inside of her.

I was on my side, Sunny cradled in my grasp, her cheeks pink and brow dewy with sweat. She licked her lip, and hunger stirred through me. I'd had little occasion to kiss those lips during today's games, and I dipped my head now.

"My pretty petal," I murmured, and Sunny arched eagerly for the kiss, moaning as my mouth met hers for a slow and deep caress. "My good girl," I growled in her ear as she shivered.

Sunny sighed as I kissed her again, opening her mouth for me to fill with my tongue, to lick and stroke against her own. My hands wandered over her skin, from the slope of her back to her rounded ass.

"Did you like my cock in your ass, petal?" I teased.

Sunny shifted in my hold, her head falling back to rest against my arm, her face and throat flushed with new arousal, eyelids drooping with exhaustion.

"Yes, beast. I love everything you do to me. Today was *wonderful,*" she said, a dreamy lilt in her voice.

I swallowed hard but was unable to dislodge the lump that appeared in my throat. So I bent my head, taking her lips more gently, nibbling and teasing them with my tongue and teeth and tusks until Sunny's hands were grasping at my chest.

She was a dangerous little creature. And I was finding myself far more defenseless than any orc had a right to be.

CHAPTER 14
Sunny

"SO WHO DID MAKE THIS?" I asked Khell'ar.

I was kneeling on a padded mat in front of a large tub, still nude and still very much plugged. Khell had woken me at some point for more sex, a rough and quick fuck with me on my belly and him holding me spread wide. Thankfully not again in the ass though, since I was still feeling that just on the fun side of too much.

Khell hummed in the tub, his enormous frame filling it to the brim, head hanging over the ledge as I followed his instructions on stroking a warmly scented oil through the thick locks. It was the first time I'd seen his hair out of the braid, and it was beautifully long and just slightly coarse. I was taking more time than necessary to brush it out and clean it, finding the act intimate and quiet after the long and exciting day.

His shoulder shrugged, and the water rippled across the surface of the tub. "The agency, I suppose. It's close to a den, but more comfortable for clients."

"How…" I hesitated over the question. Khell was usually careful to keep us immersed in the fantasy, only occasionally interjecting comments that reminded me of our position as client and professional. "How long have you worked for the agency?" I asked at last.

"Eight years," Khell said easily.

My eyes widened. That seemed like a long time. Or maybe it was just a good, professional track record. I had other, more intrusive questions—did he have relationships outside of his work, a partner at home?—but I kept my mouth shut on those, not certain I wanted the answers.

"Have you always wanted to do this?" I asked.

Khell chuckled and turned his head to catch my eye. "Fuck? Since I was a sprout, yes." I blushed, and Khell grinned at me. "I apprenticed in construction, but this was more fun."

I hummed and smiled at that, a little peek into the orc outside of the all the sex we'd been having for the past three days.

Only two left.

I brushed that souring thought aside and met Khell's eyes again, finding them narrowed on my face. "What?"

"Hmm. I have a personal question for you too, but—"

"Go ahead," I rushed out, bizarrely excited for the simple act of conversation with Khell.

"Why is this your first time trying anything like this? Not...not with a professional like me, but at all?" Khell asked slowly.

I blinked at that, the question taking me off guard. "Oh. Um...I didn't... At first, I thought some of the fantasies I had were kind of..." I bit my lip, and Khell smiled at me.

"Perverse?" he suggested evenly.

I winced and nodded, shrugging at the same time. "Yeah, I guess. Or like, dangerous. Or just ideas, but not ones I would enjoy actually going through with." Khell didn't have any judgment in his expression. In fact, it was the opposite—he was nodding in calm agreement. "And it wasn't until I was in a long relationship with someone who really wasn't at all interested in anything like this that I started to feel like it was actually something I was *missing*."

Khell frowned and shifted to sit up. "Are you still in that relationship?" There was a slight growl in his tone, and he cleared his throat immediately after. "It's not my business. You don't have to answer."

"No, I'm not," I said immediately, my eyes trailing away. "But...we split up a little over a week ago. He proposed. I said no."

I wasn't sure *why* I was telling Khell all of this, only that it was easy to speak the words, and relieving too.

"Stand up, petal," Khell said, tone firm enough that I followed on instinct.

When he reached between my legs, my cheeks went up in flames, and I let out a whimper of embarrassment as he pulled the plug free and a rush of cum ran out of me. *It's his fault, not yours,* I reminded myself as Khell reached up with a washcloth, cleaning me patiently.

To distract myself, I picked up the conversation where we'd left it. "I just didn't want to be with someone forever, wondering if I was hiding this. Or that I couldn't *ever* find out if it was something I wanted in a sexual relationship."

"Turn," Khell said, and I squeezed my eyes shut. The plug in my ass left me with a constant stuffed sensation, and I was almost terrified of having him pull it out.

But I turned and prattled on. "That wasn't all that wasn't working between us or anything, but I just couldn't shake it. My friend said I should try and find out the answer, and I thought she meant with a stranger—" I gasped and squeaked as Khell pulled out the plug, the hollow sensation shocking and vulnerable. He covered me with the washcloth, rubbing around my asshole to soothe me. "She meant a professional, and I'd seen the ads so...so I called the agency," I finished lamely.

"That was very brave of you, petal," Khell said lowly. He

tossed the washcloth away from us. "Come. Join me, and we'll wash each other."

I sighed and hurried into the water, wincing at the brief sting. In spite of the invitation to wash, the first thing Khell did was bundle me against his chest, arms wrapping around my bare back.

"I was right," I murmured. "I should've done something sooner, but I was right about myself. I couldn't go the rest of my life without this."

Khell purred, head lowering to nuzzle against my hair. "No. No, you are too perfectly suited. You are orc bait, petal."

I snorted at that and tilted my head back, but found Khell's gaze solemn.

"One of my kind would've sniffed you out eventually, hunted that pretty cunt down, and claimed you."

My lips parted but I couldn't form a word, and Khell just took it as an opportunity to kiss me, tongue stroking in to tease and twine around mine.

Did he mean that, or was it pretty words he felt paid to say? Would *he* have hunted me if we'd met in the city? If I'd seen Khell in the park or the grocery store or at a bar on a night out with Natalie, would I have been brave enough to meet his eye, dare him to come speak to me?

The honest truth was probably no.

My heart ached and clenched in my chest, and I wrapped my arms tight around Khell's shoulders, clinging to him and begging for more in the kiss.

"WE'RE STAYING THE NIGHT HERE?" I mumbled as Khell tucked blankets in around us in the deep, round pit of a bed.

"We are."

He'd turned the lanterns in the room down to the smallest

little flickers of light. Deep underground as we were, it could've been early evening or dawn for all I knew. Our bath had been slow and thorough and gentle, stirring up arousal without feeding it into another session of fucking. I'd fallen asleep and woken again in the nest, Khell settling in with a plate of food that he let me feed to us both.

Now fed and bathed, I found myself surrounded by the heat and muscle of my—

I blinked in the dark, my throat tight.

My *partner*. Not my orc. Khell wasn't mine.

Maybe so many days together like this was a mistake for my first experience. I didn't know how to accept the intimacy Khell offered for the sake of my comfort without the gestures affecting my emotions.

I didn't want to leave, didn't want this fantasy I'd *paid* for to break apart. I couldn't even imagine the reality that was only days away, and I couldn't imagine Khell as part of my real life. He was too vivid, too consuming. He certainly wouldn't fit in my small coach house bathroom.

"What's sore?" Khell rumbled into the top of my head.

I'd been growing tense, barely noticing Khell's hands stroking and soothing at my back and hips. Since "my heart" was too melodramatic an answer, I settled on, "My hips, but just a little."

Khell made that lovely growling purr sound that vibrated through his whole chest, and his arms circled me, rotating my limp and rested body slowly until my back was to his front. His legs curled up behind mine, chin at the crown of my head, making him a comically large spoon.

One hand passed over my bare breasts, squeezing them each gently in turn, and then down over my sex. His fingers slipped between my thighs, lifting one up and guiding my leg to rest over his.

At the back of my mind, I marveled at my own lack of surprise that Khell was maneuvering me for more sex. This was my role here, wonderfully simple and shockingly decadent. I was his to use.

But Khell was drawing me to lean against him, his arms around me, hands covering my hips and fingers digging in. I moaned softly at the lovely, aching relief that followed, Khell carefully working my muscles loose. There was a hint of arousal as he touched me, hands stroking the crease of my thighs and just outside of my sex, down the inner muscles of my thighs and around to return to my ass, but the day had been too long and too full of extreme sensation for me to do more than accept the gentle attention my orc offered.

There you go again, I hissed to myself, but half of my brain was already offline, exhausted and soothed by Khell's massage, and the other half was following quickly.

"You were perfect today, petal."

"So were you," I murmured, snuggling back into the warm and velvety chest at my back. "The whole time. I'm lucky it was you, beast."

Why can't it always be you, Khell?

"I'm lucky too."

I felt the words more than heard them, a whisper over the top of my head, tickling through my mess of hair, fluttering over my falling lashes as I sank to sleep at last.

I WOKE BEFORE KHELL, the den just faintly lit by the lamps, enough for me to sit up in the nest of blankets and pillows and stare down at the orc snoring softly.

I'd come to the agency, to Khell, to discover a truth about myself. But I'd accomplished that easily enough on the very first day. Now I found myself obsessed with the male before me, curious about the truth of Khell. He was a secret to me, presented at my feet, naked and handsome and sexual, but that exposure was a kind of deception.

He knew my private fantasies, every inch of my body, now some of my own history. I knew the snarl on his face as he glared down at me almost in anger, exploding with satisfaction inside of me. I knew his laughter, and I was certain it was honest. But I didn't know which of his words were true, or if what we did together was more than the base satisfaction of fucking for him. I thought he was enjoying himself as much as I was, but while this was a job, I couldn't be certain.

Did I really want Khell, or did I want his performance that was designed to please me?

I was afraid the question was impossible to answer until I knew the alternative, a version of reality far out of my reach.

Khell hummed and grunted in his sleep, shifting and nudging the blanket down from his stomach until the defined and muscular Adonis belt of his hips was visible. He was a little softer-looking in sleep, some of the tension of his body easing and making the sharp lines of his muscles less defined.

I twisted my hand into the hem of the blanket, pulling it slowly away from him to reveal his cock, the broad spread of his legs, the heavy sac resting against the mattress. I reached out to touch him, to claim him in my hand, make demands at my own whim, and then paused.

Was I allowed? I'd signed all the forms of consent, spelled out clearly that I wanted to be touched while sleeping, but Khell hadn't. It was only further proof of the line between us, the brittle reality of the joy I'd found with him, and I craved to drive forward and shatter the barrier, take what I wanted and make Khell...*mine.*

"Touch me."

I shivered at the sound of his voice, both relieved and disappointed to glance up and find his eyes open, studying me with the same focus I'd been giving him.

I took the permission immediately, my hand wrapping around Khell's soft cock by the base, holding his gaze. I fisted him tightly and pumped, working my way up to his tip and smiling as he grunted, and I found the first pool of his ample precum, helping my progress of working him in my grip.

Khell'ar groaned, his arms stretching in the nest, hips nudging up into my grip. He was a picture of surrender, and I wasn't fooled for a second. He could take the control back from me in a heartbeat. He'd already ordered me to touch him.

Rather than wait for his next command, I climbed over one thigh, making a place for myself between his legs. I wrapped both hands around his cock, now stiff with his stav starting to pump in the velvety, thick sleeve of his length. I was very fond of that delightful internal mechanism of his, like his cock was working double time to satisfy me.

His clients, a bitter voice whispered, and I brushed it quickly away.

Khell's hands reached down to scoop my hair back as I ducked and took my first lick. The rich flavor of him was immediately satisfying on my tongue, feeding a hunger that seemed to simmer constantly in the background ever since I'd knelt before him in the dungeon and taken him in my mouth for the first time.

I'd never been that excited to offer oral—and a bit self-conscious when receiving it—but Khell made such lovely sounds as I worked him into my mouth and had a flavor I was growing fond of, and now I always found myself looking forward to the act.

"Is my petal hungry this morning?" Khell asked, words rough and amused, a chuckle broken by a groan as I sucked him down as deep as I could.

"You said you would teach my throat to take your cock," I said with a gasp as I lifted off his length.

His eyes widened slightly at that announcement, and I blushed. I wanted to conquer this orc. This male. Khell'ar. I wanted to master his body as he'd mastered mine. I wanted to be his favorite, and the thought made my eyes sting with its futility, its meaninglessness. I dove back down and sucked at his cock roughly, but my throat had tightened and I gagged slightly as I tried to force my way down.

Khell grunted and his hips flexed up as I squeezed around him, but he retreated quickly and his fingers tugged in my hair, lifting me up again. "Not from this position. Up, little petal."

I sat up, gasping, and Khell moved quickly, knocking me back down into the blankets and then jumping up out of the nest to kneel at the edge near my head. His hands grabbed my ankles and yanked them up into the air. He jostled me into place until my head was hanging over the edge of the nest, his cock poised just in front of my lips, and my legs spread in the air.

"You must slap my hip if it's too much," Khell said sternly, his bright irises just visible in the dark above, before adding, "but I will motivate you to stay relaxed."

He dove down before I could answer, lips and tongue hungry on my cunt. I cried out, and the sound was muffled by a gentle thrust of Khell's hips, his cock finding its way home between my lips. I moaned and let my eyes fall shut, drawing him in eagerly, whimpering and whining as his tongue thrust into me.

Oh, he was right! His cock sank in more easily from this angle, with my throat open. I reached out and grasped his thighs in tight grips, using the leverage to test how deeply I could take him straight away. Khell snarled against me, the dark vibration wonderful on my sensitive sex, and I moaned around his cock in answer, a small rush of fluid soothing my throat. If my mouth weren't so stuffed, I would've grinned.

I would conquer my orc, but not without him returning the favor, it seemed. I could learn to live with that.

CHAPTER 15
Khell'ar

SUNNY FROWNED at the pattern on the game board, munching aimlessly on the bowl of trail mix I'd set at her side. She was swamped in the fabric of a green velvet cloak, one that was meant to be a costume of mine for today's game—a game I was forgoing in favor of one of an entirely different nature.

"Do you give up?" I asked.

"No," Sunny snapped immediately.

I tucked my grin behind my hand and glanced down at the board again. She'd picked up the rules of Ram'kurr—a traditional orcish game that I'd been told was a cross between human's chess and euchre—within a few rounds. She did well, for a human woman who'd been playing for less than two hours, but she was no match for—

"Aha!" she cried, scooping up two of her speckled tokens, scooting one of my solids, and then stealing away a speckled one of my own.

It was my turn now to frown at the board. Surely she'd broken a rule...made some novice mistake to...

No. No, Sunny had simply bested me.

"Do you give up?" she cooed in a teasing, saccharine tone.

"An orc never surrenders to the enemy," I said.

Ram'kurr amongst orcs generally ended in a physical fight, or with the loser refusing to admit defeat and the game being set aside until someone else bothered to clear it up and put it away for the next time.

Sunny hummed, smirking like the devilish little champion she apparently was, and nestled into the heap of pillows at her back, carrying her bowl of nuts with her.

Beginner's luck, I thought but refused to speak out loud.

A small, pale foot perched itself on my right knee, toes wiggling in greeting. "Well, while you search futilely for your next move, how about a foot massage?"

I growled softly, but with a glance out of the corner of my eyes, I saw that the sound didn't deter Sunny's glee in the least. Her cheeks were flushed, a sweeter pink than the one I drew out when I was fucking her breathless, and her bottom lip was caught between her teeth, trapped in her grin. The green velvet had slid aside, offering me the view of Sunny's wonderfully biteable thigh nearly up to her hip.

I snatched the foot into my grip and pulled, tugging Sunny out of her throne of pillows and onto her back with a yelp of surprise. She glared at me through rumpled golden hair, and the robe slipped yet again to reveal one breast. With my claws retracted, I dug my thumbs into the arch of her foot and smirked as Sunny's annoyance melted into approval, her body squirming closer as I circled my thumbs into weary and tight muscles.

We were meant to be back at the cottage by now. I'd originally planned on satisfying the curiosity Sunny had for being restrained and paddled—a scenario from her notes that I thought would be especially appealing in front of the large mirrors in the dungeon.

"God, that's so nice," Sunny murmured, toes curling and another sexual moan rising from her throat.

I could see her pussy now under the shadow of the robe,

red and tender. I could smell her arousal too, tart and sweet and tempting. But Sunny had soft, red scratches on her skin from my claws, and delicate bruises too. There were shadows under her eyes, and after she'd finished draining my balls dry with her mouth this morning, she'd drunk two full glasses of water in a row, not having realized how parched she'd become. Her body was rightfully tired, and while she'd paid for this experience, this stretching of her limits, the strain of being under command, I couldn't resist this backwards self-ishness.

Sunny needed care, and I was making that my only goal for our day. I'd been feeding her since we woke, making sure there was always a tempting snack close at hand. Once this massage was done, I would carry her into another bath full of salts to soothe her muscles, plus oats and milk and herbs to heal her skin. We would nap in the dark of the den, take dinner by candlelight, and I would carry her back to the cottage under the moonlight.

"Khell," Sunny breathed, nudging me with her other foot. "What time is it?"

"I don't know," I lied.

We only have one more day, I thought. *She will leave me tomorrow night.*

Sunny hummed as I pulled and rubbed at her toes before switching to her other foot. She started up her moaning again and I huffed, forcing my stare up to the ceiling of the den rather than the sensual woman in front of me.

"Are you bored, petal?" Was she wondering why I hadn't proposed our next game? The ones we were *meant* to be playing.

"Nooo," Sunny said, drawing the word out, her head shaking. "You're...you're making me rest, aren't you?"

"Yes. You need it."

I braced myself for her argument, my frown growing

deeper as I found a scratch on one of her ankles, probably from running through the woods the day before.

"I do," Sunny said on a sigh. She swept her hair back from her face and smiled at me. "Thank you, Khell."

I grunted, attempting to dismiss her gratitude, but even I knew it was useless. Sunny's skin was soft and cool in my hands, warming under my touch. My lungs were full of her scent, fresh and bright and sharp, and she was still rich on my tongue. My gaze tracked every rise and fall of her chest, the flutter of her lashes as she blinked. My ears muted the rest of the world to study her breaths, her heartbeat.

"You're so good at this," she whispered.

My hands were working their way up to her calves, an ankle in each grip. "We take anatomy classes when we join MSA. And physical therapy. Nutrition." Sexual therapy classes too. And MSA specific courses on safety and etiquette with our partners. I wasn't supposed to break the illusion by discussing any of it with Sunny, but I'd already accepted that I'd broken the usual boundaries with this woman. I'd never craved a client before. I'd never been so protective of one, either.

"I think I meant the, like…the balance. I'm not sure I'd know when or how to stop with you. I wanted to quit on the second day, and you helped me push through. After yester-day, I feel like we could've just gone on fucking forever—" I laughed, and Sunny blushed and shook her head. "What? It's —You know what I mean. And instead, you know it's time to rest."

"Will you be disappointed if we don't try every depraved idea in that deceptively sweet-looking brain of yours?" I asked her.

She snorted and sat up, pulling her legs free of my hands and wrapping the robe a little tighter around her body, cutting me off from my favorite view. But the disappointment of her modesty was quickly soothed by her helping herself to my lap, her legs straddling my hips and arms circling my neck.

"There is absolutely nothing about this experience I could be disappointed in," Sunny said softly, meeting my eyes shyly, her cheeks flushing as I helped myself to grasping her luscious ass through the velvet and drawing her closer. "Khell, thank you…thank you so much for—"

Her brow furrowed, lips parted and voice lost.

For doing my job, I thought, the notion strangely distasteful. Sunny looked more distressed the longer she was at a loss for words, and my own thoughts turned uncomfortable. What were we to one another? Nothing but sex worker and client.

I leaned forward and Sunny's face relaxed in relief, her eyes falling shut at the same moment my mouth found hers, tongue stroking in immediately, already starving for her taste again. Sunny sighed as I groaned, my arms tightening around her, her legs squeezing my hips.

I was her hired partner. Her pleasure was my responsibility, my role. We were boxed in by that reality, but it didn't prevent me from wondering. What *could* we be?

Too dangerous, I warned myself, even as another part of me whispered, *You already know*.

Sunny whimpered into the kiss, shifting in my arms, and I pulled away, brow furrowing in concern. She gasped, catching her breath, and grinned up at me, reaching between us to push the fabric of the robe aside, struggling to free herself and press closer to my skin.

I purred and smiled down at her. "We were just speaking of your need for rest, petal."

She laughed, pulling one arm free of the cloak and wrapping it around my shoulder, trying to drag me down on top of her. "I know. Which is why you should be very gentle and do all the work this time."

Resist her, Khell. She is only human. She can't overpower you!

No, in strength, Sunny couldn't beat me. But the scent of

her arousal was making my mouth water. The catch of her breath as she squirmed and fought to bare herself to me, to press her skin to mine, made my ears twitch and my instincts to *chase* rise up. The look of her, rumpled in the sheets, blushing with excitement, that bright smile curving on her lips, called to me like a siren at the cliff's edge.

Sunny moaned and relaxed again as I dove down to claim those swollen, bitten lips. My hips landed against hers, and my arm still cradling her waist tugged the velvet back until our skin met, drawing another purr from my chest, the sound vibrating down into Sunny through our kiss.

Resisting Sunny was nearly futile. She was all bright curiosity and eager surrender. She consumed pleasure with the appetite of a succubus, offered it back with the blessing of a—

I pulled away from the little temptress with a growl, sitting up and glaring down at her, my snarl rising at the picture of her splayed out for my taking. Sunny was smirking, breasts rocking with her gasps for air.

"Wicked petal."

She giggled, and my frown couldn't stand against the sound.

"You just like to see what you can get away with," I said.

Sunny sighed and scooted back, wrapping the velvet around herself again, my fingers itching to tear it away so she couldn't hide herself from me. "A bit," she admitted with a small shrug.

I rose from the nest, stepping out and turning back to scoop her up into my arms. "You forget who is in charge," I said.

Sunny hummed and leaned her head onto my shoulder. "I don't. Another bath? You haven't even gotten me properly dirty."

"This bath is larger than the one in the cottage, easier to

share with you," I said, resting her on a cushioned ledge near the wide, round bathing pool.

"If you wanted me wet, slippery, and relaxed, we could've stayed in the bed," Sunny said, her foot tapping against the clay wall.

I snorted at that and shook my head. "Orc bait," I said, thinking the words out loud.

Out of the corner of my eyes, Sunny blushed and preened, watching me work to ready the tub.

SUNNY'S FINGERS fidgeted on my shoulders as I carried her back to the cottage, my steps slow and careful with the precious cargo in my arms. Perhaps my pace was reluctant too. The cottage was one step closer to the reality now less than a day away.

Five days had seemed excessive on Monday. Now the session felt shockingly brief.

The moon was high and bright through the thinning branches of the trees surrounding us, the agency's woods quiet. There were a few other houses, but none between the orc den and the cottage that we might see, nothing to prove we were anything but alone. Sunny wasn't wearing her monitor watch, and there were no cameras or smart screens out here.

A brief and almost amusing fantasy of carting Sunny off the property altogether flitted through my head, and I let it float there in the background for far too long.

"Khell," Sunny whispered.

My arms had tightened around her, and I loosened them slightly as I turned my head to meet her gaze. She was shades of blue and gray in the dark, hints of her gold hair faint and glittering as we passed into brief patches of moonlight, and I was too busy studying the details of her face—pert nose and round eyes, the dimple on her chin—to immediately catch the expression on her face.

"Stop walking."

My feet obeyed the command without question, and I swayed in place, Sunny clasped to my chest with her legs spread. There was a rare, slight downturn of her lips and an ache in her eyes that echoed down into my chest.

"What's wrong?" I asked, ready to adjust my hold on her, concerned she might've been in pain.

She shook her head. "Nothing, I just... I want you," she said, voice so soft, it almost slipped beneath the rustling of the woods around us. "Here. Please."

My heart squeezed, as if Sunny had pressed her small hand right through my rib cage to take the organ in her grip, to force it to beat slow and hard, painfully in her possession.

"Do you want to be chased?" I asked, glancing around the woods.

"No. I just want you," she said, the thin thread of her voice breaking on the last word. "Out here. I don't know—"

I wouldn't ask her to reason with me. I didn't want to argue. I'd resisted Sunny for most of the day, and there was no battling that look on her face, the way it tore into me. I took three strides forward, into a break of the tree's shadows, where moonlight pooled on the floor of the woods like water, and then knelt.

Sunny's hands cupped my face, and she leaned in, her mouth meeting mine in a fragile kiss, skimming and brushing, breathing against one another. I had her wrapped in the cloak again, and I loosened it now to lay against the ground. I meant to lower Sunny down, but she pulled away, climbing off my lap, naked to the night sky and the woods and my starving gaze. Her hands around my jaw slid to my shoulders, barely pressing, and I rolled, lowering myself onto my back.

The moon hung behind Sunny's head, illuminating her

with a divine halo. My petal, my lusty goddess. I growled up at the sight of her, the silhouette of light outlining the slow and soft curves of her body, the tight peak of her breasts, the thin tips of her hair brushing just above her shoulder.

Sunny hummed, a sweet, small sound, and tipped her head enough for me to see one corner of her smile. Then one heel raised and her feet straddled my thighs on the ground, and the kiss of light reached between her thighs, where I wanted my mouth.

"Petal," I growled.

"I'm admiring you."

"Come sit—"

"No, Khell, please," she whispered, halting my words. "Let this time be mine."

The plea was a fist around my throat, and I nodded. Sunny remained frozen above me, traced in icy light for another moment, before finally sinking to her knees, poised above my lap.

"Whatever I say, just let it be a game." The words were barely spoken, just a flutter of her lips and likely not meant for me to hear. But orcs had keen ears.

I growled, wanting to surge up, to grab Sunny by the shoulders and force this dark mood out, to hear any words she wanted to speak, but she pressed her hot core to my cock, rocking against my length, and the growl only softened to a groan.

My hands cupped around Sunny's hips, encouraging the slow slide of her sex against my stiff cock, my stav already kicking, eager to find its way into her cunt. Sunny's breath was quick, her eyes focused down to where we touched, rubbing herself against my head, gathering the precum from the tip and using it to smooth her movement.

"Petal, bring me your mouth." She had claimed control of this union, but my words were a plea, not an order, and Sunny smiled and leaned forward, hands planted on my stomach. I had to arch up to meet her, and I thrust one hand into her hair, to hold her face to mine.

The kiss was messy, fractured by every retreat from Sunny as she kept pace on my lap, her own arousal joining mine to make me slick and ready for her. I wanted to wrap my arms around her, to roll us over so I could pin her beneath me. Sunny's teeth nipped at my lips, the excited notes of her pleasure small and confined in her throat.

"Use me," I whispered against her.

She moaned, turning away from the kiss and pressing her cheek to mine. "I want you to be mine."

I growled, my fingers tightening briefly in her hair before she shoved me down to my back again, pulling away and reaching between us. My cock was too eager to be inside her, the pound and ache of my length warring against the vise around my heart that demanded I pull Sunny's mouth back to mine, kiss her until she confessed more of her secrets.

The heat of her, the slick and easy descent of her wet and gasping cunt on my cock made us both cry out, our eyes meeting and fastening to one another. The pain she'd been wearing since she stopped our progress in the woods vanished, replaced with a gentle relief.

"Oh god, Khell, you're fucking perfect inside of me."

You are home, Sunny.

It struck me hard, at the same moment her body rose above mine and every cell of me wanted to protest. Fuck. Sunny was mine.

The ache in my chest was not a foul mood but the mating bond, weaving tighter, tying me to the woman now riding my cock like her next breath depended on the act.

My mate.

The purr rose up in my chest, as loud as a roar, even as my head spun in alarm.

"Sunny, I—"

"Fuck, Khell, I love this," she gasped, mouth open on a long moan.

I'd found my mate, her lush body soaking my cock, her hands digging into the muscles of my chest. I'd mated a client, broken the contract that protected the professional boundary meant to exist, and destroyed my career with MSA.

I'd met the woman meant to warm my bed, to give meaning to waking in the morning, to build my life with. I sat up, reaching for Sunny, and her arms circled my shoulders, equally eager to twine together, sinking down to the hilt of my cock and rocking there, already starting to flutter around me as my stav pumped to the beat of my drumming heart.

I clasped the back of Sunny's neck to draw her mouth to mine, to kiss her breathless and lay my claim first with words and then with the fucking she deserved.

"I can't believe I nearly went my whole life without this," Sunny murmured before diving forward, tongue meeting mine eagerly.

I groaned against her, my arms gripping her tighter at the same time that my heart seemed to crack in its cage.

Sunny had come to me, not for an emotional connection, not for the binding relationship of a mate, but to discover a part of herself—a part she'd trapped in a relationship she'd only barely ended. She was my client. She was young. She'd come to be set free, not bound. Well, not like this.

The words were on my tongue. Could she taste them?

"Sunny," I growled, but my throat seized and choked what wanted to follow.

"Khell," she gasped out, arching, starting to flutter along my length as she bounced. "Thank you, thank you for this."

For this.

For this week. For this experience. For being paid to be with her.

Sunny was lost in the throes of her rising orgasm and my body was tight, muscles coiling, trapped in the moment, the contract. I snarled as Sunny cried out and gave into the beast inside of me, rising up on my knees and then falling forward, my claws digging into Sunny's ass as I lowered her to the ground beneath me, onto the cloak she'd dropped earlier.

The moonlight was dressing her in pools of silver now, bared to my gaze, her expression torn with pleasure as she clamped down on my cock. My mate. My Sunny. She would always be mine now. I was permanently entwined with her. Would she feel it as orcs did? If she did, the bond would call her back to me, but if she didn't...

I threw my head back and roared with frustration, my hips slapping against her wet sex, refusing the siren call of her orgasm, demanding that she return to that precipice and fall again for me.

Sunny howled, gasped, her eyes growing wide and searching mine. Was I being too rough? No, my little mate could take me—she'd proven as much.

"Oh fuck, Khell, don't stop!"

I bared my teeth in a snarl of a grin, lifting her hips from the ground, driving deeper, harder, watching Sunny's breasts bounce with my force. She was mine, and I couldn't claim her. Not with words. But tonight, like this? I would mate her as an orc ought to claim what was theirs. My claws scratched the globes of her ass, my thumbs digging into the muscle of her inner thighs to spread her wider, to fit myself closer.

Sunny came again with a scream, her own hands flying into the grass and dirt and crunching leaves, back lifting off the cloak, throat flexing and swallowing hard. And still I thrusted and bucked, gritting my teeth against the rising heat in my spine, the swollen throb of my stav begging to release seed into my mate. Not yet. I wouldn't let this end yet.

And as if we were of one mind, Sunny's sweet and tender and exhausted body began to squirm in my hands, forcing herself against me in that same brutal beat I'd chosen, fucking herself, her brow furrowed with focus.

My mate. And yet not mine.

Say it, my thoughts snarled. *She will choose you*, another voice soothed. *When she's ready*, came a warning whisper.

"Khell!" Sunny gasped, her eyes wide, almost frightened, legs shaking and trembling.

She lifted a hand from the earth, reached for me, and I fell upon her. I took her lips without consideration for my tusks on her fragile skin. My arms wrapped around her back, crushing her to my chest and knowing she could bear my strength. I buried my hips as close to hers as she could take, stretching her to her limits as my stav expanded painfully in my cock, and then my orgasm exploded into her.

It was obscene, filthy. Sunny was crying out, her voice swallowed by my mouth, shaking in my arms as I filled her with burst after burst of seed until it was splashing against us both, spilling out between us onto the cloak. A mating's worth of cum, painting Sunny in my scent to warn others away, to mark her as mine.

Mine, and not mine.

I would let her leave tomorrow and then I would be fired from MSA, or at the very least, I would have to quit. I belonged to Sunny now.

Sunny let out a high sigh, wiggling beneath me. I grunted, and another almost painful jet of release shot into her, making her gasp.

"Holy fuck, Khell," she whispered, giggling slightly.

I growled and bundled Sunny in my arms, hiding my face in her hair, keeping us locked together. Impulsively, I tilted her hips a little higher, trying to prevent any of my seed left in her from leaving. She wouldn't get pregnant, we were both covered, but I wanted her filled to the brim with me.

Sunny moaned, a strong aftershock shuddering through her, and her arms circled my shoulders, her cheek rubbing against my throat, flushed and warm and soft.

It was on the tip of my tongue again to tell her what had

just passed, what she was to me now, if not what we were to each other.

Then she shivered, and the mating bond rallied a list of what needed done. Wrap Sunny up and get her inside, preferably all the way into the bed without my cock having to leave her silky wet heat. Get her water, food, fuck her until she couldn't speak or move, until she couldn't even think. And tomorrow, I would have to let her leave.

There was no possible reason she would find me again, although the bond would call me closer to her, so maybe—

Don't hope. Just be what Sunny needs. Until tomorrow, when she needs you to let her leave.

CHAPTER 16
Sunny

SOMETHING WAS DIFFERENT. I wasn't sure if something was wrong exactly, only that it wasn't…quite right.

"Khell?" I breathed, my voice hoarse from how much I'd been babbling and begging all day, gasping and shouting praises, whimpering and whining.

His stav was fucking me but he held my hips firmly to his, and his mouth was latched to my left breast, suckling and kissing and nibbling. I'd already come once just like this with him feasting on my right breast, and I was certain he was working me to another release. Symmetrical bliss.

My thighs were sticky with cum, but Khell hadn't suggested a bath for me once. He'd made sure I drank water and ate, and then carried on fucking me in every possible position. Not rough, not like in the woods or in any of our games. He fucked me gently and thoroughly, making sure I was never too sore to keep going.

"Khell," I repeated, tugging gently on his braid. I'd seen him wince earlier when I'd had his hair in my grip while he ate me out. Either orcs had sensitive scalps, or I *was* rough on his braid.

Khell grunted, nuzzling his tusks against my breast but

not stopping the slow draw of sucking on my nipple and then swirling his tongue in circles to soothe or torture me.

"How...how much time do we have left?"

That did make my orc pause. Even his stav stuttered from its rhythm inside of me.

"Not long," Khell rasped out against my breast, although I didn't know why his voice would be hoarse too. He wasn't the one howling at every orgasm, although he'd roared through quite a few.

I whimpered as he went back to licking and nipping my breast, but the sound was drawn out of my chest rather than Khell's teasing. Not long. Was that hours or minutes? Either way, this would be over soon.

It would never be enough.

We'd barely scratched the surface of...of my requests. Of what I wanted to do. And the list had piled higher the longer I was with Khell.

Khell's stav returned to its steady, almost metronome-like tempo inside of me, and his tusks pinched my flesh with his upper incisors, tongue flicking rapidly over my nipple until its tip was sharp and painfully tender and—

I came with a whine, squeezing on the swollen shifting rod of the stav pumping in Khell's cock, clasping his head in place, shivering and sweating and gushing on the mattress.

Khell pulled free of me before I could catch my breath. I sobbed at the sudden rush of cool air over my skin and my empty hands and cunt. His hands wrapped around my shoulders, twisting and turning me like his rag doll again, rolling me onto my belly. I was limp and too exhausted to be properly disgusted at the state of the bed, or of myself too. Khell's hands pet at my ass, and it didn't even occur to me to protest the idea of him fucking me there again.

The bed rocked slightly, and then Khell was tugging a pillow from somewhere and stuffing it under my hips. The smooth fabric was shockingly coarse against my tender clit, and it must've been insanity or a new addiction, or the starving desperation that raced through me anytime I was near Khell, that had me shifting to rub myself against it.

Distracted by the rough and stimulating sensation of fabric against my clit, and the aftershocks from the fresh orgasm rippling through me, I missed Khell'ar shifting around me until something cool snapped shut around my ankle. I stiffened and twisted my head back just in time to watch Khell shove my legs wide, and a second cuff efficiently locked around my other ankle. Between the two, a long bar spread me open, heels raised in the air.

Khell was frowning. He'd been solemn and almost surly since we got back from the woods, and I would've assumed he was mad at me except that he'd been so incredibly gentle, constantly kissing me, constantly purring, constantly petting every inch of my skin. Even now he stroked down my calves, pushing my ankles gently toward my ass.

"Wrists," he said, arching an eyebrow at me.

Hogtied. Check.

And here I'd started to think that Khell was done playing games during my visit. My breath was short and quick in my chest, but I didn't hesitate or ask any questions, sliding my wrists back until my arms were flat on the bed.

Khell shook a pair of fancy, padded cuffs, with a little digital screen glowing something unreadable from my position. "These will unlock on a timer, or when you say your safe word."

In all the time I'd been here, I hadn't even uttered a syllable of my safe word. I nodded and relaxed, wiggling my hips again and sighing at the tingle of friction on my clit. Khell had left it alone for a few hours and it was still aching, but also now throbbing with a suspended arousal he'd built up in me—constantly satisfied, constantly wanting more.

He was gentle with the cuffs, linking them around the bar spreading my ankles, allowing me limited movement while also offering a pleasant stretch in my shoulders and the sense of captivity I'd been intrigued by.

"You are mine, Sunny," Khell whispered, words rough.

I opened my lips to agree—not for the sake of our assigned roles; it was the truth now—but the words were stolen out of my mouth as Khell drew my hips back and sank home to the hilt again. His fingers found my wrists, covering the backs of my hands with his broad palms, encompassing me in his grip as he fucked me with slow and deep thrusts, pulling almost completely out before sinking in as deep as he could go.

I was breathless. The friction of the pillow, of Khell's cock inside of me, of the tug and jostle on my legs and shoulders, all a constant reminder that I was at Khell's mercy.

But he *was* merciful. Khell was kind and careful even as he was fucking me so hard it made my brain rattle in my skull.

There was pressure on top of me, tension in my legs enough to burn, and then slow, wet kisses traveled down my spine, proving my point. Khell lifted away before the position hurt, his hands stroking up and down my arms in a leisurely echo of the fucking he was giving me.

I missed his face, but maybe it was better this way. He couldn't see my eyes watering as I thought about this day, this week ending. He could hear my moans and only know that they were from pleasure, and not also the ache building in my chest. The strange tangle of relief at his touching me, combined with the rising sorrow of knowing that touch was going to be stolen away soon.

"Don't stop," I said, probably for the thousandth time that day.

Khell huffed a ragged sound behind me, his hands moving to clasp my waist, to draw me back onto his cock. My cheek was pressed against the tangled sheet. My swollen, sensitive nipples crushed and rubbing into the mattress, my clit against the pillow. The cuff rattled and slid against the bar with each of my breaths and each of Khell's steady snaps of his hips, just rough enough to clap inside of me but not enough to sting.

I love you, I thought, which was the most absurdly sex-addled thing that I could've come up with. I didn't *know* Khell. And in spite of the ledger of sexual fantasies I'd handed over to him and MSA, and the confessions I'd offered in the den, Khell didn't really know me either.

"Come for me, petal," Khell growled behind me.

From any other man, the words would've been useless. But Khell had memorized my body and its responses. He shifted up onto his knees slightly, stav stroking against my front walls, and I released a low cry into the bed beneath me as I started to shake.

Every time I thought I was too tired, too used up to enjoy an orgasm, Khell proved me wrong. Warmth sizzled through me, centering at my cunt and flaring slowly out in pulses of heat and syrupy satisfaction. His snarls of relief joined my panting whines, our bodies working together, trying to find new depths for him to plunge, a way for our skin to fuse together, our hearts to beat in union.

The release seemed to go on forever, slow and throbbing, extending down to my toes and up into my head, erasing all the heartache for the moment and replacing it with a pure, bright understanding that this was *right*. This was exactly what my body was designed for. Khell was a part of me. I didn't feel my bindings, the awkward strain of my body, the messy bed I was lying on. No, there was only the lovely pulse of relief and the knowledge that I was right where I ought to be, held by exactly whom I was meant to be held by.

And then, abruptly and while I was still shuddering, Khell pulled free of me.

I blinked and whined, the sound choked off as the tension of my legs was interrupted and they flopped to the mattress, liberated from the spreader. As quick as he'd put me on my belly, Khell turned me again, my back finding an uncomfortably wet spot on the bed, his arms cradling me so I wasn't lying on my still cuffed wrists.

Khell was looming over me, lowering himself until the image of him was blurry, too close to be studied, his hot forehead against mine.

"Close your eyes, Sunny."

I was well-trained now, and they fell shut at the command. Khell's lips were my reward, almost as chapped as my own and twice as hungry. He purred above me, but the sound was ragged, the vibration rough in my mouth as his tongue slipped in, searching and licking for every flavor of me.

I wanted to say the words to him, tell him what I'd thought while he'd fucked me, as if I might make 'I love you' sound like a joke. Would he say it back for the sake of our games, our arranged roles? Would it be sweet to hear, even if I knew it was a lie?

Khell's kiss was endless, thorough, as he nibbled and licked, fucking my mouth with his tongue and then retreating to brush his lips and tusks against me. I took every touch, soaked up our flavors mixed together, tried to return to that hazy perfect place where I couldn't find the edges between us.

I gasped as he pulled away, my lungs remembering their need for oxygen now that my lips were deprived of my orc.

"Keep them closed, my pretty petal," Khell rasped.

I nodded obediently as Khell put me on my side, giving my bound arms space. The bed jostled as he rose, and I shivered in place until a blanket covered me. *Sweet orc*, I thought, smiling. What game was next? How much time did we have? If it wasn't long, I would've rather we spent it together in the bed, touching in any way.

I waited a breath, two, a long and quiet pause. Khell could be remarkably quiet for being so massive, but then a floorboard creaked. His steps moved to the door, and I cheated for a glance.

He was leaving the room, naked and gloriously tall, his cock still shining with our release. There were scratches on his back, although I knew they wouldn't last long. They were my marks, just as the little bruises from his claws and tusks scattered over my skin were his marks, and they filled me with a sense of pride. He paused at the threshold, and I shut my eyes again before he turned and caught me staring.

There was another long stretch of quiet, a soft shuffle, and then a moment later, I heard the click of a door shutting.

My eyes opened and I held my breath, waiting for another sound within the cottage that never came. Was I imagining the whiff of fresh air floating closer? My stomach turned and I sat up with a groan, my muscles weak and sore, the room spinning briefly and then settling again.

The cottage was quiet, and now that I was sitting up I could see the sun was starting to set, the woods outside taking on an orangey glow.

It was the end of the fifth day. Khell had left.

Without a goodbye? I grit my teeth and bowed my head, swallowing the wounded sound that wanted to rise up from the gentle tearing in my chest.

No, he'd left after spending almost a full twenty-four hours in bed with me. After a glorious kiss. Five days that had changed how I viewed myself, viewed sex.

How else were we meant to say goodbye?

I sucked in a deep breath, but the wound in my chest wouldn't heal so easily. Fair enough. I rose up from the bed on wobbling legs at the same moment that the cuffs around my wrist beeped and then released, falling to the bed.

Time's up.

CHAPTER 17
Khell'ar

SUNNY WAS MEANT to have two hours in the cottage alone before she left. I only gave her one, unable to tear myself away any sooner. Even then, I remained in the woods, watching.

Sunny left barely twenty minutes after me. Hidden in the trees, I could smell her from yards away. She hadn't bathed, her skin was still coated in our release. Neither had I, too reluctant to lose her scent, but I'd expected her to want to clean up. Her hair was tangled, lips chapped, eyes hollow—

No, you're exaggerating now.

My claws bit into my own palms, my muscles so tense they burned as I planted my heels into the branch of the tree I perched on and resisted the urge to leap down to the ground and chase after my mate, throw her up into my arms and carry her...

Where?

Home.

I huffed gently and frowned down at where Sunny fidgeted in front of the cottage. A moment later, headlights appeared through the trees, illuminating her for a moment, casting her in shadow the next. She was tired, and while she'd been smiling and loose when I'd left her, the curve of her lips was tipped down now.

My heart hammered, and my body screamed silently at being held back from its rightful duty—caring for the woman below. Caring for my mate. I waited for Sunny to slide into the backseat of the sedan that arrived for her, then threw myself in the opposite direction before I could break the unspoken promise I'd made her—to let her go.

For now.

You don't know how you'll even find her again.

Which was true, but an orc would find his way to his mate. It was our nature, our imperative. If I told any of my orcish friends about letting Sunny walk away, they would punch me in the face and rightfully call me a fool. But Sunny wasn't an orc. And a sex work session wasn't the place to form a mating bond.

Astraeya would be so smug.

My own SUV was parked in the small lot up the hill, the only vehicle plugged into the electric station. The arrival of all-electric utility vehicles was the advent of orcs taking to the road en masse, treating our nature goddess as she deserved while enjoying the luxury of leg room, even at our size. The hood was dusted with fallen leaves and marked with pollen, and I brushed the mess away, ignoring the way my hand shook.

The interior was cold, the silence inside ringing in my ears —silence where Sunny's breaths should've been, her sighs and whimpers and laughter. I shook myself and started the car, pulling out and heading the back way down the hill.

Checkout was quick at MSA. Sunny would have a few exit questions in person and then a longer survey to fill out in her email. Still, if I allowed myself to bump into her in the halls, I would probably grab her with both hands—and my tusks too, for good measure—and take off running. I kept my foot off the accelerator pedal for most of the drive, giving her plenty of time to leave before I arrived and hating every second.

Astraeya was frowning at her tablet as I arrived at her office door.

"Pair of storm clouds, you two," she murmured, not bothering to look up.

I opened my mouth to ask about Sunny and then shut it again, swallowing hard and letting my claws dig just a bit deeper into my hands. "I have to turn in my resignation. Immediately."

Astraeya's head shot up at that, violet eyes wide and flaring with shock and interest. "*What?*" She stood before I could answer, thunder in her expression as she rounded her desk. "She gave you a full score, Khell, so you'd better not tell me that you hurt that girl."

If I did, I was sure to have my next ten years of life sucked out of my body in under a minute, based on Astraeya's sharpened features and the high set of her shoulders.

"I mated."

Astraeya's mouth was open—ready to eat me alive, no doubt—but her jaw dropped another inch at that announcement, hackles falling with her shoulders. She stepped back once and rolled her eyes, sighing.

"Oh, thank god," she breathed out, shaking the tension out of her body with a little shimmy. As quickly as anger had appeared, a bright giddy smile replaced her temper. "Congratulations!"

I stared back at Astraeya as her grin remained fixed but her eyes narrowed to slits.

"You don't look like a mated orc."

"I didn't tell her. It breaks MSA contract—" I said, the words dull on my own tongue.

"Khell!"

"Not to mention her trust in me as her partner," I added.

"Fucking roller coaster," Astraeya muttered, searching the

room and coming up empty. She waved her hand at me, and I thought I was being dismissed as she turned away, until she spoke again. "Fine, fine. Sit down, you great, green log of an idiot orc."

As insults went, it was well-suited. Green was untried, young. A log was useless, lifeless. Astraeya had been catching on to the way we orcs spoke to one another. She waved at the chair in front of her desk, barely large enough for me, and I moved forward slowly, my mind disconnected from my own body.

Sunny was driving away, and I was growing awkward in my skin, missing the most important part of myself.

"What did it take, all of a day?" Astraeya asked, sitting down and glaring across her desk at me.

"Four."

"Stubborn."

I blinked at her, scrunching myself into a smaller ball in the seat, my knees high in front of me.

Astraeya sighed again. "Okay. Your dismissal from MSA *is* immediate, obviously. I'll push it through HR and get you paid."

"Not for this one," I said quickly.

Astraeya scoffed. "What are we going to do, just keep it? Give it back to her?"

I shrugged. That didn't sound so bad.

"I'll get you her number, address," Astraeya said, ignoring me.

"No!"

"No?" she snapped, leaning forward. "What are you going to do, Khell? She reeked of you as she left, sure, but even for an orc, hunting her down the highway into the city is a stretch!"

So she lived in the city. It was more than I wanted to know right away, but now that I did...my lease was coming up. I'd planned to renew, but maybe being more central wouldn't be so bad. Especially now that I'd need to find new work.

And Sunny.

"Khell," Astraeya prodded, tone gentling. "She didn't want to leave. You know I can tell you that honestly."

I wasn't blind. I knew as much too. But it didn't change certain facts.

"Orcs and humans have mated before, you're not that exciting of news," she continued.

"I'm not giving up," I said. *Aren't you?* "But there are complications."

Even for orcs, it would be complicated if a mating bond snapped in place while one of the mates was fresh out of a relationship with someone else. Mating was celebratory, but it wasn't a magical influence over personal feelings.

"My offer for her information will stand," Astraeya said slowly.

"It's against MSA—"

"I know our policies, Khell. But this isn't something you did *wrong*. It's just nature. I'll deal with it on my end, don't worry about me."

I sighed at that and nodded. Sunny wasn't ready to be hunted down, reluctance to give up a sexual frenzy or not. But I would have a way of finding her now, if it became urgent.

How long could an orc go out of contact with their mate? I would find out, it seemed.

"Are you *sure*?" Astraeya pressed.

"If she…if she returns…if she *asks* for me," I started.

"I'll call you," Astraeya answered immediately. "No one else."

I relaxed a fraction more. Repeat customers were rare in the grand scheme of our work, although they made for steady money. I winced when I thought of my own two regular clients. MSA would break the news to them gently, and I couldn't regret quitting. I would never satisfy anyone but Sunny again. I would never be satisfied with anyone else.

If Sunny wanted me at MSA again, she would find me. If she didn't…

"How much time will you give her?"

"What's enough?" I asked, glancing up from the edge of the desk for the first time in minutes, like a shamed school boy. Astraeya pursed her lips, and I filled in some of what was missing. "Enough for a woman who just ended a long relationship."

Astraeya groaned and sagged backwards into her desk chair, eyes rolling up toward the ceiling. "Woof, Khell. That's not… There's no one right answer to that."

I let out a low grumble and nodded.

"Not too long," Astraeya said, tipping her chin back down to glare at me. "Less time than you think is noble. Seriously, the orcish chivalry customs make my head spin. Considerate behavior to your mate includes everything from how red you mark their ass before guests come to the home, to giving them excessive space and time to accept the mating."

A nice summer rose blush for Sunny's ass would do. She wasn't quite as hearty as an orc, and I wouldn't want her unnecessarily uncomfortable.

"A month?" I asked.

Astraeya huffed and tipped her head side to side. "A month…a month should do."

A month, then. A month to resist hunting Sunny. A month to let her find her footing in her new life before offering her a place in mine, claiming a place in hers.

Surely a mated orc could survive a month of waiting?

"Call if you need the number, Khell," Astraeya said with a grim prediction in her tone.

CHAPTER 18
Sunny

I FORGOT to ring the doorbell outside of Natalie's house. I stood on her doorstep, cool Chicago autumn winds flipping under my skirt, cum sticking my thighs together, and just stared at that old glass door. Really, I stared at my reflection.

I was a mess, hair tangled and eyes wide with shock, lips still swollen and bruised from kisses. There were marks on my throat from Khell's careful claws and gentle nips. I was dressed in a sweater and a skirt, and I hadn't realized how used to being *naked* I'd grown in just five days, but even the sight of clothes seemed wrong. The soft fabrics abraded the marks on my body, hid them.

A shadow appeared on the other side of the door, and I jumped in place, my brain shocking back into the moment as it opened and Natalie's husband Theo appeared.

"Sunn—Whoa," he said, nose wrinkling and rearing back. Theo was tall and broad-shouldered, and I'd previously thought of him as impressively muscular, but he was lankier to my eye now after being around Khell. He had shaggy brown hair that looked like he cut it himself and bright green eyes behind rounded tortoiseshell glasses. "Um…come on… Nat!" he called over his shoulder.

"Hi," I said weakly as he stepped back and gave his place at the door to Natalie a moment later.

"Sunny, there you are! Just in time for dinner," Natalie said, beaming at me.

Theo leaned in as Natalie threw the door wide for me, whispering into my friend's ear. Her eyebrows jumped, and a startled, brief laugh rose from her lips.

"Umm, why don't I take you up to the guest room and you can...get settled first," Natalie added, gaze flicking between Theo and me.

Theo hustled away, glancing wide-eyed over his shoulder at me and heading back toward their kitchen, while Natalie led me to the stairs.

"I smell, don't I?" I asked in a whisper, my cheeks flaming. I'd been sort of lost when I'd realized Khell had left the cottage and left me to my own devices. The only thing I could think to do was dress and leave.

"Eh. Weres have prissy little noses," Natalie said with a shrug, climbing the stairs ahead of me. "I didn't notice anything."

She didn't, but Theo did. Theo had opened the door and got a big ole whiff of...orc. Orc cum. Was it all the same to him, or would Khell's be—

I shook my head as we reached the landing, and the new window film caught my eye. Natalie and Theo's small Albany Park house was backed up to an apartment building, and she'd been complaining about the renters being able to see into her house.

"Pretty," I said, pointing to the frosted, almost lace-like pattern on the window.

"Thanks, we took your advice. Theo wanted these hideous stained glass decals, but Emmie and I outvoted him."

The idea of infant Emmett having interior decorating opinions brought a smile to my lips that caught Natalie's attention.

"There you are," she said, voice uncommonly gentle. "You looked kinda shell-shocked when you walked in, babe."

For no clear reason, I caught a ragged breath, standing on the landing and staring up at Natalie on the stairs. My eyes stung and then immediately watered, blurring my friend's face and her home surrounding us.

"Oh, babe! What happened?" Natalie's smear of bright, warm colors rushed toward me, and I sagged as her arms wrapped around me. "Was it awful?"

I laughed, but the sound was watery. "It was fucking *amazing*, Nat."

Natalie squeezed me tighter and laughed. "*Oh*. You poor thing. Come on, let's get you washed up. I'll sit on the toilet, and you can tell me about all the new kinky shit you love to do."

I blushed again, but this time my laughter was more sincere, full of the relief of having a *Natalie* and wondering how others managed without her.

NATALIE'S GUEST bathroom didn't have quite the collection of bath accessories that MSA's cottage did, but the water was hot and Natalie lit a candle at my request so that the glow pulsed on the other side of the opaque plastic curtain.

"Shit, you got your money's worth," Natalie said, voice foggy from my position under the stream of hot water.

I washed myself with gentle touches, exploring every tender and sore spot Khell had left on me.

"I think it's normal though, to feel that way," Natalie said.

I'd confessed to the way I'd been thinking of Khell by the end of the week, because even though it was *crazy* to fall in love with the sex worker you'd hired to make your brain explode, Natalie was a safe zone for me.

"I mean, that many orgasms and your serotonin must've been shooting through the roof," Natalie continued. "You should stay tomorrow night. I feel like it's gonna take a while for your mood to settle. That's one hell of a biochemical trip you just went on."

Boiling my time with Khell down to serotonin and dopamine created a bittersweet ache in my chest. It didn't cover the whole scope of what had happened, what had changed in me, but it was also a simpler version with a hopeful conclusion. My world would tip right side up again. My heartache would ease, and in the wake would be…maybe an amused acceptance for my lightning strike attachment to Khell'ar.

"When's Harry out of the coach house?" Natalie asked.

"Tomorrow morning, if he isn't already. But yeah, I'd like to stay with you a bit." I was wobbly, and tears kept springing to my eyes. And since I'd already been through the shockingly embarrassing experience of letting Theo smell orc cum all over me, the most uncomfortable moment had probably already passed.

"Would you do it again?" Natalie asked.

I opened my mouth to give an immediate *yes*, but Natalie rushed ahead.

"Not the whole hiring someone thing, but like, the roleplay? Getting tied up? Chased?"

And for some reason, the answer stalled now. Without Khell? Was it easier to offer him that trust because I'd signed dozens of documents and received dozens of assurances? Or because he'd looked into my eyes in that dungeon and seen me, known what I needed, what to demand of me?

That was his job, I reminded myself.

"Yes," I said, because that was the truth. Now that I knew myself in this way, I wouldn't lock these interests up again. "But I think it'll be hard to replicate. MSA makes sure clients feel really safe, and they have a lot of precautions in place."

Not that I'd used any of them when I was with Khell.

"Were you ever scared?" Natalie asked.

I took a third or fourth handful of body wash and started working gently at my thighs again. They were probably clean by now, but the phantom sensation of Khell still remained.

"Only at the beginning, and that was mostly just about whether or not I would regret the booking." I hummed and then smiled to myself. "Maybe a few other times, but that was because it was what I wanted."

Natalie cackled in answer. "Gosh. I'm so proud of you. And kind of jealous. Not for the sexathon, that sounds exhausting, and anyway, who would take care of Emmett? But like, I feel like I'm gonna have to talk to Theo about upping our game."

I snorted. "Competitive much?"

"Um, yes. You know me. I'm *very* competitive. Also, orcs aren't the only ones who like to hunt."

I grinned and took a final rinse. I did know Natalie. And now she knew me a little better too. I was surprised by how easy it was to tell her everything I'd done, everything I'd asked for. I'd been keeping those fantasies a secret, ashamed of myself. And for what?

I would've said I felt lighter without the burden, but the truth was there was still a lead weight in my chest—the absence of Khell.

I took a deep breath and lifted my face to the stream of water. Natalie would be right. The ache would pass. My brain chemicals would chill out again soon enough.

Life would go on without Khell.

THAT'S EVERYTHING. *Thanks for the time.*
No hard feelings.
-Harry

Sorry. That was curt.

I really am wishing you the best, Sonya.

-H

I tapped my finger on Harry's note, left diligently centered on the side table just inside my modest coach house entrance. His key rested at the very top of the note.

I left it there, a faint and melancholy smile on my lips as I stepped into my living room to survey the wreckage. Which, of course, there wasn't any. Harry didn't tear himself out of our home like a tornado. What there was were new small holes in the space, pinpricks, really. A club chair was gone on the far end of the room, along with the small side table between the couch and the bookshelves, my lamp now sitting on the floor without a place to stand.

It was a curious kind of surgery performed on the space, a room I'd documented the arrangement of, developed my social media following with. But what I was looking at wasn't emptiness. It was potential.

It'd been a long time since I'd been able to do more than small projects in my house, and I'd gained my popularity with my initial renovation of the coach house.

I can do it again, I realized, a brightness lighting up inside of me.

It had been a nice two days at Natalie's place, but the whole time, I'd felt a little like I was living encased inside of a thin barrier. That film over the world popped now, and I took a deep, clean breath and then hurried upstairs—*these are too narrow for Khell*—to my bedroom. *The bed's barely big enough for him.* I dropped my bag on the floor, picked up my good digital camera, and crossed into the spare bedroom that I'd given up for Harry's home office. It was especially bare now, and I had my first genuine smile in hours at the sight. A blank slate.

A project was always good news. A dozen projects was even better.

I turned on the light, stepped back in the doorway, and snapped a picture. The guest bed was there on my right, in front of the window, only a full because Harry had objected to how much space a queen would take up. The left side of the room was barren, a few dust and scratch marks on the wall from Harry's desk and cords.

I backed myself up the hall to stand outside our shared bathroom, turning on the light again, taking another photo of the space. I'd done up the bathroom before Harry arrived, and then made minor adjustments to accommodate him—a new set of shelves tucked under the sink, a longer towel rack. The space was clean and bright, but it did look a bit dated now to me, and I kept thinking of the lovely, lush bath at the cottage.

Plants would be nice, ones that liked the humidity. I could do a little demolition on my own too, just enough to make that windowsill extend around the entirety of the tub stall.

A new tub would be even better. Rip out the built-in, bring a new freestanding tub with higher walls and…and redo the tile wall…

I pulled my phone out of my back pocket and started making notes.

The coach house was mine again, and I knew myself just that little bit better than ever before.

THERE WAS something about a girl in a skirt in a hardware store.

"Need some help with—"

"I'm good, thanks," I said automatically, for what seemed like the hundredth time. I was up on my toes, reaching for the rough cut walnut four by fours overhead, and I twisted to deliver a perfunctory smile to whatever male employee had marked me as damsel in distress of the hour.

My smile froze in place at the sight of moss green skin, bright white tusks tipped with gold, and black eyes with a vivid ice blue center.

The orc's nostrils flared as our eyes met. He was dressed in a T-shirt tight enough to test the construction of the seams and a baggy pair of jeans with the cuffs rolled up. He wasn't nearly as tall as Khell, but he was even broader and charmingly squat. Or maybe the charm was the way those pointed ears stuck far out from the sides of his head.

I hadn't seen another orc since Khell left the cottage, and there was a giddy relief in my chest. I'd started to wonder if I'd made Khell up, and now here was proof otherwise. If this orc existed, so did mine.

He cleared his throat and stepped back, eyes flicking up and down my body. *Orc bait*, I remembered Khell saying. Was this orc about to—

"Sorry." he grunted. "Didn't realize."

And then he turned tail and hustled as quickly down the broad aisle as his bulky frame allowed.

Hmm. Maybe not such bait after all. I was an odd mix of relieved—he wasn't Khell—and disappointed. Did I have something on my face, or…

Oh.

I remembered the flare of his nostrils, the widening of his eyes, and my cheeks flushed with heat in the aisle. It'd been almost a week since I'd left the cottage. The same amount of time I'd spent with Khell, I'd now spent away from him. And still, that orc was able to smell Khell on me. How long would that last?

I chewed on my bottom lip and wondered if I cared. I hadn't been thrilled with arousal by the new orc. It'd been more like the comfort of seeing something familiar. My time with Khell'ar had taken my fascination with orcs and replaced it with an obsession for one in particular.

I still felt his claws digging into my ass at night, his tusks scratching their way up from my breasts to my throat, his cock pumping inside of me.

"Hey, honey, you need any—"

"I'm good!" I squeaked out, jumping in place and remembering that I was not in the dungeon of the cottage, waiting to find out what Khell had planned next for us, but in an aisle of my favorite hardware store.

I pressed my thighs together, ignored the older man who'd come to see what a young woman in a skirt was doing in the lumber aisle, and rose up on my toes to grab what I needed.

CHAPTER 19
Khell'ar

"THIS THE LAST OF THEM?" Rafe asked, nudging his boot against the boxes I'd set by the front door of the apartment.

I grunted, my back to Rafe, checking in each door to be sure.

"You're getting even chattier in your retirement," he called to me.

I grunted again and then stiffened as he started to chuckle. Raphael, or Rafe, was a fellow—*formerly fellow*, I corrected myself—MSA employee, and the only one of my non-orc friends who would cheerfully help me move from one apartment to the next. Orcs were out of the question for the time being. If any of them knew about me mating and then letting Sunny walk away without knowing the truth, they'd beat me into the ground and tell me to stay there until I was ready to try sprouting again.

All Rafe had said when I'd explained why I'd left MSA was a thoughtful, "Huh."

"Wanna get a hot dog on our way to your new place?" he asked, stacking the boxes and lifting them all at once. Rafe was tall and wiry, with pristinely carved muscle, but I had no doubt we were evenly matched in strength. In truth, he probably had me beat. Gargoyles had the strength of their stone forms, even when they walked in their flesh.

Rafe paused, shifting the boxes into one arm and reaching up to fuss the dark curls atop his head with the other, one eyebrow raised, waiting for my answer. I'd seen him eat before, and I knew "a hotdog" was really a stack of them, plus a half-dozen sides on top of that. Aside from their muscular strength, gargoyles also seemed to have exceptional intestinal fortitude.

"I'll eat," I said, forcing out something other than a grunt.

"I'll take it," Rafe said with a nod and a grin.

I surveyed the small apartment a final time. I didn't have any particular attachment to the space. I'd spent more time between the gym and MSA appointments than I had here. I'd already picked out a couple gyms near my new apartment in Ravenswood and started to scout for some trade work. I had more than enough savings, which meant plenty of time to search, and I'd taken a month to month lease, just in case.

Just in case I did find Sunny and…

I released a slow, heavy breath. It had been two weeks—a slow, dull, colorless two weeks of sitting around an apartment I'd barely used, itching to kick the door down and put my nose to the ground until I'd tracked Sunny and had her back in my arms.

I turned my back on the space and headed to the front door to lock up. Rafe was already in the driver's seat of the truck rental, and he leaned toward the open passenger window.

"Meet you at your new place. I'll pick up the food."

"Is there enough room for everything you're going to pick up?" I asked.

Rafe grinned and shrugged. "Figure I'll just toss out a couple of your boxes if I have to."

I grunted, not caring if he wanted to crack another joke for it, and headed for my own vehicle. Leaving the apartment was nothing. The only thing that mattered was already missing from my life.

Not forever. Just for now.

"I HAVE TO ADMIT, I don't get how you end up mating a client," Rafe said, wiping his mouth with a barely usable napkin.

He'd arrived with a baker's dozen Chicago dogs, two orders of onion rings, two orders of coney fries and two regular fries, four chocolate malts—three were for him—and a side salad. For me, which was thoughtful.

I wasn't keeping track exactly, but I figured he'd eaten more than two-thirds of the food already and would likely finish off the rest when I was done. Gargoyles were impressive garbage disposals.

"There's not a process to mating. It just sinks in," I said with a shrug.

My new apartment was the first story of a slightly shabby graystone, but it had high ceilings and a large shower, so it would do. Rafe and I had dropped everything off in the living room by the drafty bay window and then settled ourselves on the stoop to eat.

"Like, just randomly?" Rafe asked, frowning.

"No. It's high-functioning instinct. When that compatibility arises and the emotions click... Well, we don't really know why it happens sometimes and not others," I said, giving up on my explanation. How could I explain to someone how Sunny suited me? She suited my cock and my claws and my tusks. She suited my need to nurture another. She was strong and brave, and she submitted as easily and beautifully as she took control when she wanted.

"I guess that's my question, then. Since when do emotions

come into our work?" Rafe said. He was wearing a puzzled frown, staring across the street as a couple strolled by, their hands linked and shoulders brushing. "I can't imagine seeing a client as anything but...work."

I shrugged. "Neither could I." Until Sunny. It was as much a mathematical equation of what she asked for and how she responded, as it was the scent and feel of her or the instinctive itch in my chest to remain *near* her from the moment I'd walked into the dungeon.

Rafe hummed and then rolled his shoulders, his vast black and deep purple wings shuffling and rearranging themselves infinitesimally as he relaxed again. "Maybe it's the difference between what you do and what I do. I suppose you might get lost in role-playing."

I bristled at the suggestion but didn't bother correcting him. Rafe's work for MSA involved being available to... rougher clients. A gargoyle was about as indestructible as you could get, especially in their stone forms. And maybe he was right. The trust Sunny had granted me was personal. The act of satisfying her in a way she'd never known before was intimate.

"I miss her." I didn't mean to say it out loud, but once it was there on the air, I didn't really care.

"For the record, I think you made the right choice. Five days of fucking isn't the ground you build a relationship on." Rafe raised his hands to his side as I glared at him. "I'm not saying move on. I'm just saying, maybe take the girl out on a date and ask her about her hobbies before you tell her you're like, bound for life or whatever."

I grunted and turned away, resting my elbows on my knees and watching the neighborhood. There was a nice mix of species here. I'd been one of few non-humans in my old neighborhood. Ravenswood was full of species specialty shops—which were frequented by a wide mix of different folk

—and nice parks. The nearest to me overlooked the Chicago River.

Sunny would like it here.

And perhaps it was only wishful thinking, but the ache that had settled down into my bones seemed to have eased since we'd arrived in the neighborhood. Maybe I was closer to Sunny. Maybe she was around the corner. We could bump into one another in the elfin produce market—they always saved the best of their crops for their own markets—and I would have her against the wall in the alley before she could say hello with that bright blush on her cheeks.

I blinked and then remembered that Sunny wouldn't have signed half a dozen consent forms up front.

Fine, then. She could say hello. And then as I set her basket under the radish bin and took her hand, she could tell me how much she missed my mouth on hers. Or my stav stroking her sweet, wet pussy. And then that hand that held hers would cover her mouth to muffle her cries of relief as I fucked her in the little hidden nook between the market and the florist. I'd clean her pussy with my mouth when we'd both come—her twice—so she wouldn't be embarrassed to return to the market long enough for me to buy our groceries, and then over to the florist for her to pick out the flowers she wanted on the table. The table I would bend her over after dinner, the flowers we would accidentally knock over—

"Khell!"

I sat up straight and winced at the stiff throb of my groin and the dull pound of my balls as I shifted.

"You looked like you were about to drill a hole in that tree, if you know what I mean," Rafe said, raising one of the Styrofoam cups to his lips, an obnoxious slurping sound replacing the memories of Sunny's bright cries of pleasure.

"If I'd known you were going to be this much of a pain in the ass, I would've done the work of moving by myself," I muttered, but without any real heat.

Rafe laughed. "I just saved you from public indecency, probably, so you're welcome for that, and for the help moving too. Want me to drop the truck back off?"

I looked at the debris Rafe had scattered over the porch, empty cardboard buckets from the fries and the wrappers from the hot dogs bunched into wads, like the heads of white flowers dropped decoratively around us. I could leave Rafe to the truck, settle into my new apartment for the night.

But it would be as Sunny-less as the last apartment, and at least taking care of the truck was something to do.

"No, let's clean up and I'll go," I said, adding a muttered, "Thanks."

Rafe rose, twisting and stretching his wings out to either side, the late evening sun glowing through their dark membrane. I didn't know if gargoyles took mates or if their hearts were as impenetrable as their stone bodies, but I hoped Rafe ran into someone who twisted his head up. He deserved to suffer at the hands of romance.

I ROLLED my shoulders for the third time, my body hunched over the far-too-short grocery cart, vowing that next time, I would make the trek to an orcish grocers, if only for more aisle space and taller carts.

A young impish woman and her horde of children passed me as I pushed up against a wall of cereal boxes to give them space. She ignored me, and one of her implings—leashed to the belt around her waist and flying on tiny wings—bapped its fist against my shoulder on its way by. I stifled my chuckle and reached an arm across the aisle to grab a tub of oats.

When I turned forward again, there was a glimpse of familiar peachy pink, just visible between an elderly couple. My cart hit the corner of a cardboard display as I craned my head.

A flick of blonde hair. The fluttering skirt of a sundress in late October.

Sunny.

I narrowly avoided barreling down the display, *and* the elderly couple for that matter, as I rushed for the end of the aisle.

I'd sensed it—the slight easing of the painful tension that had simmered in my chest since I'd left Sunny at the cottage. I was *closer*. Was she here? I could collide my cart into hers. There was no convenient nook behind this big-box grocery store, but there were always the hidden places under the rails of the L train, and the roar of a train would cover Sunny's cries as I—

My steps stalled at the end of the aisle, and my nose wrinkled at the harsh edge of strong perfume. There was none of Sunny's tart sweetness, but if she was perfumed, it might've disguised her natural scent.

I pushed forward, eyes searching the aisles for three rows and then—

There! That peach!

A tall man stepped aside and there was—

Oh.

My hands were hot, crowded together on the push bar of the cart, and my shoulders sagged as I straightened. The young woman in the aisle was tall and slim. She wore a suit jacket over the dress, and her lips were the wrong shade of pink. The blonde hair I'd caught a glimpse of was two shades too light and not a natural tone, and it was braided back, the tail hitting her waist.

She glanced up the aisle at me with bright blue eyes, blinking once and then offering me a sly, secretive smile.

I turned away, hunching back over my cart and walking blindly forward. Not Sunny at all. She wasn't here.

I paused when I was safely out of the way of traffic and tried to return to the moment before I'd seen the skirt. I needed groceries. The cupboards were empty and my boxes still packed. I was only halfway done gathering everything on my list. Sunny not being here with me didn't *change* anything.

If she were here, she could push the cart and I could reach the high shelves.

I sighed, stood straight, and rolled my shoulders.

Less than two weeks, I promised myself. *Better not starve in the meantime.*

CHAPTER 20
Sunny

THE UPSHOT of miserably missing Khell'ar for three weeks was that my intense need for distraction had created an incredible uptick in productivity.

Missing the taste of orc cum as you drink your morning coffee? Better rearrange the counters and pantry.

Bent over unrolling a new carpet in the living room and start daydreaming about getting railed from behind? Switch gears and finish putting up those succulent shelves in the bathroom!

Wake up in the dead of night from a wet dream of being pinned down by massive green muscles and a fat cock, only to realize you are, in fact, alone and starting to cry? Go up to the attic to paint.

I rolled my neck on my shoulders, listening to the satisfying *crack, snap, crick*. My eyes ached after too many nights of interrupted sleep, and I was fairly sure I was working on this latest piece with my vision offline, but it was nearly done now and I...

I stepped back, reaching up with the hand still holding the brush to rub a hair away from my face. A cold smear crossed my cheek, and I sighed. Paint. Great.

The light in the attic was changing, and I winced, realizing that I'd been up here so long morning had arrived. The attic of my little coach house was actually a finished room, with a lovely beamed dome ceiling. It'd had a pull-down ladder when I'd first arrived, and I'd managed to install a set of spiral, faux-iron stairs instead. There were only three windows and the light wasn't particularly good, but it was my favorite room in the house. The beams and curved ceiling gave the space a sacred quality that made me feel safe in my work.

I blinked at the easel in front of me. I'd started something of a collection, and it wasn't hard to guess why. A dark, enchanted woods, shadows and strange greenery, imaginary creatures watching from the corners, seductive blooms that glowed with poisonous luminescence. A heroine caught in its trap, feminine figures in diaphanous dresses, branches of willows twisting around their wrists, skirts caught in the mouths of little beasts. I wanted to be the girl running through the woods again, giddy and waiting to be caught.

I missed Khell giving me baths and feeding me and hiding his smiles, although I preferred it even more when he didn't hide them at all. I missed the night in the moonlight, when I'd pretended we were more than client and partner. And a small part of me missed the games too. Being trapped and out of control. The simplicity of following orders to their delicious end.

On the canvas, a girl spun in the grass, her long braid—it reminded me of Khell's—twisting around her like a rope. The shadows were at her back, the woods quiet and peaceful there, and ahead of her was glaring brilliance and a mass of strange creatures with bright eyes and sharp teeth, perfectly crisp and clear in the light. In the midst of them was a monster, bare and naked and golden, a lion's mane and a satyr's strong legs and the dense muscles of an orc's torso all melded together. He shone brighter than anything else in the frame, his vivid white gaze on the girl, a long golden arm and articulated fingers tipped with blood red claws reaching out to her.

She was rearing back, eyes wide and lips parted on a gasp or scream, but her own hand was floating toward him too, toward the violent clarity of the bright side of the woods, the outrageous strangeness of the creatures calling to her. She was hesitating, still deciding between the dim safety of normalcy and the monstrous exposure of the light.

Before Khell, the most frightening possibility was to know myself, accept myself, and *love* myself for who I truly was. Because what if no one else ever felt the same way for me in that truth?

Now I was terrified I might sink back into those mild and unchallenging shadows.

My blog was more active than ever. I had stacks of new art to get ready to scan and have available in prints. My home was growing more my own as I played in my spaces and reshaped the rooms.

But it was as if I'd stepped into that brilliance, experienced its warmth and peace, learned every bit of myself and embraced it, and then had been promptly shoved back toward the shadowy edge of the wood.

I squinted at the canvas. The bright edge of the wood almost blended in with the creamy yellow of my walls as the sun blinked in through the window and struck them both.

I twisted, looking at the mess of my studio, at the gentle slope of the beams up to the roof, like trees leaning to cover me, at the bare, cream-colored canvas of the walls.

Inspiration struck hard, clearing some of the fog of sitting at work too long, a fresh shot of adrenaline to my brain before I grew maudlin and mopey again.

I needed more paint.

"I LOVE YOU, and part of loving you is telling you when I think you look like shit," Natalie said, leaning over the broad arm of the pedicure massage chair.

I nodded, pressing my back into the rolling knobs of the chair, pretending they were Khell's fingers as I let my eyes blink slowly shut. When I opened them again, I was back in the city, sitting in front of floor-to-ceiling windows that overlooked busy Clark Street.

"Are you eating?" Natalie asked.

"Are you practicing this kind of interrogation for when Emmett gets older?" I asked, before adding, "Yeah. Irregularly, but that's not my problem."

"Showering?"

The small woman with incredibly strong fingers, and slightly pointed ears peeking through a curtain of what I was pretty sure was bottle-purple hair, gave me a speculative glance from under her bangs.

"Daily," I said, for both their sakes.

"'Cause you have paint on your face," Natalie pointed out, and I blushed. "You haven't had paint on your face since college. Are you sleeping?"

The tears that sprung to my eyes were spontaneous but not surprising. I got weepy when I was tired, and I'd been tired for weeks now. I shook my head, unable to speak through the sudden knot in my throat, and Natalie only reached across the arm rests to take my hand.

"Okay," she said softly, our pedicurists taking care to keep their heads ducked as they bundled us up in warm, damp towels. "Do you want me to come over tonight? Theo can watch Em, and we can order food and drink wine and watch movies. You always pass out during a movie."

I smiled at the thought, and at having a friend who knew me so well. But then I thought about waking up in the middle of the night again, at the edge of an orgasm that wouldn't crash, feeling lonely and awful and horny and simmering with the urge to go and *do anything else.*

I opened my mouth to offer Natalie an excuse. If I could stall a few more days, we'd be near the full moon, and then she'd be busy with Theo and I'd be off the hook for another week or so.

Before anything could come to mind, a figure on the sidewalk across the street caught my eye. Tall and beautifully broad, a dark hoodie covering his head, a rich green fist wrapped around the handle of a gym bag. And that ass, hugged in gray sweatpants, flexing with every step toward the double doors of the Crossfit complex.

Khell!

My pedicurist squawked as I stood, feet tangled in the towel, planted in the mini jet tub. My cunt throbbed at the thought of him, the sight of him, already growing wet and ready for the orc who'd trained it so well.

He grabbed the handle of the door, and then stepped back to hold it open for a statuesque harpy exiting. His head tipped and the hood fell back and—

And it wasn't Khell at all. The orc's hair was short and inky black, and his jawline looked like an axehead, all wide and sharp. My chest panged so roughly, I fell back into the chair, aware of the glare of the elfish girl at my feet and Natalie's slack jaw, her eyes drifting to what caught my attention.

"I'm an idiot," I said before she could think it.

"You're not," Natalie said.

"You need to hold still," the girl at my feet muttered.

"Right, sorry," I squeezed out of collapsing lungs.

Because I was not going to see Khell out on the streets of Chicago. Millions of people lived in this city and plenty of them were big, handsome orcs. I couldn't freeze like a deer in headlights every time I saw one.

I was shaking in the chair, still yearning to throw myself

out, to charge across the busy traffic of Clark Street, to reach out to that orc as if I could tear his mask away and reveal the one I *wanted* to see.

"Babe," Natalie said gently.

"I'll be okay," I answered.

"No, look at me."

I watched the girl at my feet instead for several minutes. She pulled the towel away and cupped lotion into her palms, rubbing it into the soles of my feet, my calves, my toes. She was thorough and strong, and it *did* feel nice, but it wasn't the touch I was craving.

Finally, I looked up at Natalie, her expression soft and worried.

"Maybe it *wasn't* just the serotonin," Natalie said.

I blinked back the new wave of tears that tried to rise and shook my head. "I don't think it was. What do I do, Natalie?"

She shrugged. "What do you want to do?"

I bit my lip to keep from spitting out the immediate, absurd answer. "Something really stupid," I said instead.

Natalie laughed. "Will it make you happy?"

"Probably only temporarily," I admitted.

Natalie hummed at that. "Well, look. We'll take doing something stupid *once* for temporary happiness. And then we'll come back and reevaluate after, okay?"

My grin was wobbling, but it was there at least. "Okay. Hi, so sorry, I just need to step away for a minute, is that okay?" I asked my pedicurist.

Her eyes rolled, but she stuffed flimsy flip-flops onto my feet and leaned back so I could move, grabbing my phone out of my purse with shaking fingers.

I hadn't saved the number, but it came up with a quick search online.

"Monster Smash Agency, how can we help you?"

"Hi, this is, um, Sonya Bancroft, and I was interested in... booking a follow-up."

"Just one moment, Ms. Bancroft, let me transfer you to your agent."

There was a brief trill of static and music on the other line before it cut out.

"Sonya! It's good to hear from you again!" The chipper, bright voice of the succubus Astraeya was eager in my ear. "What can I do for you?"

My mouth was open, but it took me a long moment to speak. Was I really going to do this? I had the money...for now, but not enough saved to really justify spending it on something like this. What if this only put a pause on the problem? What if I became *addicted* to Khell?

As if my tongue knew my brain might deny me this moment, I spoke in a rush. "I'd like to book a night. With my partner from before."

"Excellent, excellent. I'm *so* happy you enjoyed your experience with MSA," Astraeya rattled on.

Natalie was twisted around her chair to watch me, and my irritated pedicurist was glaring at me, her small chin perched in her hand.

"Can I ask...if your partner was unavailable at the time you needed, would you be willing to partner with another?" Astraeya asked slowly.

My heart leapt into my throat, and my head was shaking uselessly. "I—No, I can do any time. I...I only want Khell, please," I whispered over the line.

"Excellent!" Astraeya said, much louder in my ear this time. "Give me just a moment to, um...check the calendar and I'll—Hold, please!" she all but shouted.

I pursed my lips and let out a slow breath, turning my back on Natalie and letting my eyes fall shut as the waiting music played lightly in my left ear. But this wait was much longer than the first, and all my slow breathing couldn't stop the worried racing of my heart or the furrowing of my brow. Was Khell really so booked up they wouldn't be able to find a place for me? He'd been available on short notice the first time. Or had he left the cottage and told MSA not to pair us together again?

My stomach turned queasily and I opened my eyes again, searching for the clock on the wall and watching the seconds tick by.

A minute went by. It wasn't going to happen. I'd given into the impulse to schedule just one little night of bliss, only to run into a scheduling conflict?

Two minutes.

My skin was breaking out in clammy goose bumps, heartbeat slowing as reality set in. Five days. All I was going to get, all I had, was those five days. It was time to move on and—

"Sonya! Hi, sorry for the wait." Astraeya's voice in my ear made me jump in place, my free hand slapping over my lips to cover my gasp. "You and your partner are all set for a night at the cottage this Friday. You can arrive at our office as early as three pm, and we'll get you over there by four!"

"Khell? Khell's my partner?" I asked, trying not to sound as though I'd just run a marathon, as though I was taking full breaths for the first time in three weeks, as though my entire nervous system had just lit up in excitement, my limbs tingling like they were waking up from a deep sleep.

"He sure is," Astraeya chuckled. "He's looking forward to seeing you again."

I blushed but dismissed the words. "Thank you. I'll be there."

Astraeya said a few more things, and I was fairly certain I answered her questions without sounding insane, but later I wouldn't recall another word of the conversation. I hung up at last, tasting the air in my lungs—sharp with the scent of the nail spa's chemicals, suddenly my new favorite smell.

Natalie and I were both beaming as I turned around and floated back to the massage chair.

"Sorry," I said gently to the young girl waiting on me.

"Forgive her," Natalie said with a nod. "You know how it is when you gotta book the good dick in advance."

I snorted out a giggle, and my pedicurist huffed and hid her smile, ducking her head and returning to her work.

"IS THERE anything specific you're hoping for with this session?" Astraeya asked as I sat in the same desk chair across from her.

I bit my lip and tried to keep from jiggling my heel, watching the clock. It wasn't even three-thirty yet. I wasn't getting to the cottage any sooner by watching the clock.

"Umm…" Touching Khell. Kissing him. Being pressed to the bed under his weight. Riding his lap as he told me I was his.

I didn't care if he chained me, chased me, or just fucked me nonstop for the sixteen hours we were together. All of the above, please.

"It's totally reasonable to say 'partner's choice,'" Astraeya said, smiling at me. "He knows your preferences and your dislikes."

I sighed and nodded, smiling. "Partner's choice."

Astraeya grinned back at me, glancing down at her tablet briefly and pressing her lips together. "You know…" she said slowly, before hesitating and glancing up at me. "Well, Khell is really looking forward to working with you again."

Maybe it was true, but the words made my smile fade a bit. It just sounded like something a business would say to keep a customer returning.

"He…retired from MSA recently," Astraeya added, watching my face.

The news struck me hard, turning off the pitiful and

familiar spiral of a moment ago and wiping my expression clean and blank. "What?"

"He's no longer one of our available partners. I brought him in for you as a freelancer."

"A freelancer," I repeated.

Khell had retired? From MSA or from sex work? Was he working elsewhere, privately with clients, or had he moved on?

"I'm sure he didn't want you to have to partner with anyone else," Astraeya said, leaning forward.

Because I had told her only Khell. I chewed on my lip again for a moment, staring down at my hands. There was a bit of paint still marking my wrist from waking up early this morning and working on the walls of my studio.

It had been surprisingly easy to get through the week. I'd thought I'd be madly watching the hours pass, waiting to return to the cottage, but instead, it was almost like returning to normal. Booking the appointment was like taking "the end" out of the back of the story and allowing it to grow again. My time with Khell wasn't over after all.

But he was *retired*.

"Is he…back in construction?" I asked.

"I think so!" Astraeya answered, beaming at me. "It's cute he told you about that."

So he hadn't moved to another company. He'd just left this work. And I'd dragged him back. Or at least gently called. I hadn't *begged* him. Maybe Astraeya had on my behalf, though.

"Sonya," Astraeya said gently, catching onto my turmoil by now. "It's not uncommon for our partners to have an attachment to a client. To want to…be there for them."

But Khell had retired. He'd left MSA.

He'd quit the job that brought us together.

Was it really right to use an "attachment" to bring him back?

For a week, I'd felt that door opening, the words waiting, the canvas stretching to make room for more beauty. And now I knew—tonight would only delay the inevitable.

This would be the last time. My end with Khell had been the evening he left the cottage.

CHAPTER 21
Khell'ar

I PACED the cottage floorboards as though I were threatening the walls around me, every step thumping, wood creaking. My eyes held the face of the clock in the kitchen, trying to force the hands to turn faster.

One month. I had waited, and my patience had paid off. Sunny had called the agency, asked for me again. Another day and I would've certainly broken, but the relief of the call soothed the fever.

Thank fuck for Astraeya. She'd marked me down as "freelancer." If MSA really wanted to dig deeper, they might have had some concerns about why their recently departed former employee came back for the last client they'd booked. I didn't care. Sunny would be in my grip in minutes. And then…

I would have to break the MSA contract, tell Sunny the truth about the mating bond, and see if there was a chance for us, for me, outside of the cottage and the bookings.

My stav was already starting to pump like I was a sapling before his first good rut—constantly hard and clueless as to what to do with the new charge of arousal always simmering in his length.

Except I knew exactly what to do with my cock now. I just

needed Sunny here with me. We had sixteen hours. I would remind Sunny exactly how much she liked being mine, and then I would find the way to offer myself to her as more than a partner in these carefully arranged meetings. I wouldn't rush. Sunny had instructed Astraeya to let me have control—of course she had—and I would use that permission to spoil Sunny with pleasure and kisses and care and my cock until she was soft and sweet and my good little pet.

Tires crunched on the dirt road, and my pacing turned to a rush to the window, long claws flicking the curtain aside. A bright yellow car bumped along the road toward the cottage. Sunny had driven herself this time.

My cock throbbed, wept in anticipation and I reached down, squeezing at myself, uncertain if I was soothing the ache or making it worse.

It was good she was alone. If Astraeya had brought Sunny here again, I would've slammed the door on the succubus' face. Not that I wasn't grateful for her calling me. But she didn't need to witness my hunger for my mate. That was Sunny's privilege alone.

Sit down. Don't terrify her, I thought, backing away from the window, moving toward the head of the dining table, forcing myself into a seat that faced the doorway.

Then again, Sunny liked to be a little scared. No, I would wait here, be the first thing she saw as she opened the door, and then—

The car stopped outside the cottage, and I held my breath, my claws digging into my thighs through my sweatpants. I hadn't changed into a costume this time. Neither of us would wear clothes long enough to make changing them worth it. I hesitated, my ears perked and twitching as Sunny opened and shut her car door, and then tore my shirt off over my head.

And maybe I would take off the pants too, let Sunny *really* get a good look.

Except her steps were already outside the door, and I was twitching in my seat, body desperate to rise and charge, to meet her. To snatch her up. To taste her again. To press her into me and dig my teeth into her flesh and *claim* my mate.

The door handle clicked, and sunlight streamed in through the crack. I growled at the shadow on the floor until the door opened enough for the shadow to reach the feet, the legs, the bright yellow sundress.

"Oh!" Sunny paused in the doorway, eyes wide on me. "You're already here."

I should've spoken. Greeted her. Told her I'd been waiting for her for four weeks, and it might've been less if she hadn't called MSA first.

I only growled, my entire body straining not to leap across the space.

Her surprise softened into something sweeter briefly, and then a little fold appeared between her eyes. Worry? Or that ache she'd revealed the night in the woods?

"Khell," she said, far too timid.

My control snapped, and her eyes flared wide again as I shot into motion, everything blurring but my need to be *on* her. *In* her.

She gasped as I reached her, my arms snatching her up off her toes, my foot kicking the door shut, tearing the glare of the sun away so that the brightest thing in the room was *my mate.*

"Sunny," I purred. I hitched her up against my hips, grinning at the instinctive part of her legs, the way her pupils darkened, her warm gaze as they widened. I rocked my hard length into her, and my purr became a growl. "Are you wet for me, petal?"

Sunny whimpered, her tongue flicking out over her lip, her body already falling into the natural motion of riding me. Just two quick motions of shoving clothes aside, and I would be inside my mate again.

"Oh god, Khell," Sunny breathed, breasts pressing into my chest, back arching and lips tipped up in invitation. Begging, really. "I don't think I can—"

"No more waiting," I growled, and dove down, taking her mouth in one bite, parting her lips with the plunge of my tongue in time with the desperate thrust of my hips.

Sunny's flavor was as sweet and fresh as I'd remembered, and I lapped at her cries. Our bodies were trying to meet in fruitless, chaotic union, rutting and rubbing every inch of ourselves together. Sunny's hands clawed at my bare back as she gasped and cried out in the kiss.

No more waiting, I assured myself. Perhaps I would go the old way, kidnap Sunny and woo her in my den until she was as happy to stay as I was to keep her. For now, I abandoned my grip on one of Sunny's thighs in favor of a brief, rough squeeze of her breast, grinning into her yelp, gentling my kisses in apology until she was biting me back for more. My hand moved south, gathering up the fabric of her yellow skirt and shoving it out of my way.

"Khell," Sunny moaned as my claws grazed her inner thighs.

"Mine," I snarled, pressing my forehead to hers.

I had to flex my hand twice before my claws would retract, and they ached in their sleeves. Sunny's underwear was wet under my fingers, and we both groaned as I shoved the little line of lace fabric aside so I could touch her properly.

Soaked and hot and slippery. Ready for me. Or nearly. It had been a month, after all.

I lifted my head to watch as I plunged two fingers into Sunny's weeping cunt. Her eyes shut on a moan, and for a moment as I stroked my way inside of her, that ache vanished, replaced by a sweet and smiling relief.

"There now, petal," I murmured. "It's better now that we're together again, isn't it?"

I dipped my head to kiss her again, sweetly this time, but

Sunny's fingers dug into my back, a whine rising in her throat.

The sound was pure pain, faint, but undeniably a wound.

My fingers were gliding easily inside of her, but I stilled them and searched her face.

Her eyes opened again, glittering with tears, pink lips trembling. "I can't do this, Khell."

I froze, the haze of desperate need clearing at those words. Was this a game? No, denial had never been Sunny's strong suit, and the turmoil on her face was far too real.

She'd been trying to say it—not *I can't wait*, but *I can't do this*. Impossible. She had *called* for me. The beast in me refused the words, refused the idea of anything but taking Sunny now, regardless of what she said. But I was not a beast, and my mate was hurting, which was unbearable.

I pulled my fingers free slowly, and Sunny sobbed, sagging forward against my chest as I sorted her panties back into place.

"Astraeya told me," she whispered, and I stiffened, trying to keep a new growl leashed. "You retired."

Oh.

I sighed, scooping Sunny up by the backs of her thighs and straightening, carrying her away from the door. "I did. But that doesn't need to worry you."

"Khell!" Sunny cried out, and then squeaked as I fell into the cushions of the blue couch with her on my lap.

"Sunny," I growled.

"You gave up this work, you can't come back for my sake," Sunny said, wrestling against me and then huffing and glaring at me. "Let me stand!"

My heart slammed in my chest. Tell her bluntly now, or try to soothe her and keep to my plan? "Sunny, petal, I *want* to be here with you. I came for my own sake."

That gave her pause, a little flicker of hope coloring her cheeks as she blinked back at me, but a moment later her head was shaking again, brow furrowing. "And what about… what about next time?" she whispered, stepping back, skirting out of the way of my reaching hands. "What about when you have another job or…or you meet someone?"

I scoffed. Maybe it would be better to explain everything to her now. I straightened on the couch and tried to speak, but Sunny was still going, still walking backwards away from me.

"It's not your fault, and I'm not going to ask for a refund—"

"Sunny, I don't give a fuck if you pay—"

"But I already let myself get too attached."

"Well, thank the old oaks for that," I growled, standing and preparing to *chase* Sunny if that was what it took.

"I can't do this, Khell," Sunny said. And my poor mate was crying, trembling in her pretty dress and sweater, head shaking, showing me glimpses of those foolish lovely ears I would bite later for *not listening*.

"Sunny," I barked, some mix of the tone I used to be the dominant and my own patience running thin. "Come here."

Sunny stiffened and swayed forward for a moment before shaking her head once. "This isn't a game, Khell'ar."

"I'm well aware. Sunny, you are mine. My—"

"Hodge podge," Sunny bit out, chin tipping up in stubborn determination.

I blinked in confusion once. "Wha—"

And then the lights of the cottage turned red, and my heart stopped in my chest. The safe word.

All the doors swung open abruptly, and my heart started up again just as fast, trying to climb its way up my throat, as if I could spit it out and leave it at Sunny's feet.

"Partner report," called a cold voice over the hidden intercoms as Sunny turned on her heel, eyes still holding mine.

"Sunny, wait," I pleaded. But all it took was one step forward from me, and Sunny spun and raced for the door.

"Partner report," the MSA help line called again.

"Fuck off," I snarled, chasing after Sunny.

It wasn't a far distance for her to go, and she'd already covered half of it in the muddled little argument. She made it to the door before me, and I thought I felt my heart race over the threshold with her.

"Sunny, *please!*" I shouted, reaching for the door.

But MSA had policies and procedures for the red light safe word. The front door swung shut, snapping and locking in place, just as my fist landed against the wood.

"Partner report, please."

"Put Astraeya on the line," I snapped, banging once more on the door. "Sunny, please, just wait outside!"

"Report—"

"Client is unharmed but had a strong emotional response. *Put Astraeya on!*"

There was a huff of irritation on the line, but the red lights turned off. The little shit agent kept the door locked, though.

"Sunny?" I called, rapping more lightly on the door, resting my head against the surface and catching my breath.

My answer was the sound of her car starting.

"Fuck!"

Every crunch of gravel and snap of a twig under Sunny's retreating car had a physical manifestation in my chest, my body trying to cave in on itself like I was the thing being crushed under those tires.

I'd just had her in reach. I should've thrust into her, told her she was my mate, and not pulled out again until we were both exhausted and in agreement.

"Khell? What's—"

"Astraeya, she ran because you told her I retired. Unlock the fucking door so I can get to my mate," I snarled, not caring now what was on MSA's tapes for them to review. It would be fine. Sunny was *attached*. I just needed three seconds to make everything clear to her.

"She *ran?*"

"Astraeya, the door!" I yelled. There was a moment of quiet, and I tried to find calm when all I wanted to do was take an axe to the cottage. "I didn't get a chance to tell her, Astraeya. Please. Open the door."

Another beat of quiet. "Okay, I'm just pulling up the controls. Invite me to the wedding and tell Sunny to toss the bouquet my way."

I snorted, but the lock clicked directly and I wasn't going to waste another second. I threw the door open and bolted down the drive through the woods.

The smell of exhaust was still in the air, Sunny's tail lights visible in the distance. I would catch her. There was only so fast you could go on a drive this bumpy. But even knowing so didn't stop the worry racing through me. That I'd just miss her. That I'd never hunt her down in the city.

No. I would. Astraeya would give me her information, or I would sniff every door in Chicago until I found her.

The tail lights grew brighter as she braked around a curve and I ran harder, breath sawing in and out of me, muscles burning. The sun would set soon, the woods bright and glowing. I was shirtless in the autumn chill, chasing down a *car* like a dog. I was chasing down my *mate*.

And I would catch her. My claws were out, biting into the heels of my palms, and the air stung in my lungs as I pushed myself harder.

The tail lights brightened again, and I'd closed some of the distance. Could she see me in her rearview mirror? A feral orc barreling down a dirt road after her. Hunting her?

She would love it.

I grinned at the thought and the sight of the brake lights remaining on. She was slowing down.

She was *stopping*.

I let out a long growl as Sunny stepped out of the driver's

side of her car, engine still running, her hands on her hips. I didn't slow my charge.

"What are you *doing?!*" she cried, her eyes growing huge as she realized as I was racing closer, not slowing at all. "Khell! We can't just keep—"

She didn't scream as I caught her up in my arms again, but her breath caught in her chest and she stiffened as I slammed her door shut.

"I retired because I met my mate," I said, holding those lovely warm eyes of hers. I was hard again, determined for what came next.

"Your mate?" Sunny repeated, and I growled at the first glimmer of heartbreak in her gaze.

"A foolish little human, with no sense of self-preservation. Who likes her orc's cum running down her thighs, and who wants to be chased through the woods and caught roughly and fucked till she can't stand up straight. And who beats an orc at his own games when she's only just learned the rules," I said, thinking of Rum'kurr, and also thinking of the way Sunny had trapped me in her snare that first day as she'd let me put her in chains on her knees before me.

Sunny wasn't breathing. Her mouth hung open but no words came out, so I bent and kissed her briefly.

"I should've said so before we ended our time together, but I thought it might overwhelm you," I admitted. "I don't know if I was cowardly or noble, but I'm *sorry*, petal. Don't run from me."

"Your mate?" Sunny repeated in a whisper.

I purred and pressed my chest to hers so she could feel the sound and the pounding of my heart. "My mate—the only woman I will ever chase or fuck or spank or kiss ever again. I've *missed* you. I was at the end of my patience when Astraeya called. Now tell me what you have to say."

"Say?" Sunny blinked and shook her head slowly, face blank.

I chuckled and reached up, wrapping a hand around the front of her throat, pressing my claws into her pulse. "Yes. What does my petal have to say about taking her orc's cock now?"

"Here?" Sunny was breathy, wiggling against me again, and she had an almost drugged expression on her face. The shock of the news was strong, but it seemed to be relaxing her at last.

"Here," I rumbled, tightening my grip just a touch, forcing her head back so I could tower over her. "What does my *mate* say?"

Mate. Sunny mouthed the word, gazing with wild wonder up at me for another moment before licking her lips. "I missed you too. *So* much. It was like I was living in a glass jar. I couldn't touch the world around me."

I nodded, and Sunny softened in my arms, her pulse beating wildly against my claws. Still, she hadn't really answered me yet.

And then she did.

"Kiss me again."

My mouth was on hers before she'd finished the words, our tongues tangling. I slid the hand on her throat to the back of her neck, claws scratching up into her hair. Her legs wrapped around my hips, and her hands slid down, pushing at the waistband of the sweatpants I was wearing.

Thank fuck.

It didn't take much adjustment. I shoved her skirt up again, caught the edge of her damp panties with my thumb claw, and tore them apart, earning a gasping laugh from Sunny. A few wiggles from her, and my pants were down far enough to free my cock, the fabric briefly scratching at the dripping head.

"Fuck me," Sunny managed to gasp out, my tusks scratching at her jaw. "Oh god, I've needed you."

And by some miracle, I managed not to simply shove

myself into her with one thrust, although it was a close call at that first wet kiss of pussy to cockhead. Sunny wrapped her arms around my shoulders and leaned back against the window of her car, all the tangle and tears just a memory on her smiling face.

"Petal," I breathed, hips rolling slowly forward.

Sunny's moan was high and strained, her cunt tight around my cock as I sank in. She needed more stretching, but after the confusion at the cottage, I was impatient. Still, she was wet and my cock was leaking eager precum, and the journey was a slow but beautiful reunion of flesh.

Sunny was fully dressed and I missed her skin, but it was cold in the woods.

"What are you—Oh!" Sunny hiccuped as I sank in to the hilt, stepping back from the car so she was seated fully and only on my cock, gravity making the connection *deep*.

"We need better accommodations," I said, grinning and nipping at Sunny's nose. She was mine now.

Oh, there was more to be spoken, of course. It would come after we did.

"You'd better not be jogging back to the cottage," Sunny said, and then laughed as I pulled her backseat car door open. "Khell, we won't both fit!"

I wouldn't fit sitting down on my own, let alone with Sunny on my lap, but that wasn't my goal. With her head cradled in my hand and my arm around her hips, I leaned forward, bending my knees and ducking us both into the shelter of the car.

Sunny laughed as I laid her down on the bench seat, her motion teasing my length. I still was barely able to get my shoulders inside, and I certainly couldn't sit up, but I wanted to be pressed to Sunny, not separated from her.

I started to rock, just in and out of her by a small inch, and Sunny's eyes fluttered shut, her own hips nudging back against me.

"Oh fuck, your stav is already so thick."

It was painfully swollen and pumping fast and rough in my length, stroking Sunny from the inside as I slid my hands under her skirt and started to work her dress up over her head.

"I need your skin, petal. Need to taste every inch of you."

Sunny whined but arched her back and helped me wrestle her out of her dress, breasts caged in a lace bra. I left her to finish the work, my head lowering to suck on those perfect breasts, teasing her nipples through the lace and wrapping my hands around her hips, pulling her more roughly onto my cock.

"Fuck, fuck yes, beast," Sunny murmured, tossing her dress over the top of the passenger seat. Her fingers found their favorite spot, tangled in my braid. "Fuck, is anyone going to find us like this?"

If they did, it would take an army to get me to stop. Well, an army or a request from Sunny.

"No," I growled. Astraeya would probably cover for us. "You're mine now, petal."

"Say it again," Sunny whispered in my ear, tugging on my hair to draw my mouth back to hers.

Her lips were swollen, eyes still a little red from crying. I noticed suddenly how tired she looked. She hadn't been getting her sleep.

"My mate," I rasped out, drawing slowly out, watching the worry bloom in her eyes and then explode into nothing as I slammed deep inside of her again. "Mine now."

"Yes!"

The praise was quiet, tenuous. I'd sprung a big piece of information on her, and we would have work to do together. But she *was* mine now.

I stroked my hands down her hips and thighs, to her knees, clasping behind them and pushing them back, Sunny's eyes popping at the stretch.

"Brace your feet on the inside of the car," I said, grinning at that pretty little blush of nerves on her cheeks that appeared whenever I gave her an order that frightened and thrilled her.

Her knees hugged my ribs, one foot braced almost up at the roof of the car. It opened her sex to me, and I sank in deeper on the next thrust, making Sunny shout and my stav jump in my length.

I braced my hands on the far side of the car. Her old car might need its alignment checked after this.

Worth it.

I would take care of her now.

I drew back and then drove forward in one steady, endless drive of my hips. Sunny shouted, back arching, and my mouth fell to her breasts again. The car squeaked as I picked up an even, exhausting, thorough pace, the body of the vehicle rocking with Sunny and me as we fucked.

"Oh god, yes! My beast," Sunny cried. "Oh fuck, Khell, I'm so close. Bite. Harder. Fuck me."

I grunted at the orders and followed them all, biting and sucking on the nipple in my mouth, slamming home in my mate a little rougher, faster.

Sunny's knees pinched my ribs, one hand scratching my shoulder blade, the other twisting my braid in her fist.

"Again, again, again—Oh, *yes!*"

Sunny squealed and thrashed under me, a wet splash striking my hips, kissing my balls. I roared in triumph, attacking her other breast with my lips as she clasped and quenched my cock with her release.

The pleading pulse of her cunt around me would always be my weak spot, but I tried to resist the call until Sunny's eyes opened again and found mine.

"Mine," I snarled, rearing up over her, and she answered the word with a soft smile and a squeeze of her legs and arms and sex around me.

I arched, my head hitting the roof of the car, and came with a bellow, a month's worth of impatience and tension spiraling out of me as I kicked my hips and filled my mate with my scent, my seed.

Sunny moaned and fluttered as I filled her, sagging beneath me, giving me the sweetest, softest place to land, my lips finding hers automatically for lazy, licking kisses. Her legs softened around me, her heels on my ass, and her hands tucked around my shoulders to hold me on top of her. The car engine made a huff of effort, as if in camaraderie.

Sunny's lips were clumsy against mine, but constant and gentle, passing and brushing and sipping, carrying the kiss on for long minutes before she seemed to have found her fill.

I attempted to twist us, to give her body a break from my weight, but she grunted her objection and squeezed her knees around my hips until I fell still again.

"Don't move," she mumbled, pressing her face into my throat, humming happily as I nuzzled her head and my tusks caught in her hair. She always seemed to like that.

"You're bossy now that our roles have changed," I chuckled, then sighed as she stiffened. "Petal?"

"Just thinking," she mumbled from beneath me. "But also not quite ready to start thinking yet."

That suited me if it kept her calm, but I purred on top of her until she was limp again.

"What now, Khell?" Sunny asked.

I lifted up slightly until I found her face in the shadow beneath me, her hair a mess of golden tangles and slightly staticky from the friction against the car upholstery. "What would my mate like now?"

Her eyes lit up briefly and then skirted away just as quick.

Yes, we still had talking to do. She still had to accept this new shift. We barely knew each other yet.

But we would and it would all come at my mate's pace, or as slowly as I could stand to allow. It was impossible not to feel confident of this with her warm and soft and wet with satisfaction against me.

"I don't want to go back to the cottage," Sunny said slowly, eyes still tilted shyly down. "Would you..."

"Ask, petal," I said when she hesitated too long and started to twitch with fretting.

"Would you come home with me?" she blurted out, gaze flashing up at me.

I grinned at her and purred roughly. I was still hard, buried inside of her. I wanted to fuck her again just for asking. But her car was running, and MSA *might* have objections to our unplanned activities in the middle of the road.

"Oh yes, mate," I rumbled, bucking just a bit to satisfy the urge and to make Sunny gasp. "Take me to your little nest. Have your way with your orc in your bed. We'll tear your sheets and fill them with our scents, just as it should be."

Sunny's cheeks flushed bright red, her breasts pressing to my chest with her quick breaths, and she pulled my face down to hers for a rough kiss.

Maybe one more orgasm before we left...

CHAPTER 22
Sunny

"ARE you doing that to touch me, or because you're worried I'm going to hit the car in front of us?" I asked, as Khell's fingers—clawless—tightened around my thigh.

Khell'ar was stuffed shirtless into my tiny yellow car, the passenger seat pushed all the way back to make room for his long legs.

He was here. He was with me.

When I'd asked if he wanted to drive separately back to my house, he'd growled and said, "If it's up to me, I don't want you out of reach. But I'll defer to you."

So we'd simply driven off together, Khell making a quick call to Astraeya on my phone, the MSA monitor watches left on a stump.

I glanced at him out of the corner of my eye, turning onto my street. His knees were up to his chest and his shoulders up to his ears. He was comically large for my car, and I almost wished someone had been able to catch a picture of Khell's ass hanging out of the backseat as he'd fucked me twice in a row.

"Both," he admitted, smiling.

So Khell'ar was a backseat driver. Or a passenger seat driver. Whatever. Maybe that would be annoying later, but for now it was wonderfully mundane. Real life merging into fantasy.

"We're almost there," I said.

"I knew you would be close," Khell murmured, ducking his head to look out the window. "I moved. I'm just in Ravenswood."

One neighborhood away. Khell'ar was close. We could *date*, if that was something mates did. I wasn't sure yet.

I opened my mouth to ask, but Khell beat me to speaking. "I want to cook for you soon, but tonight, I won't be able to keep my hands off you. What do you want to order?"

Takeout and sex. Khell was just *speaking* these things rather than teasing me with hints or telling me he was in charge. He was so open now. *I won't be able to keep my hands off you.* Said so simply and honestly.

"You choose, please," I said, turning down the side alley to reach my garage.

Khell purred and patted his hips. "Ah. My cell is at the cottage. Oh, well."

I glanced at him again, half-wondering if this was the same orc and knowing immediately that *yes*, he was. But now there wasn't a game. And it wasn't disappointing at all, it was just *real*. Except it didn't quite feel that real yet.

I stopped my car outside of my garage, hitting the button to open it, and then pulled my phone from the cupholder and unlocked it, passing it to my orc.

Khell's hand on my thigh slid up high, and I hit the brakes a little roughly as I turned and parked in the garage, his fingertips rubbing against the crease of my sex before pulling away. He had one hand scrolling my phone and the other lifting up to his nose, a purr rattling in the dark of my car as the garage door shut behind us.

"We'd better get inside quickly, Sunny. Your cunt needs me."

Fantasy. Reality. It was all jumbling together into something even more impossible than the week in the cottage.

"Unless you'd rather try to squeeze on my lap in here?" Khell teased, gaze glowing.

I jumped out of the driver's side and rushed for the garage door that led to the yard, Khell taking a little longer to unfold himself from the passenger seat.

The coach house sat to the right of the garage, behind the great old house that had been divided into apartments. I shared the yard with the tenants, including a small veggie garden that Khell examined with mild interest before following me. I glanced up at the windows, wondering if any of my neighbors would be surprised to see a giant shirtless orc in the garden, and then hurried to my front door.

Khell's shadow covered mine on the door, and I shivered at the sight, then sighed as his hand clasped the back of my neck.

"We'll make an early night of it. You need rest. And we have time now," Khell said gently. "I'll stay as long as you want me to."

Meaning it wouldn't be over at ten in the morning tomorrow. We weren't on an appointment now. This was...

Except I wasn't sure what it was. Dating? That seemed small for the word *mate*.

"Sunny," Khell prompted.

I twisted the key in the lock and then stepped inside, holding the door open for Khell. My ceilings were high, that was good. But the doorways were narrow, the stairs and halls too. Khell just barely fit.

He was still using my phone as he stepped in, the screen illuminating his face, but his eyes were focused on my coach house, lips curling up as he took in my space.

"Smells like you. Feels like you," he said. "Curious and playful. Quit hovering at my edges, petal."

I shut the front door, barely remembering to pull the key

from the lock, and then ran after Khell into the living room. His arm snapped around my waist as I leapt at him, pressing my face into his throat and wrapping my arms around his shoulders.

"You're here," I whispered, taking a deep breath of him.

"Until you toss me out. And then I'll just convince you to let me back in," Khell said. He found my large couch, turning on my vintage lamp that now had a home on a newly refurbished vintage console table. "There. Food's ordered. Close your curtains and undress for me, petal. I want our skin touching, whether we talk or fuck."

I laughed against Khell's neck. "If we're both naked, you know it'll be fucking."

"It can be both," he said, jostling me with a soft shrug.

I leaned back, my arms still looped around his neck, and studied the lovely sharp angles of his face, reaching up to brush his tusks with my fingertips. Khell was patient, smiling, calm. He was the orc who had untangled my hair and washed me in the bath, and something more too, because he was holding my gaze and waiting for me to choose.

"I don't want to be distracted from either of those activities," I said, rising off Khell's lap and reaching behind him to grab my curtains.

He helped himself to handfuls of my breasts, leaning in and resting his chin in my cleavage as I stretched.

"And since we have time...I just want to enjoy being with you again first," I said, mulling over my answer for a moment before looking down at Khell. His eyes were hooded, and I caught him just as his long tongue flicked out to taste me. "We have time?"

Khell purred, rubbing his cheek against the top of my dress above my collar once and then guiding me back, his hands scooping under my skirt to help me undress.

"We have time, mate. And we will make the most of it together."

I bent and Khell stretched at the same moment, our lips meeting, the flavor of the kiss so beautifully familiar. My skirt was up over my waist, Khell distracted from stripping me as his tongue plunged into my mouth, my ass exposed to the cool air of the room. He had my torn panties in his sweatpants pocket, his massive hands circling my waist, his tusks framing our kiss.

This is not a fantasy. This is not a fantasy, I chanted to myself as I settled on Khell's lap.

He managed to finish pulling my dress over my head as he kicked his sweatpants off, my sex and his cock rubbing together briefly before the clothing was tossed away, and we took a moment to breathe.

Khell's braid was already lopsided from my grip on it earlier, his dark gaze warm and avidly studying my face.

"Do you wish I'd told you then?" Khell asked, tipping his head. "That I'd mated you."

I blinked. Mated. Like it was done and settled, but I still didn't know what it meant. I reached down between us, my breath catching as I stroked the head of his cock against my clit, and then moved it to my opening. Khell's throat flexed as I sank onto his length.

"A little," I admitted. "But you can make it up to me now."

Khell purred, his beautiful, hard face solemn, and he drew me forward for another kiss, every tendon and muscle relaxing in me with the brush of his lips on mine.

I WOKE in the middle of the night, just as I had for weeks now, a heavy but comforting weight over my waist. I wasn't frustrated this time, though. My heart wasn't hurting. And while my sex was warm and slightly throbbing, it was undeniably from satisfaction, rather than a lack of it.

Still, it took me a moment to orient myself. I was in my

bed, and the great lumpy mountain of muscle I was embracing was Khell. My Khell.

My…*mate.*

I could guess the meaning of the term, but Khell and I hadn't taken the time to really discuss it in depth yet.

Mine.

The word echoed in my head, a mix of both our voices.

I fumbled my hand over to my bedside table and found my phone. It was after five, and I was fairly certain Khell and I had collapsed in the sheets before midnight. Six whole hours of uninterrupted sleep in one night? Not bad.

I rolled in the cradle of Khell's arms, my pillow stuffed in his armpit for me to rest my head there. He was flat on his back, spread out over the majority of the queen bed. I bet even his feet were hanging over the edge. My gaze was studying the profile of his sleeping face, my hand sliding over his chest to find the tail of his braid, twisting it around my hand. His tusks were bright in the dark, his lips slightly parted and breaths heavy.

For the first time in weeks, I was comfortable. I was wide awake, my thoughts still cataloging everything that had happened last night, and Khell was fast asleep. His cock was half-hard, tenting the sheet we were under, and I was pretty confident that if I took him in my hand, Khell would be more than happy to meet my demand.

It was a tempting distraction. But also for the first time in weeks, I wasn't jittery with desperation. It was like finally having ownership of my body back.

Khell was here. He would stay until I told him to leave, whenever that was. He lived nearby. Being with Khell could be normal. As normal as it was to be with an orc twice my size, whose impatience had run out before we reached the top of the stairs, so he'd put me on my hands and knees and rutted me right there. As normal as it was to finally make it into the bed, to kiss softly and say goodnight and then both decide we needed each other once more, with me riding him until my thighs burned and I forgot to breathe through the orgasm that struck like lightning.

Khell slept through me sliding his arm aside and rising from the bed. I wasn't falling back asleep, and I wanted to take advantage of this new version of my normal. I snuck out of my bedroom, cleaned up briefly in the bathroom and grabbed a robe, and then tiptoed up the spiral staircase to my studio.

My studio had been the main subject of my blog for the last week, as I slowly worked on a mural over the walls. I was painting the subject of my recent work, the enchanted woods, on the sloping domed walls of the room, from the dark shady corners around to the bright sunlit glades.

I filled up my palette with bright tones and wheeled my cart of water jars and towels and fine-tipped brushes over to a tree laden so full of strange birds that the branches sagged toward my floor. I'd worked out the rough base of colors for this section of wall already, but I'd been looking forward to the challenge of details—tiny golden beaks and iridescent feathers and blood tipped claws. Having actually gotten some decent rest meant I could enjoy my work this morning instead of using it as a survival method.

I worked in silence, trying to bring the beautifully jeweled and ferocious little creatures of my imagination to life on the wall. I'd done a great deal of work before I heard Khell's heavy footsteps from the floor below.

"Sunny?"

The sun was rising out the window, just a soft glow in the sky, and I turned my head toward the stairs. "Up here. I can come down."

"No, I want to explore," Khell answered.

I stared speculatively at the small opening. "Will you fit?"

There was a grunt from below, and a creak from the stairs,

but Khell's head appeared a moment later, his glowing eyes glaring at me. "Are you teasing me?"

"Am I allowed?" I asked back, definitely teasing now.

Khell grinned. "Yes. I like it."

I beamed at him, and for a moment we were just staring at one another. Then Khell blinked and took in the room around us, lips parting. He twisted, forcing his shoulders through the narrow opening of the stairs, and then stepped the rest of the way up, turning in place. He hadn't dressed at all, and he looked huge and wild against the dark backdrop of my newly painted walls—one of my illustrated beasts come to life in front of me.

"Your imagination is even more impressive than I realized," Khell purred. He stopped and moved forward, hunching to study a canvas.

"It's not just kinky fantasies up here," I said, tapping my head with the end of my brush.

Khell was busy examining my art. It was the piece with the golden monster reaching out from the blinding light. He took a quicker look at a few nearby canvases before straightening and studying the room again.

"Girls and beasts in the woods," he said.

"I don't know if it's a metaphor, or a product of reading too many old fairy tales growing up, or—"

Khell's arm reached back, hand open, and I grabbed on, allowing him to draw me to his side. "It's you, petal. Your wonder and your hunger. I like them very much."

I pressed my face into his side to hide my blush. I'd tried to keep my illustrations sweet and pretty, welcoming, and left my darker work for my own personal enjoyment. Fusing the two was a relief. Another part of myself integrated fully. And as much as it wouldn't have changed my mind, it was a warm relief for Khell to like them.

Khell's arm tightened around me, his hand rubbing the

threadbare cotton of my robe against my back. "Do you have more work you want to do?"

I shook my head, stroking my cheek against that velvety texture of his skin, my eyes falling shut and my lungs filling up with the rich, earthy scent of my orc.

"Are you hungry, little mate?"

"Not yet," I said. I wrapped my arms around his waist and pressed my hips into his thigh, tipping my head back until I found the sharp light of his eyes glowing above me. "I couldn't decide whether I wanted to stay in bed this morning or come up here. Somehow, being able to walk away made this feel…more real. Less like another…"

"Appointment," Khell said, nodding and looking around the room, his lips curving up.

Khell's easy smile certainly was new and delightful. It was no less precious now for being granted frequently.

"Does it not feel real now?" he asked me, gaze glittering.

"Mostly real," I said. *A little too good to be true*, I added privately.

Khell twisted, pressing his half-hard cock against me, his hands circling my neck gently to hold my head. "What about now?"

My lips twitched as he thrust his hips forward, the head of his cock leaking his interest through my thin robe to leave a sticky mark on my skin.

"That helps," I said, nodding slightly.

"Mmm. And this?"

Khell's hands smoothed down my throat and then under my robe, shoving it down my shoulders to trap my arms, pushing until my chest was exposed. His cock jerked and nestled itself between my breasts. I lifted my hands to hold my breasts together, and Khell's lips parted as he stared down at his cock cradled there, his hips shifting again, another drip of precum sliding down to my skin. I dipped my chin and lapped at his tip with his next thrust, smiling at his grunt.

"A little more," I teased, and Khell blinked, eyes lifting to mine, his grin stretching.

He untied the robe's belt, and I released my breasts to let him push the fabric down to the floor. His right hand tangled in my hair, pulling me up to the tip of my toes for a kiss, and his left caught me between my thighs, stroking at my slit. I moaned and then gasped as his claws appeared on my sex, gentle and dragging.

"And now?"

"That helps," I said, nodding rapidly.

Khell laughed, and I whined as his claws left me, his left arm twining around my waist to lift my feet from the floor. "Which wall is safe?"

"Safe?" I asked, still squirming after the touch of his claws.

"I don't want to smudge your work."

"Oh." *Oh!* I waved behind me to the wall near the eastern window. "There."

Khell carried me around my cart of paint and a table stacked with prints to ship before pressing me to the wall and dropping to his knees in front of me. I laughed and leaned back. Khell on his knees was still a giant, and he leaned in, kissing and licking at my breasts, cupping one in his large hand and gazing up at me as that long, dark tongue circled my nipple.

"Did I help inspire your art, petal?" Khell growled, his claws burrowing between my thighs again.

I sighed and spread my legs, nodding slowly. "Yes."

"Good. Let me inspire you again."

He crouched, his free hand scooping me up by the back of my thighs and lifting me off my toes. His shoulders made room for themselves between my legs, and I cried out as I went from standing on my own feet to sitting on Khell's mouth, his tongue plunging in, claws and tusks holding me open.

"Oh fuck, Khell!" My feet braced against his back, hands taking hold of his braid, my shoulders pressed to the wall to keep myself from tumbling forward.

Khell's tongue was like a lovely, sinuous, lively cock in my cunt, thrusting and searching and licking at my walls. His nose was breathing and nuzzling against my clit, a dull tease, but effective stimulation as I rocked on his mouth.

"I think—fuck, fuck yes, please—I think this is less real than ever," I managed, breath short and rapid, hips churning as Khell's hot tongue fucked me playfully, his purr vibrating against my sex.

He chuckled, and I moaned. The wall scraped against my back and the room spun, and Khell was halfway up, his hands holding my ass in place, before I realized he was standing.

I screamed—partly in shock and partly at the punch of his tongue against what I suspected was my G-spot—and my hands slapped the ceiling, stretching to brace against the beams. A hysterical giggle escaped me, a gasp of surprise, and a low whine of need.

My studio looked wild from this angle, the woods I'd painted on the walls lit perfectly by the morning sun, coming to life. And here I was with my beast, caught in the air like a bird, being feasted on.

"Khell," I pleaded, uncertain what it was I was asking for. *This isn't the fantasy*, I reminded myself. *This is real*. But there was panic fluttering in my chest, as if this scene might break if I weren't careful. Or maybe that tremor was the rise of my next release, Khell's tongue determinedly seeking out my most sensitive places, his claws digging into my ass to hold me in place.

I refused to let my eyes fall shut as I came, refused to blink and lose sight of my surroundings, of the dark russet braid in my grip, of the amber eyes watching me fall apart. I shuddered and sighed at the rush of heat and electricity that took over my body, but I held my eyes open, held Khell's gaze, tightened my hold on him before he could escape.

His tongue lapped me from hole to clit as he leaned back, breath ragged. "Relax," he soothed. "I have you. This is real."

I was relaxing anyway, an inevitable result of Khell's efforts, and he shifted me slowly, letting me slide down the wall into the circle of his arms, right down onto his cock, then further until he was inside of me to the hilt.

"There now, petal," Khell purred, his shadow now covering me, his warm mass supporting me.

This stretch. I'd walked around with the absence of this after the cottage, and it was like being made complete again.

"I missed you," I whispered, blinking up at him.

Khell nodded, brow furrowing, stepping in closer, his hands fastening my ankles at his back before one held my hip and the other my throat and jaw. "It was awful," he agreed. "It's over now. I'm sorry, Sunny."

I kissed his chest and squeezed my legs around his hips, and Khell purred, hips flexing and stav pumping inside of me.

"It's all right," I said, thinking of everything I *had* done in the past month.

I had been miserable, yes. But I'd made my home my own. I'd grown closer with Natalie, more honest with myself. I'd missed Khell's presence terribly and accepted that while we'd spent a week having sex and maybe that shouldn't have meant much, Khell made the act personal and intimate and more than just physical release.

"Look at me, petal."

I obeyed immediately, and my entire body perked up at the fix of Khell's gaze on me.

"It's over now. This is real."

I smiled up at him and Khell purred again, rocking gently into me, stav pumping steady and opposite of his thrusts.

"It is. Kiss, please."

Khell had to hunch for us to be able to kiss in this position, but his mouth was eager, coated in my flavor, and his claws pinched my jaw, holding me in place. He pulled my hips away from the wall, tilting me for a deeper angle, and I moaned into his mouth, his tongue mimicking the motion of his cock.

My hands held his ass, enjoyed the flex of his muscles as he fucked me, and the kiss continued, breaking for brief gasps of air.

"Mine," Khell growled, his hips starting to snap, the punch of his cock flaring bursts of pleasure inside of me, the warning of the rising release.

"Mine," I answered.

Khell huffed and his head bent, tusks biting my shoulder gently, hand tightening on my throat, holding me in place for his taking.

"Yours," he snarled, the word muffled around my flesh.

I hung onto Khell like he was my anchor as the orgasm tore through me, my shout buried against his shoulder, my teeth grabbing on in a mirror of his. He roared, plunging deep and holding himself there as his stav stroked us both through his release.

We remained there, tied together, for a long moment, catching our breath and shivering through aftershocks as his stav bucked, milking him to completion. I kissed the spot I'd grabbed with my teeth, smiling privately at the temporary marks I'd made. Khell released his jaws slowly, his tongue flicking over my skin.

"Yours," he said again, turning his head and pressing his lips softly to mine, lingering there until our racing hearts slowed and matched time.

CHAPTER 23
Khell'ar

SUNNY TOOK her coffee with an absurd amount of coarse brown sugar. I'd watched her tear one packet after another and pour it into the cup she'd ordered at the little breakfast diner she'd chosen. We'd been seated across from one another, and I'd given up my seat before we'd ordered our food, moving to squeeze onto the same bench as her, wanting to feel her close.

Now I was missing that view of her face.

"So you didn't choose to be mated to me," she said, her head tipped down so I could only admire the golden crown of waves in her hair and the shadowy view of her breasts down the collar of her sweater.

She'd dressed in jeans that hugged her full ass and thighs beautifully, then laughed at me. "Maybe if I'm not in a skirt, we can keep from fucking in public."

I would've attested to my ability to control myself, but Sunny was right—the inaccessibility of pants was a necessary protective measure. So was eating out in public instead of at Sunny's modest dining table.

"I did choose you," I said.

"You said it was instinct," Sunny said, looking up, face set without expression.

Sunny had usually been so open, transparent even, during our week with MSA. Now I kept hitting these walls. It was understandable, and the reason I'd hesitated in telling her about the bond, but I didn't need her to accept the reality of it yet. I just needed her here at my side.

"The bond forms under the information our instinct provides," I said, nodding. "But I chose to think of you outside of the role of my client while we were together. To share my name, truths about myself, to deviate from the itinerary—"

"*Itinerary?*" Sunny tried to whisper the word, but it came out as more of a strangled squawk.

I laughed and nodded, sinking lower in my seat until my knees hit the bench opposite us. My arm was draped over the back of the booth, pressed to Sunny's shoulders.

"MSA provided me with a daily recommended schedule. I could tweak it based on what you seemed to enjoy most, but I more or less gave up on following the ones they provided for you immediately. They were too safe. I knew you could take more," I purred, dipping my head to nip Sunny's nose, her stunned eyes crossing before I pulled away.

"And your name..." she pressed.

"I usually don't offer one," I said, shrugging. "Or I make one up. But I wanted to hear you screaming *mine.*"

Sunny blushed and leaned into my side, that reserve fading at last. "I didn't realize you weren't supposed to give your name."

"Well, I wasn't about to tell you how unprofessional I was being," I said.

Our breakfast arrived at that moment, my plate piled high with my double order of breakfast scramble, and Sunny's plate of savory waffles steaming.

The waitress stared at us both as she set down two gravy

bowls, one eyebrow arched as if in doubt of our ability to finish off all the food we'd ordered. She must not have served orcs very often.

"Can we get three sides of bacon?" I asked.

Sunny snorted, stealing one of the gravy bowls for herself and pouring it over her waffles.

The waitress turned on her heel.

"My house isn't big enough for the fridge you're going to need," Sunny murmured.

I stared at her, waited for the light remark to sink in, smiling as her eyes widened when it did. She turned bright pink and glanced up at me, looking immediately away.

"Not that you'll want—"

"I will want," I said, wondering if it would interrupt her appetite to continue our discussion on mating. "The bond is permanent, but we'll take the developments at your pace. And I'll make do with your fridge when you're ready."

It was small and charmingly vintage, but I could always get us an industrial freezer. Sunny had a decently sized basement.

"Your bathroom, however," I said, patting Sunny on the back as she choked on her sip of grapefruit juice. *Too pushy*?

"Oh god, how will you even fit in the shower?" Sunny muttered, shaking her head.

I tried to take a bite of food, grinning at my plate at how easily she asked the questions. Sunny worrying about how I would shower wasn't exactly long-term commitment, but it wasn't refusing the idea, either.

"It's like marriage, isn't it?" Sunny asked softly, taking a bite of her waffle and chewing it slowly.

"When that's what you want it to be…yes," I said, just as quiet. "It's…it's the knowing, Sunny. Knowing where the path leads."

Sunny stared into space, and I wondered if she'd paid

attention to my answer, or if maybe it had shorted out her brain, or—

"Okay, so we start with dating," she said, her words clear and her shoulders squaring like she was about to go into battle. "Like we skipped the awkward first dinners and coffee, and we sorted out the conversation where we're exclusive, and now we're in that committed but not—"

I caught her chin in my fingers and planted the kiss over her words, humming with her as our lips connected and helped themselves to sips and gentle sucking. Dating was the tip of the iceberg of mating, perhaps, but at least it wasn't a rejection.

"I accept," I said, fighting the urge to corner her and draw her onto my lap, make a mess of her in front of everyone in the restaurant.

Sunny blinked at me, cheeks swelling with her smile, and leaned up for another peck. "Okay. Now let's eat, I'm starving. My orc boyfriend wore me out."

Sunny squirmed in her seat as I purred for her.

***

SUNNY STARTED five projects in a day and finished two. She shed her socks in random places throughout her house— at the stove while she was cooking pasta, the dining table, tucked inside of the bathroom cabinet—and then put on whatever pair was closest the next time her toes were cold. She scowled as she used a power drill and smiled any time she got to pick up a paint brush, whether it was for a canvas or a wall.

She woke up in the middle of each night. If I was sleeping, she would drift up to her studio, but if I woke in time and caught her—

"Unnngh, Khell, yes!"

I grinned through my growl, bucking my hips up to meet

Sunny's. Her arms were stretched over my head, hands clasped around the top bar of her wrought iron headboard, bracing herself as she rode my cock roughly.

"Oh–oh god," she cried out, eyes widening as she stared down at me.

I reared up, my hands sliding up from their grip on her hips to stroke her back and draw her closer. Sunny was nearly there, and it was my job as her mate to throw her over the edge. My mouth found one of her breasts, my hand taking hold of the other, and I sucked hard, my tusks digging into her soft flesh.

Sunny's hands released the headboard, grasping the back of my head and holding me in place as she came with a high cry, her cunt tightening on my stav. I purred as she clasped and fluttered around me, my heels digging into the bed, bracing against the siren call of my own release. Sunny joked about me wearing her out, but I knew how much she could handle and I liked her to sleep late into the morning so I had time to make her breakfast.

As her shuddering settled and she breathed the long sigh of her completion, I rolled us on the bed, cradling her in my arms, laughing at the look of surprise on her face. Why was my little mate always surprised to find I wanted more of her?

My stav was still pumping in the sleeve of my cock, and I fixed myself deep inside of Sunny, letting it stroke her as I bent and kissed her flushed cheeks and full lips.

"You should know better than to think I would be finished with you so quickly," I murmured, pinching the lobe of her ear between my teeth.

But Sunny didn't shiver and whine. "Khell, what are we doing? This isn't normal, is it?"

I blinked, and then leaned back. I had turned the lamp on when I'd snatched Sunny back into the bed, and I was glad of it now. She could see my face as well as I could see hers.

Sunny was chewing on her bottom lip, a line of worry marked between her brows.

"I don't think cowgirl is that advanced," I said, wincing even as I made the joke.

But Sunny let out a puff of a laugh and shook her head. "It's been a week."

It had. A very good week. Astraeya had dropped my car off on the street in front of Sunny's house on Sunday. We'd driven it back to my apartment and christened my bed before packing me a bag of clothes and walking hand in hand back to Sunny's. I'd finished the installation of a vintage lamp over Sunny's dining table on Monday. On Wednesday, I'd mitered the corners for the shelves Sunny wanted in the bathroom. On Thursday, we'd put a shelf up in the kitchen window for potted herbs.

To be fair though, we'd had more sex than productive projects.

"Do you want to take a break?" I asked. Sunny stiffened and I growled, unable to resist dipping down and kissing her firmly. "A break from fucking, mate. Or a night where I go to my apartment? So it feels…normal."

Human normal, I thought. We were absolutely normal for newly mated orcs.

"I…" Sunny trailed off, and her hands stroked down my back and then back up again. She didn't mind my weight on her, I was confident of that now. And I was fairly confident that even if she did want to slow down for a moment, it wouldn't last long. Sunny was as aggressively eager as I was.

Her brow furrowed as she stared up at me, her thighs tightening around my hips as if in objection to the question.

"I…" She huffed and shook her head. "Jesus, what am I talking about? I don't *want* normal. Come here, beast."

I leaned back out of reach, chuckling at Sunny's resulting pout. "No normal for my pretty petal?"

"Don't tease me, I'm still adjusting to being a deviant."

"Maybe you need to be reminded what kind of deviant you are, petal," I purred.

Sunny's cheeks flushed. "What do you mean?"

I withdrew from her slowly, reveling in her soft whine of protest. "You're my pretty little pet. Mine to fuck, to fill, to use as often as I like."

"Then why are you moving so far away?" Sunny said, lips twitching, proud of herself for talking back.

I was proud of her too. She hadn't played the brat much in our time at the cottage. It would be fun to toy with her when she was like this.

"Because you're misbehaving."

"I'm not!" Sunny cried, sitting up on her elbows as I stepped off the bed. I snatched her ankles up in one hand, her hip in the other, and flipped her over onto her belly. "Oh! Khell!"

With a quick spread of her legs, I was climbing back on the bed, plunging home into Sunny's wet cunt. She was on her elbows again, about to turn to snap at me, when I thrust in. She arched up, shouting, and I reached for her hair, taking a fistful and twisting it in my grip.

"Fuck!"

"Yes," I snarled in agreement, rearing back before snapping forward again, my force knocking Sunny flat onto her belly with a howl.

Her hands were yanking at the sheet, trying to find purchase as I set a hard and heavy pace. I used my free hand to haul her hips up, leaving her unbalanced and at my mercy. She couldn't plant her knees, and I didn't give her the time to catch her breath, to sit up on her hands.

"Beast," Sunny gasped, and I held my breath. Would she ask me to stop? "Yes, more!"

I grinned and twisted her hair again, reveled in her cry of relief, her voice muffled into the mattress, gasping and moaning.

"You don't worry about what's normal, pet. You only worry about your orc's cock and when it will fuck you next."

"Yes, beast," Sunny squeezed out through a high-pitched keen, the note broken with every slap of our bodies together.

"And you tell your master when you need to be fucked."

"Yes!"

"And when you need to be pet and tended and fed," I growled.

Sunny writhed on the bed, hands gripping the edge of the mattress, ass bouncing against my hips. She was still shy about being spoiled outside of sex, but that was all right.

"And when you need my claws and my tusks."

"Always," Sunny moaned.

I released her hair, leaning forward and wrapping my arms around her, taking the tight point of a nipple between two claws, and the tender folds of her sex with the other. Sunny buried her cries into the sheets as I fucked and toyed with her, my stav painfully swollen in my cock, pumping and thrusting, warning release.

"Petal," I gasped into Sunny's hair, resisting the urge to take her shoulder in my teeth, not certain I could hold back from biting too hard.

I caught Sunny's clit with my claw, circling the little nub with the dull tip, and Sunny came with a scream. I followed, pinning her down in my hold, giving into the sweet demand of her cunt, flooding her with my release. She would start the laundry this morning and forget it by the afternoon, but I would move everything into the dryer. If Sunny's kink was the games we played in bed, mine was completing her half finished projects throughout the day.

Sunny's face was red and sweaty as she turned it to the side, panting for air. I started to lift myself and her hand reached back, swatting at my side.

"Don't move," she gasped.

"Do you want rest now, pretty petal?" I asked, kissing her hot cheek.

Sunny groaned and shifted under me, spreading her legs wider, toes curling into the bed. "I want...I want you to make me beg you to stop."

CHAPTER 24
Sunny

"YOU'LL BE RID of me soon."

I froze in place, spoon in the ricotta mix for tonight's lasagna, eyes on my new kitchen backsplash. "What? Why?"

Khell appeared in the narrow doorway, his phone in hand but too far for me to read the screen. For a moment, I forgot what we were talking about. Khell in street clothes scrambled my brain. They were always so *fitted,* and he seemed to favor sweatpants over jeans since it was easier to find his size. Which meant it really wouldn't take much effort at all to tear them off of him.

"Job offer," he said. "Built-ins for a new yarn store in Andersonville."

"Oh," I said with a sigh, my shoulders softening. "Congrats! I told you reference photos would do the trick."

Khell purred and inched closer. My kitchen was a tight fit, but we'd already made it work a couple times. My counters were the perfect height for me to perch on and for Khell to slide right inside of me.

You're out of control, I told myself, but then Khell appeared before me, crowding me between my cupboards and the stove, pressing me up against the back wall and bending his knees until our faces were level.

"Did you think I meant permanently?"

I blushed. Khell's teasing was warm and prickling, constantly tearing at the little defenses I put up to try and make our situation seem less sudden and extreme than it was. He'd been more or less living in my house for two weeks. We'd been fucking like rabbits. We'd already picked out a new tub for the upstairs and had plans to demo into the guest room to expand the bathroom's footprint nicely.

"Sunny," Khell purred, skimming his lips against mine.

"It just caught me off guard," I admitted.

"You're not losing me," Khell rumbled, claws digging into my hips.

"I know," I said, nodding, flushing at his resulting smile.

"Do you need reminding?" he asked, words crisp.

When he used that voice, I *wanted* reminding, but—

"The lasagna," I said, words thin and breathless and Khell's grin growing. "Natalie and Theo will be here in an hour. We have dinner."

Natalie had been kind of pushy about meeting Khell. I didn't blame her, but I was feeling sort of funny about how much I'd already confessed to her. She knew everything we'd done together. She even knew I'd nearly told Khell I loved him, something I hadn't confessed to Khell yet, although I was getting close to blurting it out lately.

"Mmm, that reminds me. Orcs have a custom amongst mates when it comes to house guests," Khell said.

"A custom?" I asked, blinking.

Khell hummed and finally leaned back, turning to the lasagna. "Mmhm. Of course, since we're dating, it might not apply—"

"Quit baiting me," I laughed, joining him as he scooped out the filling and spread it over the noodles.

Khell, and apparently orcs in general, ate primarily vegetables and high-protein grains and only occasionally meat. Since Theo and Natalie were both eager carnivores, I'd opted for a veggie lasagna with meatballs on the side. Khell had grabbed us a bottle of some small batch pepper moonshine from a mothman he knew. It'd been a long time since I'd had any kind of dinner party, and I was equal parts excited and nervous for tonight.

"I love to bait you, just as you love to bait me, petal," Khell answered, twisting and bending to kiss the crown of my head as I added the sautéed veggies to our lasagna and then draped over another layer of noodles. "Get this in the oven, and I'll teach you the custom."

I narrowed my eyes up at him briefly. Teaching me the custom was not *explaining* to me the custom, but I was too curious to argue.

"When does the job start?" I asked.

"Monday. Will I… Will you want me to…"

Khell was almost never nervous or hesitant, but I could guess the question.

"If it's easier for you to get up and go to work in the morning, I could come stay at your place tomorrow night," I offered, focusing on the food in front of me.

Khell purred at my back, his body framing mine easily as I smoothed another layer of cheese into the dish. "You won't mind trading on and off?"

"Can I do some decoration at yours for my blog?"

"You can do whatever you like, mate."

He always used that word carefully. *Mates* were allowed to decorate their partners homes. *Mates* got to sleep in and were fed breakfast by hand. *Mates* found their laundry dry and folded hours after they'd forgotten it in the washing machine.

Being "petal" was playful and naughty and sweet. Being "mate" was being cared for and reminded of belonging. I loved both roles.

We finished the lasagna, and Khell moved out of the way so I had room to slide it into the oven. The meatballs were simmering in the crockpot, and Natalie and Theo were bringing roasted potatoes and good bread. Everything was ready. And I was…jittery.

"Would it be bad if we broke into the moonshine before they got here?" I asked Khell as he led me by the hand out of the kitchen, through the dining room and back to the living room. "I'm too nervous to sit still for an hour."

"I have a cure for that," Khell said.

"You can't fuck me," I rushed out, mostly to convince myself. "Theo will smell it on me, and then he'll be awkward all night."

Khell grinned. I'd told him about Theo's face when he opened the door of his house the day I left the cottage, and also about the orc at the hardware store. He'd been obnoxiously proud of himself.

Khell moved ahead of me, planting himself on the center of my couch, his knees touching. He patted his lap and arched an eyebrow. "Sit."

I glared back at him. "Khell."

"Pet," he bit out, drawing a shiver from me.

Being "pet" meant I obeyed and I liked it.

I sighed and stepped forward, reaching out to grasp his shoulders, but Khell swatted my hands aside and took my hips. He turned me away from him and drew me back until I had to stumble and spread my legs for his to fit between.

"Khell, we really can't fuck before dinner," I warned, but I didn't sound convincing, even to my own ears.

"We won't," Khell said, drawing me back to lean against his chest. His hands petted down my front, skimming over my breasts. "I won't even undress you, petal. Would you like to know the custom?"

"I'm not sure. Is it…like, a custom for the house…like lighting candles at the windows?"

Even I knew how unlikely that was.

"Orc dens don't have windows," Khell said, stifling a laugh. "It's a custom for your ass."

"Khell!" I cried, trying to leap up, but I was fastened in place by his massive arm around my waist.

"When a mate is receiving guests into the home, they get spanked," Khell said, grunting as I squirmed on his lap. "Keep moving like that, and you *will* be fucked, pet."

I stilled for a moment, blushing, and then only moved enough to shoot Khell a glare over my shoulder. "You're making this up."

"The mate is spanked, their ass turned red and hot, so that all through the visit they feel that attention from their partner. The reminder of touch and the promise of being alone together," Khell purred.

"Only you could make a spanking sound romantic," I teased, my lips twitching. "It's usually known as punishment."

Khell hummed and frowned slightly. "I admit, orcs are heartier. A spank isn't really about pain so much as high sensation for us, the heat pleasant. If you want this, I'd make sure to adjust. But since we're only dating…"

"Oh, and if your friends were coming over tonight?" I prompted, rolling my eyes.

"I should make you a paddle before that happens," Khell said, tusks glinting in his grin. "Otherwise, you might hurt your hand."

I blinked at him. Was he joking? And why did it irritate me so much every time he said "only dating"?

"You'd really have me spank your ass?" I asked, tipping my head.

"I'd want you to. It would be up to you," Khell said with a shrug. "You know everything is always up to you, Sunny."

I blinked again. "And it's not a punishment?"

"It won't feel like one."

Damnit. This wily, clever, sexy, beastly orc.

"If I find out you've made this up—"

"I haven't. Oak's honor."

"—I will absolutely find a paddle and make you bend over for it every time *anyone* comes over. Even the mailman!"

Khell was shaking with laughter. "We don't have to."

"Oh, we're going to. I wouldn't want to disrespect your customs," I said primly. Which was true. And also, if Khell wanted to spank me and he promised I would enjoy it, then… well, it would certainly keep me from being nervous until Natalie and Theo arrived. I paused and raised a finger. "But I'm observing this custom on a case by case basis. You're not spanking me before my parents come to visit next month."

Khell laughed and blushed. "Fair enough. You're sure you'd like to try it now?"

I nodded and squared my shoulders, maintaining the semblance of my own pride, when really there was nothing Khell could ask of me that I wouldn't want to try with him. "Is there a special position I'm supposed to observe?"

"I mean…I have a preference," Khell answered, still grinning. He grabbed one of my large decorative pillows from the corner of the couch and then leaned forward, spreading his legs wide—and mine too, for that matter—and placing the pillow on the floor.

I stared down at it for a long moment before it clicked. "Beast," I muttered.

"But I offered you a pillow!" Khell teased.

"Don't you dare let me fall," I grumbled, leaning forward slowly.

"Mate, I would never," he purred.

And his arm around my waist supported me as I tipped forward, planting my hands in the pillow and then, at the nudge of his other hand on my back, lowering myself down to my elbows, hanging upside down from his lap.

My thighs were spread and stretched, and the position

made my core feel hollow. Fuck. Was sex *entirely* off the table?

Khell shifted and I squeaked, but he didn't let me fall. His hands grasped the back of my thighs, already exposed from the awkward position, and then he smoothed his touch up until the skirt of my dress flipped down at the waist, brushing against my hair and the pillow under me.

"We should try this position another time," Khell mused. "Does it hurt?"

It wasn't comfortable, but the tension was the sort I enjoyed. I shook my head and asked, "How many times do you spank me?"

"Until I like the color," Khell said mildly. And then his claws hooked into the waistband of my underwear, pulling it down to leave it stretched just beneath my ass, probably pushing my cheeks high and round. "It's a good thing we leave your curtains closed now. This view is mine alone."

I blushed, annoyance and humor warring with the urge to preen at the praise.

And then there was a *crack!* of sound and a sharp spike of sensation against my right cheek, and I screamed at the first slap of Khell's broad palm on my ass. His touch returned to soothe, stroking my bare skin, a deep burn following the first strike.

I took a breath, ready to remark on his lack of warning, only to be cut off.

Crack!

I gasped, and Khell chuckled, squeezing both cheeks in his two hands, massaging the flesh. And of course, he was right —the heat of the slaps went right down into my cunt, making me achy and warm. The pain was brief and it only left heat and awareness behind.

"Pink now, but that won't last long," Khell said, mostly to himself.

"Is this meant to discourage house parties?" I joked, but

the catch in my voice made it a pretty obvious lie. If anything, this might mean I needed to find more friends to invite over regularly.

Crack!

I moaned and let my head fall forward.

Crack!

"Ahh!"

Khell started massaging me immediately again. "I didn't know the custom as a sprout, but my parents hosted parties at least once a week. And we were always going to some. Orcs are very social."

I laughed at that, then cried out again as Khell spanked me once, twice, and then again and again until I was shaking and trying to drag myself away. He held me by my waist and softened the repetitive slaps with strokes and squeezes from his hot palm until I was soft and sagging.

"Do you need another pillow?"

The angle was awkward and the floor was still hard under the pillow and rug, but...but I liked being uncomfortable. I shook my head.

Khell rewarded me with two quick smacks on one cheek, before switching hands and evening me out.

My ass was fire hot, and I was panting and babbling at the floor. And my sex was wet. I could feel the air against my clit, the pulse of arousal.

"Make me come," I whispered.

"Hmmm." *Crack!*

"Khell!"

"I don't know..." *Crack!*

I arched and tried to tilt my hips down, as if I could force contact.

"Well now, look at you. Your cunt is begging," Khell said, chuckling, the bastard.

"Beast."

"Pet."

I whined and scratched at the rug in front of me.

Crack! Crack! Crack! Crack!

I shuddered, and Khell growled.

"Be honest, you'll come just from this," Khell said.

He was probably right, but I wanted his touch on my clit. I wanted his cock inside of me.

"Fuck me," I said, an order in the words. Surely he wouldn't turn down—

He laughed. "Not a chance, petal. No, I'm going to make you sit on this cherry red ass all night, leave you thinking of being stretched out and under my hand. And then later, after our lovely dinner and a nice long visit, when your friends have decided that I'm an acceptable sort of orc to let you stay with and they've called their cab and left us alone again… then you can have my cock."

I moaned and slapped my palm against the floor. "I'll tell Natalie to fuck off and let me get laid the second I open the door," I said.

Khell grabbed my waist and let out a belly laugh, shaking me on his lap until I was giggling too. He shifted, pulling his hands away, and I thought he meant to let me slide away.

But of course not.

Crack! Crack!

These ones were harder, and I screamed in earnest, the sensation sharp and intense. But the moment Khell's hands grasped my cheek, the pain settled again, softened and burned into me, leaving me limp.

"There, that's pretty. That should do for the first time," Khell murmured, framing my ass in his hands and pressing my cheeks together, then spreading them apart. "Fine. I want to make a good impression, so I'd better have you relaxed."

My head was still spinning from the last two spanks, and then the room was spinning as Khell pulled me up from the floor. He turned me face-up on his lap, and I groaned at the burning flames that covered my ass. Sitting would be an adventure tonight.

"Wait, let me ride you—" I cried.

"I said no cock, pet," Khell growled.

I gaped at him, my brain too full of the heat on my ass to catch up to his plan. His hand was under my skirt, shoving my panties aside, and then his fingers were plunging deep, stroking every sensitive, aching, needy inch of me.

It was embarrassingly quick. Khell had barely started touching me before I was orgasming, and it was like having all the joy of the release stolen from me. I'd missed the fun of the climb.

But Khell wasn't a one-and-done sort of lover. His mouth found mine, swallowing my voice as he continued to fuck me with his fingers, his thumb searching out my clit and making quick, firm circles. I gasped for air and found his tongue against mine, thrusting as fast and thoroughly as his hand between my legs.

The second orgasm was nearly as sudden as the first, but sweeter and longer, the fire of the spanking tangling with the explosion of release. Khell gentled his touch but kept it constant as I shook and shuddered in his arms, only pulling away when the aftershocks settled.

I was sweaty, my ass was burning, my panties were twisted and probably wet, and Khell was beaming down at me, cradling the mess he'd made like I was precious wreckage.

"Beautiful," he said. "Stand up for me and turn around."

He had to help me up, but he probably wanted to see my legs shaking.

"Raise your skirt."

I sucked in a breath but did as he said, and I was sure that my face went as red as my ass as I waited for him to speak. His claws traced the marks on my flesh, and I bit down on the moan that wanted to rise. I failed to stifle the sound when he leaned in and *licked* over the spot.

"I went a little darker than I'd planned," he rasped out before licking up another stripe.

Was licking his apology?

"I liked it," I admitted, turning to smile at him. "It's a good custom."

"HOW HARD DID he fuck you before we got here?" Natalie hissed in my ear. We were in the kitchen serving up flourless chocolate cake and whipped cream, and Natalie was swaying back and forth, possibly to the music playing in the next room or maybe just to her own internal rhythm.

Pepper moonshine hit *hard*.

"They can both hear you," I whispered back. Theo was a werewolf and orcs had big ears, so I figured that probably made them roughly equal.

"I don't care. It'll be a competitive incentive for Theo later."

I snorted. I didn't think Theo was half as competitive as his wife. "He didn't," I said. Natalie's eyes narrowed at me, and I squirmed. "Not exactly."

She blinked, then grinned and nodded. "Creative. Nice."

"We do more than have sex," I said, somewhat defensively.

"Well, duh. The house looks great. Did you buy the little baskets for all your grubby socks, or did he?"

I blinked and glanced down. Khell had brought me a stack of small woven baskets and left one in every room. And... yup, sure enough, socks I'd abandoned earlier were now tucked inside. Which meant *Khell* was going around tidying up my socks.

I swooned and cut an extra thick slice of the cake for my orc.

My *mate*.

I giggled, and Natalie punched me in the shoulder. "Ow!"

"I'm happy for you!" Natalie shouted at me.

"Fists aren't love, Nat," Theo called from the living room.

Natalie scoffed, leaning up against my refrigerator and watching me arrange the plates. "She's fine," she called back.

A massive figure appeared out of the corner of my eye, Khell looming in the doorway with his arms crossed over his chest. He'd put on a pair of dark blue jeans that hugged his ass like a lover and a fitted black sweater. I wanted to climb him.

"Are you antagonizing my—" Khell blinked and stuttered briefly.

"Mate?" Natalie suggested, biting her teeth around the *T*.

I glanced at Khell and smiled. He wasn't aware I'd told Natalie about our situation, and I watched as he puffed up with pride.

"I'm no rougher with her than you are, buddy," Natalie said, offering Khell a feral grin.

Sometimes, Natalie had more of the wolf in her than Theo did.

"How's Theo picking up Rum'kurr?" I asked before Khell and Natalie could poke at each any further.

"Losing!" Theo called.

"But respectfully," Khell said, before flashing me a smile. "He doesn't have your skill."

Khell still beat me at Rum'kurr nine times out of ten, but he always looked especially giddy whenever I did manage to best him.

"Here, take these." I passed Khell two plates of dessert, and he took his cue to leave after leaning in for a quick kiss.

Natalie watched it all with an eager stare, but her smile was calm as we were left alone again. "I am happy for you," she repeated, thankfully this time without a punch.

"Me too," I said, nodding and passing her a plate of her own. "Thank you for all the advice."

Natalie's eyebrows ticked up. "That's right. This was all my idea, wasn't it? Ooohhh, Khell, you should be *very* grateful," she said, turning on her heel and weaving back to the dining room table, sliding into her seat next to Theo.

Khell had made me a new set of dining room chairs—probably because the ones I'd had before seemed a little flimsy for his frame—and I walked in to find that one of the four had been pushed into the far corner of the room. Khell watched my approach with a wicked tilt on his lips.

I could, of course, retrieve the banished chair and have a seat for myself. I didn't.

Khell purred as I approached his left thigh. His arm circled my waist to offer me support as I settled on his lap. With the first brush of my ass on his thigh—muffled through our clothes—my cheeks went up in flames at the reminder. Heat rushed in, along with a deep but not unpleasant soreness. Natalie and Theo were both humming over the cake Khell had made, offering their compliments, and Khell was calmly nodding and thanking them. But I knew what he was thinking about as his hand slid down to my hip, squeezing just around the swell of my ass. I hid my moan around a bite of cake—which deserved the sound anyway.

"Do you like it, petal?" Khell purred, leaning in so his lips were near my ear.

Sneaky bastard. "The cake is wonderful," I said, turning my head away from our guests to glare up into his eyes. "Beast," I added in a whisper.

He grinned and scratched my tender flesh with his claws through the fabric of my skirt.

The truth was I probably didn't need to be spanked to be eager for my orc's touch. It was next to impossible to avoid being drawn in by him. When Khell described how being mated felt—as if I'd latched on to him, embedded myself deep in his chest—I'd immediately recognized the sensation. And now that we were together, it didn't even hurt. It was just as if the entire world seemed to tilt in his direction, and gravity always led me back to his side.

But if my orc wanted to spank me and tease me before a dinner party, I found I had no objections.

CHAPTER 25
Sunny

I HEARD Khell's footsteps coming up from the basement as I returned home from a trip to the art supply store, and I rushed to meet him at the door.

"What are you doing down there?" I asked, Khell's eyes wide with surprise as I appeared in front of the cracked door.

He slid out through as narrow a gap as he could manage, using his bulk to hide the view below from my gaze. "Have patience."

It wasn't my first time asking, and it wasn't the first time I'd received the same answer.

Khell had been working on a secret project down in my basement for over a month, in between our work on the upstairs master bath and the various jobs he was finding via word of mouth. It'd been almost two months together, and he more or less lived with me, something I was planning to make official before this next month was up. All we really needed was to finish the bathroom so the coach house was more comfortable for him.

And maybe we needed to say a few things we'd been tiptoeing around a bit too.

"We need to get ready," Khell said, taking my arm and steering me away from the basement door.

"I'm not the one covered in sawdust and dirt," I teased, brushing at the mess on his chest.

"You're about to be," Khell rumbled, reaching for me.

I yelped and ran ahead of him to the stairs, huffing as his laughter echoed after me.

"We don't have time for you to make a mess of me," I called over my shoulder, heading for the bedroom.

"I have a guess why you're always so eager to go out," Khell said, following me up the stairs at a slower pace. "I think you don't want my friends to come here because you're afraid to paddle my ass."

I blushed. He was partly right. "We barely fit you in here. How are we going to fit...you know, a whole bunch of orcs and gargoyles and satyrs?"

Khell laughed and veered into the bathroom. We hadn't gotten the new wall up, but the much larger tub and waterfall showerhead were both installed. It *was* tempting to join Khell, but it also meant we'd probably be late to meeting everyone at the bar.

Khell's most recent commission was a massive bartop at a new trendy bar owned by his mothman friend, Elias, whom he'd met through MSA. I'd met a few of his other friends in the past couple months, but this was going to be a big group of them together for Elias's opening night.

I hung my purchases on the stair railing and then changed in the bedroom, debating briefly over a pair of jeans or a dress. Khell and I had nearly been caught fucking in public a couple of times now. Jeans *might* deter him from coaxing me into a dark alley corner, or they might just make it harder for me to redress in a hurry. And did I really want to deter him? I smirked to myself and chose the dress, pulling on a pair of thigh high socks.

It was better to be prepared when it came to going out with Khell. Two months later, and we still couldn't really keep our hands to ourselves. Which suited me just fine.

ELIAS'S BAR, Nightlight, was located in the heart of Wicker Park and perfectly suited to the overly glossy shop fronts and music venues. The entire space had a warm, golden quality, with high-polished wood and dim yellow bulbs in stylishly arranged clusters and vintage chandeliers. It matched the tall, brilliant man behind the bar with the yellow, brown, and black wings and the thick ruff of soft, golden fur peeking up from the open buttons of his white dress shirt.

I'd met Elias briefly before, and he'd mostly spoken over my head to Khell, ignoring me. Tonight, he waved cheerfully at our arrival, shining brightly under the carefully angled hazy spotlights. The room was full of all sorts of species, and I was one of only a handful of other humans. Khell guided me to the bar, and I was surprised to find Elias beaming at me.

"Sunny, I have an experiment I'd like you to try," he greeted me.

"You poison her, I'll tear your wings off," Khell warned, strangely friendly in tone considering the threat of the words.

Elias shrugged and turned to his amply cluttered shelves of dubiously labeled alcohol.

"Do you make most of what you sell?" I asked.

"Maybe half. I only bring in the best," Elias answered over his shoulder. He pulled down a glittering gem of a bottle, filled with a brilliant fuschia liquid up to the wax and cork seal.

"Natalie and Theo came," Khell said, pointing out my friends at the other end of the bar. "Oh, and they've met Rafe. Natalie will challenge him to a drinking competition."

"She'll lose. She's a lightweight, she just won't admit it," I said.

Elias poured me a small sample of whatever was in the bottle into a champagne glass and then slid it in my direction, crossing his arms on the bar top and watching me.

"What is it?" Khell asked, and this time it was his turn to be ignored by the pretty mothman.

Elias's antennae—like lovely, glittering gold ferns—twitched as I picked up the glass and took a sip. Bright, tart sweetness struck my tongue first, and the next sip went down easily before the heat of the alcohol hit my chest.

"Ooo, that's dangerous," I said, grinning.

"Lychee hibiscus," Elias offered. "Here, I'll make it a cocktail so it doesn't knock you flat before the end of the night."

I passed the glass back, and Elias added a soda water and a bit of ginger syrup.

"We'll call it the Sunny Day," Elias said with a wink in my direction. Khell growled and finally caught his friend's attention. "I haven't forgotten you. I picked this out specifically for you," Elias said, pulling up a bottle from under the counter.

American oak single malt. Khell was purring again in less than a minute, and then Elias was off to charm someone else without another word.

"Did he stop working for MSA too?" I asked Khell.

"He's a snob. He picks and chooses his clients," Khell said. "I think he just does the work for fun, but Astraeya says he's good. Come on, my cousins are here."

SEVERAL HOURS and many cocktails later, I'd been introduced to what I was sure was everyone in the bar. Khell was losing gracelessly to Natalie at a game of darts, and I found myself comfortably ensconced in a conversation about orcish customs with Khell's old co-worker, Eck'am, and his mate, Lenata.

"Mating outside of our species isn't so rare," Lenata said with a wave of her hand. "Male orcs are three to one and trees are hard lovers."

Apparently, jokes about fucking trees were fairly common in orcish humor.

"Khell'ar was always good mate material. I worried for him at the agency, thought he would miss his chance. But the fates sent you in the right direction," Eck'am said, reaching out to slap me roughly on the shoulder.

The couple was apparently a duo at MSA. For "advanced" clients, according to Lenata, whatever that meant.

Maybe it was my specialty cocktail from Elias, or the cheerfully casual atmosphere of the group where everyone seemed to know how Khell and I met and no one cared in the slightest, but a strange urge struck me.

"I have a question," I said, drawing the couple's focus. I blinked at them and then to the back of the room where Khell was roaring over a new bullseye. "What is 'orc bait'?"

Eck'am and Lenata blinked at me, and for a moment my mind went blank. Why had I asked that? They didn't even look as though they knew what the words meant.

Then Lenata tipped her head to the side and frowned. "Well...I mean, aside from the obvious—"

"What is the obvious?" I pressed before sucking down more of my liquid courage.

"Good enthusiasm for fucking," Lenata said, shrugging and then hesitating. "*Usually* orcs like someone tall."

"And strong," Eck'am added with a wince. "Good for wrestling in bed."

I nodded, smiling brightly. "I'm not very strong or tall."

"How fast can you climb a tree?" Lenata asked.

"I can't climb a tree at all," I said, my grin growing.

"I'm sure you have other nice qualities," Eck'am said, reaching out to slap my arm again.

"Maybe," I said, laughing and finding Khell in the crowd again. "Excuse me."

Lenata hissed in Eck'am's ear as I left them, probably remarking on what a strange human I was, but that was fine.

I wove through the crowd, waved at where Theo and Rafe were watching Natalie and Khell's match, and then found my orc. I wrapped my arms around Khell's waist and pressed my cheek to his broad back, just as he shot another dart at the target.

"Arghh!" Khell growled, a bright clack of the dart going wild and hitting the wall.

"HA *HA!*" Natalie screeched. "I *win*, you massive log!"

Khell turned, and I stepped closer as he glared down at me. "Petal," he snarled, but his hands helped themselves to possessively cupping my ass.

"I'm not orc bait," I said, snuggling myself as close to him as I could.

Khell blinked. "What?"

"I'm not orc bait. I'm not tall and I'm not strong and I can't climb a tree," I said. I *was* enthusiastic about fucking, but Khell knew that already.

Khell's brow furrowed, face twisted comically in confusion.

I rose to my tiptoes, which was still several inches shy of reaching my orc's lips, and wiggled provocatively against his groin. "I'm *Khell* bait."

His confusion melted away into warm humor, and he chuckled and squeezed my ass roughly as he ducked his head to kiss me. "That you are, petal."

I let him lick and kiss my mouth for a moment before pulling away and smiling up at him. "Take me home, *mate*."

"SUNNY!" Khell's voice was rough, gasping. His fingers were tangled in my hair, his groan of pleasure vibrating all the way down to his cock where it was stuffed in my mouth. I moaned around his length and Khell growled, pulling roughly on my hair, warning me.

I flexed my throat, now well-practiced at taking Khell's cock, and licked my tongue against the pumping stroke of his stav.

"Fuck! *Mate*," Khell snarled, his hips bucking just slightly, the thick spurt of his cum coating my throat, hot and slippery and soothing.

His back was pressed to the front door, feet splayed wide to fit me between. I bobbed my head on his length, and he rocked with my sucking until the tip of my tongue was playing at the slit of his cockhead.

"Enough," he growled, tugging on my strands.

I leaned back with a gasp, licking my lip and gazing up at the bright stare in the dark above me.

"Wicked little petal," Khell murmured.

"Take me up to bed, mate," I pleaded with a hint of intentional whine, leaning in and rubbing my cheek against Khell's hip.

I'd been using the title to torture Khell the whole drive home. And also maybe a little bit of over the jeans fondling.

Khell growled and moved his hands from my hair to my armpits, hauling me up from my knees and then throwing me over his shoulder. But he didn't head for the bedroom.

"Beast!"

"It's time for your surprise," Khell said, carrying me through the living room and over to the basement door.

"Did you build a dungeon down there?" I asked, twisting as Khell entered the stairwell. But he kept me over his shoulder, so all I could see was the dim light of the living room growing fainter as we traveled down.

"Why now, petal?"

"You're the one doing your big reveal in the dark—Ow!" I jerked in Khell's hold, his firm slap against my ass sharp but brief.

"Why call me 'mate' now?"

"Oh." We stopped at the bottom of the stairs, but it was too dark down here to see. Still, there were clues. It smelled earthy and herbal, and also like freshly cut wood. It smelled like Khell, really. I softened in his hold and he shifted me, cradled to his front. I found his jaw in the dark and kissed along the strong edge. "It's been time. I thought I was being sensible by not rushing. But pretending that we're going slowly doesn't change the truth. You're mine."

Khell grunted in agreement. "And you're mine."

I nodded against his throat so he could feel me, and kissed his pulse.

He hummed and then we were moving again, a short trip down into a soft, cushioned mattress and lots of thick blankets. Khell was crawling on top of me, fabric shifting, and I found my hands on his bare chest, my fingers digging into his muscles greedily. A moment later, my dress was being peeled off over my head. We undressed in quiet, lips occasionally finding a place to land before we had to shift and remove another layer.

Khell hadn't fastened his pants after I'd finished him off, and I heard them hit the floor a moment before his hands were around my hips, drawing me to him. His cock sank in easily, a few thrusts to tease me, and then our bodies were joined, hot skin kissing.

I'd already started to guess what Khell had done to my basement, when finally, there was light.

I gasped at the sight above me, Khell's face surrounded by green vines weaving over the ceiling. There were little strands of lights, flowers and dragonflies and mushrooms and plain bulbs, all twinkling faintly from above. Khell rolled us, and then I was sitting atop him, able to look around properly.

The walls had buckets overflowing with herbs and flowers, as well as floating shelves decorated with obscene toys. There was a stockade hidden behind a sheer curtain, and a sex swing hanging near the corner. Khell and I were sitting inside of a round pit of bedding, and near the stairs there was a water pump poised to fill a large brass tub.

"It's the woods and the den and the dungeon all at once," I whispered, eyes still flashing to every new detail. There were mushrooms growing out of sacks near the sex swing, which was a sort of baffling sight.

"I couldn't decide between the three," Khell admitted. "You don't mind me doing all this without asking?"

It might've been a fun project to blog about, although the explanation of what this space was seemed intimate and personal. Anyway, there was really only one answer.

I leaned down and kissed Khell. "I love it. This makes it *our* home."

Khell's purr was a roar, and his arms wrapped tightly around me, holding me in place for his kiss and the gentle bucking of his hips. He tossed a little remote aside—that must've been what controlled all the little twinkle lights—and used his free hand to grasp my ass and bounce me on his length.

"You're sure you're ready?" Khell rasped out, brow furrowing, his other hand sliding up to cup the back of my neck as he grazed kisses over my lips.

"I'm positive," I whispered, before sucking on Khell's full bottom lip. "You're my mate, Khell. I choose you, and at the same time, it isn't even a choice. You're *mine*."

Khell's purr vibrated all through his body and into mine too, my eyes falling shut at the thrill.

"I'm going to take such good care of you, petal," Khell said, and he sounded so winded it made me grin.

I sat up and opened my eyes again. The play room he'd built us was whimsical and dark, like one of my illustrations. It was perfect.

Khell was perfect for me.

He hogged the covers and always bought more than we needed at the grocery store, and it was absolutely useless offering to drive because he was such a control freak. He brought home fresh flowers every time he went out and was building me a cabinet just for all the bath products he approved of. He made me feel like the most precious woman on earth, while also the filthiest and most sexually deviant.

"I love you, beast," I said, one hand planted on his chest over his drumming heart, the other cupping his jaw.

Khell's eyes flared fire-bright, his nostrils flaring, and I gasped at the kick and swell of his stav inside of me. "Petal," he growled, and then seemed to choke on the words, surging up instead and crashing his lips to mine.

The kiss was deep and desperate, our tongues twining and tasting, our moans chorusing together. Khell worked me on his length, from his tip down to his base, filling me and fucking me until my entire body, my heartbeat, seemed to pulse in time with his rhythm.

"I love you," he gasped, pulling away. "I'm going to tease you and torture you and chase you and claim you for the rest of our lives."

I buried my laugh against his throat, scratching his back with one hand and twisting his braid around my palm with the other. My knees dug into the mattress of our lovely nest, and I joined him in the riding and grinding union of our bodies. Our pants and groans and breathless cries grew loud and rushed in my ears.

Khell's hands clasped around my hips as he rose up to his knees, holding me in midair, thrusts reaching deep, skin clapping hard. I moaned into his neck, heard his gasp as I yanked on his braid and dug my nails into his back. His claws gripped my ass, tusks scratching my shoulder, stav swelling to the size of a fist and pounding inside of me with every stroke of his cock.

"I'm going to fuck you until you come screaming on my cock, and then put you over my knee and turn your ass red for making me wait to hear you say that," Khell growled. "Say it again."

"I love you. My mate. I'm yours," I babbled, not sure which part he wanted, my voice bouncing with his forceful fucking.

Khell snarled promises, a wicked plethora of the things he would do for me, and I begged for more and repeated the words.

I love you. My mate. I'm yours.

"We're going to stay here until I'm satisfied," Khell purred in my ear, licking the shell and then pinching the lobe with his tusk and lip. "And petal, I won't be satisfied for *days.*"

I whined and sucked on his throat, trying to push my desperation into Khell so he would finish me off. My teeth were scratching his skin the way he often did to me, and my jaw ached with the need to bite down, like I'd become as much a beast as I teased Khell for being.

"I love you, mate," he whispered.

And then he tilted just so and the pound and stroke of his cock and stav dug inside of me, setting off the explosive chain reaction I'd been begging for. I did scream, just as Khell had said I would, tightening and bearing down on the pleasure.

My scream was feral, my hands rough on Khell, and he roared as the tease of my teeth became brutal.

I'd bit him.

I'd bitten Khell!

There was a hot and unexpectedly sweet taste in my mouth, and I nearly scrambled out of his arms to apologize, when suddenly the world turned and I was on my back in the nest, Khell rutting wildly on top of me.

"Petal! Sunny!" he snarled, his hips bucking and clapping into me. "Fuck, fuck, fuck. My mate. Mine!"

His urgency was shocking, but the grind and pressure of him on top of me only added fuel to the fire of my release, and I came again. I arched this time, releasing Khell's throat from my bite, only to find my shoulder pinned in his jaws.

The flood of hot bliss rushing through my veins, and spilling into me from Khell's release, sharpened with the sudden strike and burn of pain, Khell's tusks and teeth breaking my skin. His roar was buried in his bite, and the little twinkle lights overhead flared and glittered as the dizzy turn of the orgasms swept through me.

Khell continued fucking me, but his strokes grew softer and slower as I caught my breath. His throat was wet against my cheek, and my shoulder ached in his grip. His tongue swiped around the edge of his teeth, and I sighed at the warm tingle that soothed the bite.

"What—You didn't—" My chest was heaving, brushing against Khell's, and he pulled away slowly, licking the wound he'd made again. When he sat up above me I found the largest, brightest smile on his face. I blinked and stared up at him. "That was…bonding?"

He laughed, gaze glittering, and rocked into me a few times, the easy and gentle pace as soothing to my aftershocks as his licking had been to the bite.

"We were already mates," Khell said, ducking to lick me once again, nuzzling his head against my cheek. "Bites like these are…proof of pride. Proof that I please you as a mate. I should've asked, but you caught me by surprise, petal. Does it hurt?"

He was licking me again and *no,* it didn't hurt. It felt… explicit, like his tongue was actually on my cunt. I squirmed and he chuckled, guessing my answer.

"Not now," I said. "I didn't actually—" I paused, and Khell leaned back to meet my eyes again. Did I want to say biting him had been an accident? I *was* proud he was my mate. He *definitely* pleased me. He pleased me to a point of feral desperation and urgency that left me…biting him. It made sense now, in an orcish way. I hadn't bitten him to prove my pride, he'd *earned* the mark. And so had I. "I didn't even realize. Does yours hurt?"

I wasn't sure if I wanted to lick the wound, if I were honest, but if it would help the way his tongue did for me, I'd do it.

"No, petal," Khell said, licking his own lips before dipping down for a soft brush of a kiss over mine. "I like the sting of your little teeth. I'm going to wear your mark on me for all to see."

My eyes widened at the animal joy that burst in my chest. "Is it permanent?"

Khell purred, wrapping his arm around my waist. "It is, but if you want to give me more marks, I'll accept them."

"More?" I squeaked as he rolled us in the nest. I'd noticed before that he liked me on top when we were resting and chatting, but as soon as we got rowdy and started fucking in earnest, he usually had me on my back.

"There was an orc in the town where I grew up. He had five visible bites from his mate, and more we couldn't see. He had the reputation of the best lover an orcess could ask for."

I laughed at that and reached out to touch the mark I'd left. His blood was already congealing, healing quickly. "So you want me to bite you up so everyone knows I'm getting the good dick, huh?"

Khell's brows waggled. "Aren't you?"

I grinned at him. "You're going to have to earn your bites, beast."

He purred, and I had no doubt he would succeed. His hand reached up, guiding me back down for him to tend the bite he'd left. Which reminded me that the bite thing went both ways, and now any orcs I met would know I was more than satisfying my mate too.

"I'll be gentler next time," Khell whispered, kissing and then tonguing the wound. "And perhaps I will keep some of your bites secret."

I snorted and rolled my eyes. "We'll see."

Khell growled playfully and rolled us again, hitching my legs up to fasten around his hips. He peppered kisses over my cheeks and jaw, down my throat as I arched for more, across my shoulders.

"What happened to turning my ass red?" I breathed.

"Mmm, we will get there. But I've forgiven you for making me wait. A bite is a very good mark so soon in a bonding."

Maybe it was an accident, maybe it wasn't. I'd certainly never bitten anyone else I'd slept with. Maybe I needed to keep following instinct.

"I really love it down here," I told Khell, my breath hitching as he started to suck on one breast, using his claws to play with the other. He purred in answer and continued his work. "But we're going to need a bigger house, don't you think?"

"I will live on a boat, if it's what you want, petal," Khell muttered.

Orcs were decidedly *grounded*, so I knew that was a joke.

"And a new house will give me new projects," I continued, riding Khell from below as he continued to tease my body.

"I would like wider halls," he allowed.

"I'd like somewhere in the country."

Khell paused at that, stretching above me again so I had to tilt my head back. "Would you?"

I nodded. "Not too far from the city. But maybe with a little bit of woods?"

Khell grinned and rolled his hips, drawing a gasp from my lips, his stav starting to slowly pump again. "I will chase you through the trees."

"Yes," I breathed, tightening my legs around his hips.

His hands found my wrists, drawing them above my head, pinning me in place. "I'll build us a little room there. Hunt you and then lock you inside with me. Chain you to the wall and fuck you until you can't stand."

My eyes widened and my heels dug into Khell's ass, trying to urge him on. "Yes, beast."

"My wicked petal needs room to play her games," Khell growled, bracing his feet in the nest, turning into a long wave on top of me, stroking out and driving in.

"*Our* games, mate," I corrected.

Khell grinned and laughed at that, stopping briefly to lean down for a feathery soft kiss. "Oh, but *mate*, unless it's Rum'kurr, you *always* best me."

I arched into his kiss, sucked on his tongue, and worked myself against him from below until Khell pulled away again.

"Then perhaps you need more practice," I said, grinning up at Khell.

He growled again, gaze flashing hot, and I knew I was in exactly the kind of trouble I'd always wanted.

EPILOGUE

SUNNY - SEVERAL YEARS LATER

THWACK!

I gasped at the impact, burying a cry behind my lips.

Khell released a low, frustrated growl. "*Harder*."

My eyes narrowed at my orc. His hands were cuffed in metal and leather, drawn up with chains above his head, faint light bleeding through the shutters of our little one-room cabin, striping his arms and face with shadows. I stepped back, studying the shape of him, legs spread and pants pushed down to his knees. His head was high, turned to grin at me over his shoulders, eyebrows waggling.

I tightened my grip around the rubber handle of the wooden paddle Khell had made for me. For me to spank him with.

I drew my arm back and then swung.

Thwack!

The crack of sound made me jump, and this time I managed to draw a grunt and a huff of breath out of my orc.

His shoulders flexed in his tight button-down, and he let out a soft laugh.

"We both know you can do better than that, petal," Khell purred.

I rolled my eyes. "We both know you're trying to top from the bottom."

Khell laughed and shrugged, unrepentant. I'd been shy of paddling him once upon a time, but those days were long gone. I knew exactly how hard to spank my orc, and I knew if he got his way, he'd be spilling his release all over the place. I'd wondered once if Khell and I might ever run out of things to learn about each other's pleasure. We hadn't yet, but I'd also discovered that although our games were familiar now, sex was never dull with my mate.

"You're going to need to bend over, or you'll make a mess of your dress pants," I said.

Khell chuckled and waited patiently for me to adjust the chains. I had to stand on my tiptoes to reach, and Khell took my nearness as an excuse to lean in, rubbing against me. I batted at his cock with the paddle and laughed as he gasped.

"Behave, beast," I hissed.

We had more than enough room after we'd moved to the country—including the little plot of woods we'd dreamed of—but one of Khell's first projects had been this cabin. It was lowered into the ground, hidden from view by a hill that covered one side, and it had become our favorite place for rougher games together. Ones that required paddles and chains.

I moved a padded platform away from the wall to the center of the room. Khell bent forward, winking at me as he rested his elbows on the surface, his back arched and ass high. When Khell was meant to be the submissive between us, he *always* played the brat.

I settled in at his side, pushing his shirt up his back to rest my hand at the base of his spine, pausing for a moment to simply savor the warmth of him. And the view of my favorite butt in the world, tight and braced for its spanking.

"Sunny," Khell prompted.

The paddle came down, sharp and sudden, and this time I caught Khell by surprise, an honest bark of shock and pleasure bursting from his lips. I didn't hesitate, striking one cheek and then the other, high and low, back and forth. Paddling Khell always left me breathless, partly from the effort it took and mostly from the heady power moments like this gave me. The sound of Khell's grunts dissolving into moans and whines was an aphrodisiac. Watching the color of his green flesh turning ruddy and dark and browned made my own cheeks flush.

And like clockwork, the moment Khell started to buck, body squirming and hips flexing forward, I grew wet and hot between my thighs.

I caught my breath, pausing in the paddling to step back and admire my work so far. There was a small glossy puddle of arousal on the concrete floor, and I shifted to allow a little streak of light to land on Khell's cock. Watching his stav work in the stiff sleeve of his length, the swollen glide up and down, always mesmerized me.

"More," my mate rasped. Khell's back was heaving with breath, head bowed down to his arms.

"We need to get back to the house," I said, shifting the paddle to my left hand so I could press my right to the marked flesh of his ass.

Khell groaned, pushing back into my bare palm. "Finish me, please, mate."

I pursed my lips, brushing my fingertips up and down Khell's ass. "Hmm...I don't know."

"Sunny," Khell growled—a warning.

To be fair, he usually took care of me after a spanking and before guests arrived. But somehow when he got his way like this, I always felt like he was still in charge, still leading the game.

"I don't think I will," I murmured, tiptoeing my fingers between his cheeks and rubbing them down his crack to his hole.

Khell gasped, his entire body trembling at the minuscule touch. "Petal, *please*."

And this time, his begging was in earnest.

"I'll make a deal with you," I said, a grin growing on my face. "You can come…if you can catch me."

Khell stiffened, head lifting and turning to glare at me. "Catch—"

"Are you ready?" I asked, backing away from him slowly.

"Sunny, I am chained—"

"Get set."

Khell stood and glared down at the chains that he and I both knew he could get out of with little effort.

"Go," I whispered.

I darted for the door of the cabin, and Khell let out a snarling laugh behind me. I would give myself a decent head start, maybe thirty seconds, maybe less. And we still had a good twenty minutes before anyone might be expected to show up. It was risky and ridiculous and entirely the kind of game we liked to play.

I left the door hanging open, darting up the stairs and into the woods, gasping at the roar that echoed from the hidden cabin behind me. We had a good ten acres of woods behind our house—situated just far enough from Chicago to afford us real space—and no neighbors directly next to us. It was private enough for an orc and his mate, and perfectly suited to Khell and me.

I ran, giggling already, heading directly for the house, and I knew the moment Khell had escaped. He made no effort to sneak up on me, growling and grunting and snapping fallen branches under his stamping feet. My legs and lungs burned as I bolted down the path, heading for the brilliant edge where the shadows of the woods broke into our backyard, rosy and glaring with the setting sun.

I was nearly to the edge of the woods when I saw the metallic gleam of a car roof bumping along our driveway.

"Damn eager orcs," I muttered, my feet stumbling as I slowed. Either our friends had set out early, or Chicago traffic had been forgiving for the first time ever.

I spun to warn Khell, but I was too late. My orc was on top of me, wild and grinning, scooping me off my feet and throwing us both against the base of a massive tree.

"Khell, the guests—" I gasped out.

Khell's eyes barely flicked beyond the trunk of the tree. "I see them. I caught you."

"We can't now," I whispered.

Khell smirked at me, his hands clasping the backs of my legs and wrapping them around his bare hips. How had the sneaky bastard run with his pants down?!

"We will," he growled.

"But they'll *know*!"

"They will," he said.

And then his thumb caught the edge of my underwear, tugging it aside. He plunged inside of me, clapping his hand over my mouth as I cried out.

"You made a deal with an orc, petal," Khell snarled in my ear, not waiting a moment before thrusting, fucking me against the tree. My arms tangled around him, fingers gripping at the once tidy shirt. It would be wrinkled from my sweaty fists when we finally greeted everyone.

His hand moved from my mouth, claws digging into the trunk near my head, fastening us in place.

"Fast and hard," I said, bucking my chin up, challenging him with narrowed eyes.

Khell grinned, tusks gleaming. "Hold tight to me, mate."

"Always."

Afterword

Welcome to the Monster Smash Agency!

I started writing this story in the fall of 2021 to feed the fluffy, smutty, potato chip eating fiend in my brain. This series is a fun new model for me where I post in progress chapters on my Patreon and then later reword, edit, polish and publish the series wide!

I am currently drafting and will soon be posting on Patreon the follow up in the series, Howl for the Gargoyle! Howl for the Gargoyle features a newly and involuntarily turned werewolf heroine named Hannah, and none other than garbage disposal stomached Rafe the gargoyle! As is pretty typical for me, Howl is pretty tonally different than Games so far, but the steam still scorches no matter what!

If serial chapter reading isn't for you, I promise to bring Howl for the Gargoyle to bookshelves later in 2023!

Also by Kathryn Moon

COMPLETE READS

The Librarian's Coven Series

Written

Warriors

Scrivens

Ancients

Standalones

Good Deeds

Command The Moon

Say Your Prayers - co-write with Crystal Ash

Secrets of Summerland

The Sweetverse

Baby + the Late Night Howlers

Lola & the Millionaires - Part One

Lola & the Millionaires - Part Two

Bad Alpha

Faith and the Dead End Devils

Sol & Lune

Book 1

Book 2

Inheritance of Hunger Trilogy

The Queen's Line

The Princess's Chosen

The Kingdom's Crown

SERIES IN PROGRESS

Sweet Pea Mysteries

The Baker's Guide To Risky Rituals

The Knitter's Guide to Banishing Boyfriends

Tempting Monsters

A Lady of Rooksgrave Manor

The Company of Fiends

Sanctuary with Kings (coming 2023)

Monster Smash Agency

Games with the Orc

Howl for the Gargoyle (coming 2023)

Acknowledgments

Every acknowledgements page ought to grow longer than the last because the more I write the wider my community and support stretches. I'm so grateful to everyone who's joined me on this journey, guided me, propped me up when I wanted to wobble, and read my work!

Special thanks in the Games with the Orc crew includes my babe Whoop for being my brain. My beta babes, Helen, Ash, Jess, and Amanda! Jess and Meghan, for taking turns editing and tidying my words. Both Daqri and then Sophie for two amazing and inspiring covers. All of the incredible artists who provided art (shared on Patreon) and most especially my patrons who were willing to take a chance on a weekly chapter update model.

As always, thank you to my family and friends, my readers, and my little furry supervisor, Coraline.

Kathryn Moon is a country mouse who started dictating stories to her mother at an early age. The fascination with building new worlds and discovering the lives of the characters who grew in her head never faltered, and she graduated college with a fiction writing degree. She loves writing women who are strong in their vulnerability, romances that are as affectionate as they are challenging, and worlds that a reader sinks into and never wants to leave. When her hands aren't busy typing they're probably knitting sweaters or crimping pie crust in Ohio. She definitely believes in magic.

You can reach her on Facebook and at ohkathrynmoon@gmail.com or you can sign up for her newsletter!